THE
MADNESS

For additional books by Dawn Kurtagich,
visit her website, dawnkurtagich.com.

THE
MADNESS

DAWN KURTAGICH

GRAYDON
HOUSE

GRAYDON
HOUSE®

ISBN-13: 978-1-525-80981-1

The Madness

Graydon House
22 Adelaide St. West, 41st Floor
Toronto, Ontario M5H 4E3, Canada
www.GraydonHouseBooks.com

Printed in U.S.A.

For my husband, who showed me that there *are* good men in the world

"The world seems full of good men—even if there are monsters in it."

—Bram Stoker, Dracula

PROLOGUE

Rain lashes the shop windows, long since closed for the evening. In her miniskirt, she feels every icy sting. Her makeup, so carefully applied, will no doubt run, leaking ivory and crimson into the puddle at her feet. They are both veneers—one hiding her fear, the other draping the world in moonlit crystals, obscuring the ugly parts.

The black 4X4 arrives with a whisper of tires. The door clicks open, a maw of darkness.

She can't see the man inside but knows he is there. Can sense him watching her.

Everything in her screams, *Run*.

She glances back only once, then takes a breath and climbs inside.

1

I wake with a scream on my lips, the feel of hands groping my flesh.

The phantom of a face hovers over me, its features distorted, indistinguishable. Inhuman.

In the fractured umbra, I'm momentarily disoriented, but then I catch sight of my bedside clock glowing orange like a doomsday eclipse and the room sinks into normality once more: 3:33 a.m. Even through my fading fear and the *whump-whump-whump* of my heart in my ears, I appreciate the symmetry.

Four hours before I have to head out, but there's no chance of more sleep. I've never been one to nap, or to languish in bed with a book. Siesta is a foreign concept, terra incognita; even the taste of the word sours in the corners of my mouth. *Tempus fugit*, Mum always used to say, clapping her hands as she hustled me up for school. So I guess I took one thing from her. Time is a commodity, after all, and we're destitute, every one of us.

I slip from bed in the silent darkness, wincing at the coolness of the floor, and walk the one, two, three, four, five, six, seven, eight, nine steps to the en suite. My foot lands wrong on five and I have to go back to the bed and do it all over again.

Three squirts of hand wash for my ablutions, three minutes

brushing my teeth, followed by a hot shower that lasts thirty minutes and thirty seconds. Afterward I use three capfuls of bleach to wash the walls, scrubbing all 393 six-by-six-inch tiles— I had one removed and replaced with a steel plate, affixed with nine dots of cement—in my forty-eight-square-foot space with a spare toothbrush set aside for just this purpose. By the time I am finished, my skin is itching and my nostrils are aflame with the tang of sodium hypochlorite.

Clean.

Moisturizer containing extracts of verbena is applied from the left side of my body to the right, except for my face, which is applied right to left. The apartment is cool and still, the chill of autumn seeping under doorframes and windowpanes. I shrug on a woolen jumper and switch on the gas fire in my open plan living room. It's not the rustic inglenook I grew up with, but the fire still soothes me.

While I wait for the space to defrost, I switch on the kettle and reach for the glass container of Welsh verbena-and-nettle tea, scooping more into the cup than normal, still shaken by a dream I can no longer remember. It lingers like an almost-scent. I keep trying to catch hold of it to no avail, but it is the embryo of new obsession. If I don't stop thinking about it, picking at it like a hangnail, it will become a new tic. A new chaos I can't control.

I drink the bitter brew in my window seat, looking out on the nothing of the world outside, shadows of a semblance of shape and form beyond the glass. My breath fogs it up and fades, over and over, fleeting evidence that I am here.

I am, I am, I am.

After the tea, I pull on my running uniform: black leggings and a light, long-sleeve Lycra top with a high collar. I secure my hair in a French twist while damp, check to make sure my neck is covered and grab a Lucozade Sport drink from the fridge before heading out for my run. If I'm not moving, life gets away from me. Sinks into a big Nothing that I have panic attacks over. Worse as I get older. *Tempus fugit, Mina.*

Kensington is pleasant this early. The sun won't rise for another hour, but the sky is already ripening like a juicy grapefruit. For the next forty-two minutes—four and two is six is three twice—I pound the pavement, hearing nothing but my increasingly labored breath and the *smack-smack-smack* of my trainers on the road. A man setting out his morning papers calls a greeting and I lift a friendly hand, even though I'm annoyed that he pulled me from my rhythm and have to go around the block and start again.

The dream's hangover lingers in my body. The details are obscured—I only remember feeling cold and helpless. Trapped. Even now, as I try to pound out the feeling, I'm still on edge.

There are other terrors too. This is life.

I fear men walking, heads bowed beneath hoodies, even if they are innocently avoiding the rain. When I cross the street I pull out my phone, 999 ready to go, help only a green button away.

I have my keys firmly wedged between index and fuck-you finger, hooked and crooked with my thumb. Still. I measure his stride, his heft, his length from shoulder to shoulder. Brawn, speed. What chance would I have against that? And all of this in the split second as we pass. He doesn't look up, but I still walk faster, hoping he can't keep apace. The amygdala, hard at work.

When I get back to my flat, it's twelve minutes past six, and my alarm is blaring from the bedroom. I shut it off and repeat my bathroom routine, this time donning my work uniform when done: a black turtleneck jumper of thin merino wool and straight-legged, wool-mix black trousers. I zip on my boots, left, right, and redo the simple French twist, wet again, secured with a smarter comb. This is me, Mina Murray. This is my life. Over and over. Safe. Known. Predictable.

I control the chaos. I tame the fear.

I prepare freshly ground coffee in the kitchen and clean out the filter while two eggs cook. I eat them in the center of a square white plate, biting from one and then the next, left to right, in an orderly fashion, putting the plate in the dishwasher when finished.

A perfunctory check of my person, then I grab my briefcase and leave the flat, remembering to lock the door once, twice, thrice for luck and balance. It is a good day and I only check it twice.

2

Brookfields is a government-funded psychiatric facility and I have been called in to assess cases that fit my remit for the last year. Women with extreme trauma. The money isn't as good as my earnings from private Harley Street clientele, but this feeds my passion rather than just my bank account.

"Need to update your ID fob," the man at reception tells me.

"Update it?"

"New photo."

"Is that really necessary?"

"Been a year," he says, his tone dismissive, bored. "Look here."

He points to the small black webcam to my left. I hold still and try not to fidget.

He faffs about with his computer and the printer whirrs to life.

"Right you are, Doc," he says, handing me a new pass.

I check the photo and cringe. Fawn-like eyes, unruly brown hair, and a small mouth with lips that are too short and too thin give me a perpetually startled expression. A cartoon character made real. I glance at my reflection in the glass behind him, reminding myself to lower my eyelids in order to shake that impression, but, as always, I only manage to look languid.

Get it together, Bambi.

"Strange one today," the registrar tells me when I arrive at intakes. Ron Wexler is a short man with a balding spot on the back of his round head, but he has kind eyes and I know he treats the patients well.

They are always strange ones if they've called me, but I don't tell him that. Women manifest trauma in unusual ways. What I discuss with the clients assigned to me here, or the ones I take on out there, is entirely privileged. Unless, of course, they are a danger to society or themselves. And yet, all too often women's traumas are treated as a kind of madness, something that takes a life of its own, thereby exonerating the society that made them that way. *Watched you break me, now you blame me.* Faouzia's lyrics blasting in my head.

"A young Jane Doe," Ron continues. "Found wandering the docklands raving about the walking dead and a coming apocalypse. She was brought in with no identifying documents and with no clothing."

"She was found naked?"

"Yep." Ron shuffles from foot to foot. "Maybe you ought to begin when she's sedated? Dr. Seward might be in later to assist."

My hackles rise. Dr. John Seward is, in my opinion, the least qualified doctor to deal with female trauma, despite his barrage of bestselling books that say otherwise. For him, it's a parlor trick, not a vocation.

The titles of his books alone make me cringe. *To Walk Alone: Female Delusions of the Mind*; *The Tower Hamlet Killer: When Women Go Mad*; and *Murder by Numbers: Count It Betty*—bestsellers all.

I smile faintly. "That would defeat the purpose. But thank you for your concern, Ron."

Ron furrows his brow. I have always inspired two distinct things in men: a protective instinct, or a perverse lust that seems never to be sated. I steer clear of it all. Love is something I preach but never practice. For Ron, I might as well be his five-year-old daughter. I can see the pigtails he imagines me wearing in his puffy, kindly face. The way he bites his lip, eyes shadowed as we walk the anemic hallway.

At the security gate, I hold out my hand for Jane Doe's folder. "I'll take it from here."

I have to suppress the urge to laugh when he hesitates. If he could be witness to some of my more intense intrusive thoughts…

At last, he hands it over.

"Be careful."

I don't dignify that with a response. Instead, I turn and let myself into the gate and march down the pristine hall, my boot heels clicking across the floor like a ticking clock.

No one would know I am counting every step.

Jane Doe is slumped in a corner of the small triage personal safety room, facing away from the door and viewing pane. Milky light from a dreary day seeps in through the single window, casting meager patches across the floor, splashes of it barely reaching the walls. The rest of the room, draped in veils of shadow, stands sickly and sad. The overhead light is off, and when I check my notes, I see she is photosensitive. A muggy red glow from the CCTV camera lends the scene a lurid air.

I observe for a long time, noting the twitches, the murmurs, and trying to catch any distinct words. I make out "orchid," "help," and "master." I note everything in my journal.

I've always been good at watching. At eleven, watching the village boys rip off the corner shop, so smug about their pocketfuls of penny sweets. At thirteen, watching the sunrise on Tylluan beach while kids snogged or shagged behind grassy knolls. At fifteen, looking for my father's tell when we'd play cards— a crease near the corner of his lazy eye. "The mind of a man, you've got there, Mins," he'd always say after my victory. His highest compliment.

After a few minutes, I ask the orderly to allow me access. He does so but gives me a handheld buzzer for emergencies, which will send him back quick-time. I pocket it without comment.

The orderly eyes me warily, just like Dr. Ron, but leaves me to it.

I sit down across from Jane Doe and fold my legs. The shadows looming from the corners unsettle me; my imagination conjures threats where there are none. I focus on the girl instead. I sit quietly for some minutes. I forget to count. This is the only time, when I am absorbed in another person, when I am helping a woman heal, that I can fully slough off that persistent tic. When I can leave myself behind. Eventually Jane Doe turns in my direction, revealing a startlingly young face and bloodshot eyes. Her ample lips are cracked, skin peeling away like melted plastic or chipped paint.

"Why are you watching me?" The voice too is very young. No more than eighteen or nineteen, I would guess.

"I want to get to know you."

"What's your name?"

"Mina. What's yours?"

She hesitates, and a fat tear leaks out of her left eye. She whispers, "Renée."

"It's nice to meet you, Renée. How are you feeling today?"

Renée frowns and withdraws into herself, but I am patient. I know that she has no idea how or what she is feeling. She is, to me, a giant question mark covered in bruises. She is pulsing with pain so fierce I can almost feel it. She licks her lips, eyes glancing left and right, then over to the window behind me. I resist the impulse to turn.

"Would you like some orange juice?"

That gets Renée's attention. She stares at me, evaluating, and eventually nods, the strands of her dingy, wheat-colored hair wobbling like greasy rat tails. She smells like old sweat and menstruation, but I've smelled worse.

I press the buzzer in my hand and the door swings violently open.

"Can we both have a cup of orange juice, please?"

The orderly, a big man, stares at me. "The buzzer ain't for deliveries."

"That will be all for now," I say, smiling. I stare until, uncomfortable with my wide-eyed scrutiny, he sighs, shakes his head, and saunters out, locking the door behind him.

"How did you do that?" Renée whispers.

"What?"

"How did you...get him to listen?"

"Have they not been listening to you?"

Renée shakes her head and I note with horror that lice are crawling through her hair. I sit still. Very still. I am in control.

"I've been asking for water." She draws invisible pictures on the padded floor with cracked nails.

"And they refused?"

Her finger moves from the floor to the air, swirling around and around. Renée leans forward as though to tell me a secret. "No one listens. But Master is coming and he will make them pay." Her voice drops an octave. "In blood."

I suppress a sudden urge to laugh. "I see. Well, they should have brought you food and water, and I'll make certain they do so in the future."

"I have food," Renée says, smiling like a child.

"You do? Can you show me?"

She shakes her head and curls in on herself. "No! No-no-no-no-no-no-no."

She's like a four-year-old hiding stolen crayons.

"Please?"

She considers, her eyes roaming my face, my hair, my hands, and my crossed legs. At last, she nods and crawls closer. The stench of rot and old blood grows. Slowly, she removes a clenched fist from the pocket of her hospital gown, grinning. "Look," she whispers, and I have to force myself not to flinch at the sewage of her breath.

She uncurls her fist, revealing the broken bodies of several flies, spiders, and beetles. Then, as I watch, she stuffs them into her mouth and crunches on them with an expression of such ecstasy that I almost lose my composure.

Renée pauses, staring at me, and then spits some of the half-masticated bug-feast into her palm and hesitantly offers it like a gift.

"You're very kind."

I must establish trust. It is vital, or everything I've built with this girl in the last few minutes will crumble. With my heart hammering in my throat, and a fever like acid rising up my neck, I reach for the slimy mess and pluck out a fly. A string of mucilaginous saliva glistens between the bug and Renée's palm.

The orderly opens the door and plonks two plastic cups of orange juice on the floor and then retreats.

"I have to go now, Renée," I manage, getting to my feet. "You can have my orange juice, since you were so kind to share your...meal."

Renée grins, black bits of bug in her teeth and tears on her cheek.

I wait until I'm on the other side of the door and hear its telltale click—safe—to drop the bug. My hand begins to shake and a terrible, familiar itching, burning, *gnawing* begins to rise, to spread from my fingertips into the palms of my hands.

I turn down the corridor and it judders like a Slinky. A nurse approaches, words falling from her lips, jumbled together.

I hurry past, bumping her accidentally, murmur, "Sorry," and try not to run.

I rush into the nearest patient toilets, the door crashing into the wall as I stumble to the sink and turn on the hot tap, pumping harsh medical-grade hand soap into my desperate palm and starting to scrub. I wash. I scrub. I rinse. I wash. I scrub. I rinse. I wash, I scrub, I rinse. The flash of an infected insect burrowing through the flesh of my palm sends another shock wave through my mind, and I shut my eyes and scrub harder, letting the water scald me. Clean me. I count every bleached tile of the room in my mind until my racing heart quells.

"Get a grip, Murray," I say, squeezing my red-raw hands into tight fists. "Get a bloody grip."

My name is ████████

   I think that's it. I'm... I CAN'T remember.

I live in ██████ though, I know that's true.

   Woke up ██████ this morning.

Feathers in my teeth. Coppery taste in my mouth.

   My brain is itching and I'm hungry.

      I'm so HUNGRY. And cold.

Lost my shoes in the night. It's getting worse.

   My name is

         My name...

               ...is...

I.

This.

    This is what it was all for. The pulse of the music, the flash of the lights, the hum of life under her heels. The night-club thrums with vibrations. She's intoxicated with the dizzying newness of it. She feels free. Unshackled from the stifling control of her clinical world.

She walks—saunters—from the loud multicolored dance floor over to the quieter side of the pub. It's a seedy place, and she delights in the filth of it. At the bar she orders a rum and Coke, holding a tenner folded between two fingers like she's seen on TV. Drink in hand, she wanders back toward the pulsing dance floor.

On the way, a guy hits on her. He's not the first. She laughs and walks past him. Power indeed.

Another man watches her from the shadows. He has been for some time. When he finally comes over, she's not surprised.

"What's your name?"

She has a reckless impulse to tell him the truth. "Jennifer," she lies.

He smiles like he's in on the secret. He watches her in that way again, and she almost feels a slink of unease climb her spinal column.

Then he hands her a black business card, held neatly between two fingers, a better impression of her at the bar. "It's a job opportunity." He smirks when she takes it. "If you want it."

It's blank, save for a glossy black logo on the back and a phone number on the front.

She frowns, turning back to him. "What do I say—"

But he is already gone.

Dear Dr. Murray,
I thought you might like to see this one. It came in via your website contact form.

Best,
Kerry Andrews
Secretary to Dr. Mina Murray
Harley Street, London

From: LucyH@Greysons.com
To: Mina Murray Contact Form
Subject: Please I need your help

Dear Bambi,
I promised myself I wouldn't do this, but I've reached a point of desperation. I've become the saddo that googles the people who've snubbed her. I still think you're a shit person, but I need your help. You're a psychiatrist, you work with women—and I need your professional help. The doctors don't know what this is. I don't want to put too much in writing. My contact information is attached.

I hope to hear from you.

Sincerely,
Lucy Holmswood

3

I sit in the driver's seat of my car in the parking bay outside Brookfields, staring at nothing. All thoughts of Renée Doe flee my head in the wake of Lucy Westenra's—now, apparently Holmswood's—email on my phone. And then I choke back a sob as a memory of Lucy rises in my mind, fresh and alive, her smile spread unselfconsciously across her face on so many of the afternoons we spent by the sea.

Lucy sweeping a lick of blond hair from her face and taking another drag on a cigarette, staring out at the incoming tide. Her eyes a steely sleet, the color of the Irish Sea in winter. Me, the skinny brunette beside her. The days were frigid, but neither of us had anywhere better to be. We daydreamed, mostly, and the topic was always the same: getting out of that dead-end town. Lucy was more earnest than I, even as she pretended nonchalance and flicked away her cig. Maybe that was because we both knew I had the better chance. I reassured her that we were both leaving, that neither of us would be pulled into the gravitational well of Tylluan, that no one would be left behind. She scoffed and asked if she could stay at my house, like she did so often, and I, of course, agreed. There was no need to ask, but she did anyway. She was my best friend, my closest self, and I knew we would escape together.

And then I ran away and left her there.

She texted me. Phoned me. Left voicemails begging me to come home, and then, later, to explain, and later still to never contact her again.

Twelve years went by in a flash of roaring silence.

I could never explain. Could never find the words to tell her, or anyone, the terrible thing that had happened to me that night on the beach. How could I find the words to describe what he did?

I shut my eyes and I push it all away.

Yet, Lucy's face haunts my dreams, and other faces too. The faces of the people I left behind, the faces of the people I let down. I dream of Wales. Of home. Of Tylluan beach, staring over the fire at Cysgod Castle, Lucy's hand warm in mine. The time she dared me to swim in the sea naked before the sun rose and, when I begged her to retract the dare, the most sacred of challenges, she had done it herself, stripping down in the half light and racing for the water with a look on her face like she wanted to challenge the ocean itself to try to stop her. Her piercing shriek as she hit the water and kept going. She went under and just when I began to panic that she'd drowned, she popped back up and waved, beckoning me to join her. I never did. Her girlfriend, Quincey, was always game. More times than not, I watched them gallivant around together, coaxing me to live a little. To dare a little. Too timid to run the gauntlet, I never joined Lucy in any of her wild, brilliant, harebrained schemes.

Twelve years safely inside my comfort zone. Twelve years free from the briny smell of the streets near the promenade, twelve years free from the slow people and the polite, abrasive smiles of happy locals. Twelve years free of friendship.

A tickle on my cheek alerts me to tears already fast-falling.

I broke so many hearts that day, including my own. I'm not certain I've ever really recovered. Not fully.

I reopen my phone, intending to get rid of the email, but my finger hovers, never actually pressing Delete.

I frown at her message. The doctors don't know what this is.

Lucy is sick. Sick enough to put aside her pride. Sick enough that the risk of humiliation is smaller than what's at stake.

I took an oath when I became a doctor, long before I chose to specialize in psychiatry. Doing nothing is paramount to doing harm. What Lucy's asking me for is something I would give to any other woman who needed help. It's what I do. The fact that it's her shouldn't matter. But, of course, it does.

I open Google and type in "Lucy Holmswood." I quickly find a wedding announcement and a photo of her with her husband, Arthur. He has ginger hair, tired eyes, and a kind smile. Together with her glamorous features, they look like a postcard. But that's not the most surprising thing about the photo. He's British nobility—a baron.

I laugh through my tears even as a spark of some ugly, unidentifiable emotion rises. I'm a doctor, living in London. Lucy married into the aristocracy. We both, I realize, got exactly what we wanted.

Just not together.

I start the engine and pull out of the Brookfields parking bay more aggressively than I intend. The car I nearly hit beeps at me and I wave an apology, heart thumping a compulsive rhythm in my chest.

By the time I've reached Marble Arch, traffic is at a standstill. I switch on the radio, but it's *Women's Hour* and the last thing I want is to be thinking about what women need. What *she* needs. I flick over to BBC Radio 1 and hum mindlessly to the music.

I still think you're a shit person, but I need your help. I curse under my breath. I have a life here in London. A real life. A safe, rational life. I have a successful career, I have a new patient that needs me, I have everything I always wanted. Everything I worked bloody hard for... And by the time traffic begins to move, I know that I will put it all aside to go and help someone that I abandoned. Someone who loved me and trusted me. Someone I left to rot.

I pack light. A pair of dark heritage check trousers, two Richmond cigarette trousers, one in black and one pin-striped. Three black sweaters, two merino wool, and one cashmere. Heeled leather boots, and one flat pair, just in case, plus a pair of loafers. I select my best simple yet professional jewelry and I put on my watch—the Bulgari—knowing, but ignoring, the fact that I am doing this to impress her.

I make a list after that. Of everything I will need to feel safe. I pack three toothbrushes, only one of which is for my teeth. I include everything for my ablutions, including my verbena-infused moisturizer and my favorite perfume. Next: bleach, sodium bicarbonate, and white vinegar. Soap. A large supply of my Welsh verbena-and-nettle tea and, finally, my laptop and charger.

By the time the clock strikes noon, I've packed every necessity I can think of and I'm ready to go. There is no one to inform of my trip. No appointments to cancel—I can check in on Renée remotely if needed, and for the week I'm away, Ron, the kindly registrar, will do well enough. I am free to do this, or not, as I wish.

So why are you doing it? For a memory? For a shadow?

Another shadow rises from my past. Mum, this time. I remember the last voicemail she left me. A rehearsed message, brief and impersonal.

Hello, Mina. I hope you're well. I can't make it down to London for Halloween. Maybe Christmas, though, yes? Take care.

I knew my mother well enough to know why she wasn't coming. Why she almost never came. As the years passed, she was less and less inclined to make the journey, not when I never returned the favor. Did she think I didn't remember? That Nos Galan Gaeaf was one of the busiest times in her craft? I spent years following her around the stillroom, listening to her talk about each plant and its magical properties, hanging fennel over the door to repel the devil, chewing on spicy cloves of garlic to ward away *pwcas*, tying a sprig of mistletoe to the rowan lintel— not for unexpected kisses, oh no—to protect against *y Gwyllgi*, Satan's hound. Every season she brought the priest to the house to bless the access points, to anoint them with holy water and say a prayer. She would take the sacrament at these times only, insisting I do the same. I was raised by a mother who prayed to a Christian God, while banishing a headache by tapping a rock on my forehead three times during the first thunderstorm of the season like a good pagan. Only in Tylluan could a priest and a witch speak the same language.

Your mum's the batty witch up on the hill, inn't she?

Voices taunting.

Lucy is tied up with memories of my mother, as inextricable as salt from seawater. So if I want to save what's left of my relationship with my mother before she casts me off for good, then maybe helping Lucy can bridge the gap. It is enough of a reason to return to Tylluan.

I count to 333 as I load the car and begin the long, 250-mile drive back to North Wales—and a past I worked very hard to put behind me.

4

As I near the place of my birth, first on the M6 toll road and onto the M56, passing town after town, city after city, one emotion lingers above all: dread. I am willingly returning to a place teetering on the side of the British map, a place I vowed never to return to as long as I drew breath.

The road twists and bends, labyrinthine and so very *green*. I forgot how tiny the roads here are, hemmed in by verdant hedges that feel claustrophobic in the way that an uninvited touch does. Halfway down the long lane leading to the cottage, I meet a tractor pulling a livestock carrier full of sheep and have to reverse up a hill for a hundred yards. The man in the tractor smiles and calls, *"Diolch, cariad!"* I grumble and wave as he passes.

I stop on the sloping hill out of sight of the house beside the proud old yew and pull out my phone, tapping in Mum's number.

"Yes," she says, her voice low, and I want to hang up right away.

"Hi, Mum."

"What is it?" she says.

"I need to stay with you for a few days."

A pause. "Has something happened?"

"No."

"What's wrong?"

"Nothing, Mum. Can I come stay?"

"When?"

It's now or never. I put the car into first and pull up to the house. She is standing in the conservatory on the handheld.

"How about now?"

She lowers the phone as she spots me, and I can't make out what expression crosses her face. She's not overjoyed, that's for sure.

When she comes to the door, she looks me up and down. "The house is a state." She says it like an accusation.

The house was always in a state, full of books on all manner of subjects from practical uses for herbcraft to tales of the *Ellyllon* elves, jars of various teas, dried bundles hanging from curtain rails and wooden beams, beeswax candles in various stages of dip and roll, and an assortment of scarves, tapestries, and macramé.

She'd be classed as a first-level hoarder—the kind that collects beautiful things that smell nice, as opposed to some of my clients who lived in manmade towers and tunnels of old newspapers, animal feces, and shopping bags, who've had to be forcibly removed and put into county care.

I follow Mum in through the open conservatory doors, noting that her step is still whitewashed to keep the Devil from entering. The smell hits me like a nostalgia brick thrown full force at my face, scents tripping over themselves to reach my nostrils, where they rip deeply buried memories from the mothballed linen closet of my mind's attic. Evergreen jasmine, peppermint, tea tree, and lavender roll through the house in waves. And of course, verbena. The only thing I took with me when I left.

The plants have taken over the entire space. One particular striped tomato plant is heaving with fruit, bent and sagging under the weight.

"It's teeming with life in here," I say strategically.

Mum touches a fern to her left and smiles like she might at a newborn. "Yes. I saw the first daffodil this spring."

I try to keep from rolling my eyes. In Welsh legend, seeing the first daffodil in spring means the rest of the year will be bountiful, full of silver and gold and all manner of prosperity. Then again, she also believes that if a daffodil droops when you look at it, it forewarns of a coming death.

"That must be it," I mutter. I refrain from informing her that the bulbs are one of the most frequent causes of accidental poisoning in all of Britain, and what does her superstition say about that?

I heard so many excessively credulous warnings throughout my life—*cursed is the man who kills a robin; break a wren's nest and never know heavenly rest*—that they became normal. But having been away for so long, living in the real world, my mother's oddness is inescapably obvious.

Once, to prove to myself that I was my own person, not bonded to superstitious captivity, I had even—though I would never tell my mother—taken a hawthorn spray in flower inside the house, which was utterly forbidden, and no shadow of doom had stricken me down.

"Did you carry a sprig of rowan in your pocket?" Mum asks as we enter the kitchen.

I remind myself to be patient. "There aren't any rowan trees where I live, Mum."

"What about the necklace Dad and I made you?"

I flinch, bile rising in my throat. "No."

She heaves a sharp sigh and clucks her tongue then fills a copper whistling kettle with water and places it on the Rayburn.

"You still don't have an electric kettle?"

She waves a hand. "Wasteful things. Nothing wrong with heating water the old-fashioned way."

Except the time it takes. Which means conversation. The last time I saw her was a couple of years back when she deigned to come down to London for Christmas, and I can't remember our last phone call. The Christmas didn't go well, and we haven't really spoken since, both leaving short voicemails with apologies about missing each other and meaningless promises to "get together soon."

"So," she says, leaning against the counter. "Tell me."

"Tell you what?"

"Why you're here."

Welcome home, Mina. How have you been, Mina? How's work, Mina?

"I heard from Lucy. Thought I'd come and see her."

She can't stop the surprised laugh that escapes her. "You've not seen Lucy in over a decade, Mina."

"I know, but she emailed me. So I'm here."

Her nostrils flare a little as she takes this in and I can almost read her mind: *Don't you go hurting that poor girl again, Mina.* Something in her expression frightens me, tells me that Lucy really is sick—and not just a little poorly.

"How have you been?" I ask quickly, hoping to distract her, to get onto better footing.

"Do you care?"

"Of course."

"Not enough to give me a proper phone call in two years."

"It hasn't been two…" Well. Maybe. "I'm sorry, okay?"

She folds her arms, seems genuinely hurt, and I feel bad.

"What's…what's been going on around here?" I try.

"Nothing good." She sniffs and opens the cupboard, rummaging inside. "Not that it concerns outsiders."

"Is that what I am?"

She says nothing. Nothing at all.

Mum was the kind of parent who encouraged my fears of the boogeyman, telling me that, not only was he real, but he was *likely* to come and get me, whether I was good or bad. Her blind faith in the old ways was ingrained deeper than any maternal feeling she had and frequently overruled that instinct. I often wonder if that's why, for the first seventeen years of my life, and on and off for a few more after that, I was timid as a mouse, never speaking up for myself, always following the lead of others. My mother taught me fear from the cradle.

The kettle begins a slow climb to a scream, and Mum gathers it off the hob with a ragged kitchen cloth, setting it down on an iron tea stand she's had since before I was born. I watch her busy herself pouring boiling water onto tea. The smell of Welsh verbena and other herbs rises, and a wave of calm descends over me.

"And what's going on with you?" Mum asks when we're settled at the cluttered conservatory table with our mugs. "Seeing anyone?"

"No." There hasn't been anyone since Jonathan. Even now, that particular wound still smarts. Losing both Lucy and Jonathan in one fell swoop has been the defining pain of my life.

We speak two different languages, my mother and me. We always have, really. Only now I own a proper voice. I don't need to listen to her rants about giant birds who understand human language or monsters of the lake. I can ignore her tales of bloodsucking demons and wraiths with corpse candles. What's more: I understand the appeal of her delusions now, more intimately than she will ever know. I understand the psychology behind her need for them, and it's almost enough for me to pity her.

But willful ignorance was always a difficult vice for me to swallow, and here, in this last forgotten place, so backwards that the locals speak of dragons and giants and the fair folk of Wales, the *Tylwyth Teg*, as though they merely vanished from their shores instead of having never existed at all, ignorance is rote.

"Not wild enough for 'em," said Mr. Swales often when I was a child. He was the farmer who rented our cottage to us. He up and died, demanding to be interred in the proper Welsh way. He had a list of instructions, which, of course, my mother carried out with a focused devotion that seemed odd to most of the town. They, no doubt, suspected the two had been lovers, but that wasn't it. They simply shared a proud and profound belief in the old ways, an affinity for a Wales long gone and a Wales that had, perhaps, never existed. They were both stubborn in their belief and practice.

One night, well after sunset, Mr. Swales came to our door, his face ashen. "I've seen a *toili*, Van," he said, stepping over the threshold. "I saw the *canwyll corff*...the flame was red."

My mother went pale but said nothing.

"I'll hear the *Cyhyraeth* tonight. I feel it in my bones."

My mother shooed me away and went to fetch her secret stash of whiskey and she and Mr. Swales talked low and close by the fireplace late into the night. Later, when I asked my mother to explain, she said that a *toili* was a phantom funeral—a procession of the dead.

"And the *canwyll*?"

She grew solemn. "The *canwyll corff*. The corpse candle, carried by the dead. If the flame burns white, it foreshadows the death of a woman. If it burns red, it foretells the death of a man. If it glows only faintly, then a child will pass."

Even then, I had laughed, and my mother scolded me, telling me to respect "what I had no mind to understand."

Later, I learned that the *Cyhyraeth* was a skeletal wraith, an ill portent, said to expel a disembodied moaning. Those who were marked for death would hear it echoing through the night, far in the distance, but also right at their ear.

Mr. Swales passed away the next week, but rather than believe his grim prediction, I felt he had, in all likelihood, spooked himself into a heart attack. Rationality has always been my greatest gift.

Mr. Swales had no family, and so it fell to me to wash his old-man body as it was laid out on our kitchen table, while my mother hurried through the house covering mirrors and closing curtains. When I was done, about to throw out the mucky dead-man water from the bowl, she caught my wrist at the sink with a sharp gasp.

"Never throw out the water," she whispered fervently, her eyes wide and scandalized. "Place it beneath the table. After he's in the earth, we can wash it away."

I had rolled my eyes again and done as she commanded, hating with every fiber of my being her silly, superstitious fears and rituals. Couldn't she see this was all ridiculous?

She burned sweet sage and lavender from the garden and brought me fresh lemongrass to tuck all around Mr. Swales's sagging body.

Because the corpse was never to be left alone, not even for a moment, and because no one came to pay respects to the old farmer who, like my mother, was considered a little batty, it was up to us to sit with him in shifts, one after another, for almost three whole days. In the evenings, my mother insisted we sit together and drink mulled wine or honey mead and eat bread and cheese.

"In his honor," she said, dry-eyed. This was no emotional tribute. It was simply tradition and must be adhered to. Duty. Obligation. It seemed so cold and empty to me, a lie's benign sister.

He began to smell. At first a subtle sour flavoring of the air, which my mother failed to notice. But then, it got worse, and he gained a sheen over his skin that made me dry-retch every time I saw it. I was horrified and fascinated and when my mother took over the deathwatch, I went to my room to research the phases of decay. It was summer then, and by the morning of day three, a blood-tinged foam had begun to leak from Mr. Swales's orifices. Only then Mum announced it was time for the funerary services to be called. That morning, we knelt by his body for the *Gwylnos*, a ritual usually held the night before the funeral in which stories of the good nature of the deceased would be passed around like Christmas presents. Instead, we spoke a few rote prayers.

After he was taken away, the house reeked for weeks. We never used the kitchen table again, and eventually, after scrubbing the stubborn wooden fibers failed to get me anywhere near it, Mum had us chop it to pieces and burn it in the adjacent field.

"It's a little Scandinavian, isn't it?" I asked on the night of the burning. "The fire? Would Mr. Swales approve?"

My mother's lips thinned but she didn't give in to my barb and I regretted it. Mr. Swales had been her friend, in his strange way. And she was mourning in hers. We learned, in the months following, that he had sold off his farmland and left the cottage and garden to my mother.

His funeral was small and quiet. Along with us, a few straggling members of the village attended, perhaps feeling guilty for not honoring the requests of one of their own, or maybe fearing his revenant. That afternoon, my mother sat alone on the front step of the house, as tradition demanded, waiting for members of the community to bring bread, butter, or beer as tribute, ready to reply, *"Diolch a cymerwch attoch,"* but once again, no one came.

The whole thing was sad and lonely and horrible and even now, standing here as a grown woman, I find myself heartsore for the isolated, empty life Mr. Swales led, wondering if my own mother will have anyone besides me to do the same for her.

When I die, I'll leave instructions for a quick cremation. No fuss. No burden. No torturous ceremony, no superstition. Just a body and a fire.

I try once more to make conversation. "How are you, anyway? How are things here?"

She clatters around with the dishes in the sink, but mutters over her shoulder, "Same as always."

No kidding. She's not making this easy.

"And money? How are you doing financially?"

I should get an award for bravery, for willfully stepping into this rabbit hole.

Mum's shoulders tense and I hold my breath. Here it comes. Some comment about Dad, about his death, about my abandonment...

"Fine."

"Fine? Really, Mum?"

She sighs. "As good as can be expected, Mina. What do you think? Without your father's income..."

"I could help," I offer quickly, knowing that this is something I *can* do, some way I can make amends.

She slams a pot into the soapy water in the sink, splashing herself and me. "I don't *want* your money, Wilhelmina."

My mother, as stubborn as ever. Once, when I was eleven or twelve, she walked around the house for a week with an iron nail in her mouth, even eating and drinking around it, as vengeance against a gossiping neighbor—who never spoke again.

"Okay, fine. Then maybe I can do things to help while I'm here."

She turns to consider me. "And how long might that be for?"

"I don't know yet. A week maybe."

"Aye, aye," she mutters, wiping her hands on her apron. "Except I have things perfectly under control. I've learned to get by alone."

I nod, knowing all too well just what she means.

5

When Lucy and I were kids, we'd look up at Ifori Estate and wonder what kind of people lived such an enchanted life. What did people who could afford those sweeping grounds and manicured lawns, who could live in a house with eighteen front-facing windows, and an indoor pool (or so we assumed) actually *look* like? They couldn't be from Tylluan, we decided. Surely they had to be a transplant from London or Paris, or far-flung Morocco?

"Filthy rich," Lucy said one particularly hot afternoon. Her arms were poking through the gates, which sat more than half a mile out from the house. Her arms were slung languidly across, as though by touching the air on the other side, she could somehow absorb their wealth via osmosis.

I leaned against the gate and wiped my forehead. "Bet they have a mini golf course."

"'Course they do. God, it's obscene."

I grinned at her. "You love it."

"Well, yeah." She grinned back, her eyes flashing. "One day, Mins. One day I'm going to live in that house and then I'll know I've made it."

"I believe you," I said, but I didn't. Not really. Aiming for

Ifori Estate was like aiming for Mount Olympus. We were mere mortals, for one, and for another, Olympus was a myth. People like us didn't get to places like that. Girls like us, especially. Somehow, I think she knew it.

But now, as I drive up the same private road we used to stare at with lazy, perfect longing, I'm hit with the amazement that Lucy did it. Lucy got into *that house*. She lives there. Here. She *is* those people now.

The drive leads to the white house everyone in the village can see from the bridge, a house we all know and recognize. Up close, however, it's even more impressive. Eighteen front-facing windows, yes, but two wings slightly behind reveal that the home is much larger than many locals suppose. Sweeping in every sense of the word. I imagine Lucy floating in that (probable) indoor pool, in designer swimwear, sporting sunglasses far too large for her face. Bug-like. I imagine her attending galas and making generous donations to all kinds of needy organizations. She always suited that kind of lifestyle, even when she didn't.

I lift the knocker on the door and let it fall, expecting a butler to answer like some old film, but it's Lucy who opens it. Her lips fall apart at the sight of me, and she blinks dumbly for several seconds. The air whooshes out of me and I can't do anything but stare.

"Fuck me," she says at last, crossing her arms.

She looks the same, and yet completely different. It's her face, but she's dressed it up differently. Gone is the bright purple lipstick and crimped hair. Now she is wearing pale white trousers and a white shirt. Her hair is pulled up in a loose bun, tendrils of blond framing her face, the picture of a "Tory wife."

"What are you doing here?"

"I got your cry for help."

"I beg your pardon?"

"The email you sent?"

Something flickers across her face—something I can't decipher. Then she nods. "Of course."

She smells of expensive moisturizer, subtle and elegant, but underneath I think I can still detect the briny scent of a wild ocean. Maybe she hasn't been tamed utterly.

"Well," she says, swallowing. That tiny movement of her throat is the only indication that she feels anything other than confident about my presence. This close, I notice that she's a little drawn in the skin, pinched beneath carefully applied makeup. She's gone heavy with the blush, but there are deep burrows beneath her eyes. She's thin.

"Well, come on then," she says, ushering me inside with a sweep of her arm, her eyebrows so high they could be hitched to her hairline.

She leads me down a bright hallway painted a pale yellow, fringed with startlingly white cornices and moldings on the ceiling. Glancing back, she catches me looking.

"Yes," she drawls, continuing on. "All original. The house is Georgian, but parts of the property are far older. The section we're in was rebuilt in 1710 by the Chancellor of St. Asaph.

"That fireplace," she adds, "is marble. Also an original feature, designed by the architect Joseph Turner. The plasterwork is in the style of Robert Adam."

When her back is turned, I roll my eyes. A young woman in uniform rounds the corner. She catches me and suppresses a smile as she passes.

"Cariad, dear," Lucy says, stopping her. "Have some tea brought to the blue parlor."

The girl curtseys. "Yes, ma'am."

Does Lucy really think I've forgotten she's the same girl who drew on the Arriva bus with permanent marker and was subsequently escorted off by the police? Or that she and Quincey used to have competitions to see who could yack their spit the farthest? One point for hitting a rock placed three feet away, and two points if your gob could stick to the window of the corner shop.

We continue on, then turn left into a pale blue room. The aforementioned blue parlor, I suppose. It's sparsely furnished; two white sofas with blue throw pillows contrast with the pale blue walls, and one darker blue armchair sits in the corner for a pop of definition. Pale gold wall sconces sit mounted beside individually lit gild-framed oil paintings. And, yes. Another "original marble fireplace," just like the one she so smugly told me about in the corridor. If it weren't so fucking elegant, it would be gauche.

Lucy raises her eyebrows even farther, smiling in that new, self-satisfied way, and gestures for me to take a seat.

I take the white seat Lucy offers, looking around at the space. I wonder how much of it is the same as when we were children and how much of the decor is her own doing. I can't tell. Here and there the room is elegantly touched with pottery and house-plants in warm beiges and hints of peacock blue that make the space seem alive. Having never known Lucy as a grown woman, I have no way of knowing if this is her taste or not. At seven-teen, she tended toward tawdry colors and patterns, purposely mismatching everything to stand out and, no doubt, aggravate her mother, who didn't give much of a monkey's arse about any-thing or anyone unless it was screaming in her face. So, Lucy screamed with colors and fabrics.

We sit somewhat uncomfortably, waiting for the tea to arrive.

"I was drinking," she says eventually, after a too-long silence.

"Pardon?"

"When I sent the email."

"I see."

A pause.

"I googled you," she says.

"You said. I googled you too."

"Were the results entertaining?" She cocks her head, chin

lifted in a challenge. She sniffs and flicks a strand of hair in a way that is entirely new—did she pick that up from her husband, I wonder?

I gesture. "Mostly it was about Arthur and Ifori."

The barb is there, and she feels it.

"I didn't find anything about your husband," she returns, leaning back, waiting expectantly.

"Oh God." I laugh, leaning back as well. "I'm *far* too busy for a husband."

"I see."

She plasters a rigid smile on her face as the same young woman from the corridor rolls in with a trolley with tea and *bara brith*.

"Thank you, Cariad."

Cariad nods and throws a little smile in my direction. "Enjoy."

"Help yourself," Lucy says, picking up the teapot and pouring two cups. Proper again. "I don't have any of that bizarre tea your mother used to make us drink, but Darjeeling should do."

"It's fine, thank you."

I take the cup she offers, ignoring the milk and sugar. She adds both and we sit back to drink and eat, observing each other. I can hardly summon an appetite, but I force myself to chew, swallow, chew and swallow. Delicate china, finer than my expensive but practical gray set. We're like two amateur actors in a play we don't recall auditioning for.

After a long silence populated only with the sounds of quiet lip-smacking and self-conscious sips, I lean forward. "Why did you ask me here, Lucy?"

She laughs dismissively. "It was a drunken message. They happen."

"If you were drunk it means your inhibitions were down. I was obviously on your mind."

"Psychoanalyzing me?"

I shrug. *"In vino, veritas."*

Lucy laughs derisively. "All of a sudden you give a shit?"

A pricking at my neck and an itch in my left palm alerts me to a tic rising. "I'm just trying to be a friend."

Lucy laughs. "I've got friends."

I sigh and a silence falls, thick and heavy between us. "What do you want from me? Am I here to grovel or to help?"

She's breathing heavily now. "I want an explanation."

Of course.

This was all a ploy to get an answer for why I left all those years ago. Why I abandoned her.

The only way out is through. I know this because I'd give my patients the same advice, and Lucy is my patient now. "Something...happened to me before I left."

Lucy frowns, some of the anger leaving her face. "What do you mean?"

I swallow, the palms of my hands and the scar on my neck itching. "I prefer not to talk about it." I say nothing, but this is Lucy, my former best friend and partner in crime, the person who once knew me better than I knew myself. Something changes in her face, some kind of understanding—of me, of the past, of events that took place more than a decade ago. A realization that none of this was about her at all.

"Oh my God... Mina." Before I know what's happening, she's pulled me into a hug. "Why didn't you tell me?" she whispers.

"It's in the past," I declare as convincingly as I can, but there's something so comforting about being back in her arms. I realize all this time I've been afraid of telling her, of how saying the truth aloud might tear me apart. But with Lucy, I never had to say anything at all.

"You stupid wally," she says into my shoulder. "I would have helped you leave."

I close my eyes and let myself feel the warmth of her embrace.

When she pulls away, there are tears in her eyes. "Life isn't always what we expect it to be, is it?"

Jonathan Harker's face flashes in my mind, but I shove it aside.

Since then, I've spent the last twelve years scheduling my days with regimented efficiency. Nothing happens that I don't plan on first. Not anymore.

"Now, why don't you tell me what's been going on?"

Her sigh is short and heavy, and for a moment I really think she's going to make a joke, brush it aside, deny it. This was all just a ploy to get me to finally come home. What else could she do, after all, when I refused to answer any of her calls and then went silent for more than a decade?

Lucy sighs and seems to make a decision about something.

"I'm sick. I'm… I think. I'm not sure." She holds herself, a gesture I've seen on so many of the women I've treated, and now she has my attention. My brain begins to note things I'd missed before because she's, well…Lucy. Holding herself. Scanning the room at intervals. Checking the access points. A twitch in her lower left eyelid. And then, of course, there's how thin she seems. The thick makeup and heavy-handed blush. Lucy was a dab hand at makeup, always was. What is she hiding?

I sit back. "Tell me what's happening."

Her hands squeeze her upper arms and let go, squeeze and release, over and over. Self-soothing patterns.

"I'm losing blocks of time," she says. "I'm always tired. I have nightmares. I wake up in strange places, sometimes out in the garden. Last night I woke up opening the latch on the full-length window in my bedroom. If I hadn't woken, I might have…" She swallows and glances away, her eyes glazing over. "I have a weird rash on my body, and I'm so frazzled and alarmed all the time. Skittish. I never want to go out. And… I'm just… I'm… so weak."

I'm not entirely astonished when she bursts into tears. I get up from the sofa and go to the door, gently closing it so we can be alone and she can feel safer. Her parlor is now my office.

"Have you taken any new medication lately? Anything that could cause side effects or an allergic reaction?" I ask.

Lucy shakes her head no.

"What you're describing," I say, coming back to the sofa, "sounds like stress responses." People are always less alarmed by stress being the cause of their pain.

She wipes at her tears, smearing makeup. "I don't... I don't know what that means."

"It could mean that you're trying to process something that's happened. Something painful. It could be PTSD," I offer. "Losing time, weakness, fatigue, nightmares...those are classic trauma symptoms." I pause. "Has anything happened lately? Anything you've found difficult to manage?"

"I... I don't remember."

"That's okay. Tell me a bit about your life. Just day to day. Tell me what you do with yourself. Catch me up."

Lucy exhales, apparently glad to move on to easier topics. "I wake at eight and see Arthur off to work. Then I get ready for the day. I usually have meetings to attend or events to organize. That might mean going to the club for lunch with the ladies on the committee, or it could mean emailing organizations from my home office. I can get rather busy."

She adds the last part with the air of someone trying to prove herself, and once again she rubs at her arms. "We host a lot of charity dinners and events. I have to ensure donations are made, catering is organized, locations are approved, press informed... there's a lot to it."

"I'm sure there is," I say, genuine. "I once attended a medical charity ball. The planning it must have taken..."

"It's a full-time job," Lucy says, laughing, but more tears fall.

"Is it stressful?"

Again, her arms wrap around herself. I note that her manicure is chipped, like she's been biting at her nails. "No more than I would find any event like this."

"I'd find it stressful," I offer.

"I suppose...the frequency of them is a bit much sometimes.

I mean, how many galas can you really get away with throwing in a single year? And sometimes Arthur wants them held in different countries last minute to better suit a client or benefactor. I once had to organize a gala in Dubai with two days' notice. It was a nightmare trying to sort things out. And the prices…" She laughs faintly. "Although that doesn't worry him."

"That sounds like a lot."

"If there were less of them, or if Arthur and I could take some time away…it might be nice."

I had wanted to phone Lucy so many times over the years. She was never far from my mind, even when I wanted her to be, even when I knew I deserved her to be. The life I imagined she was living isn't far from the one she's describing, only in my mind she was incandescently happy. A perfect rags-to-riches cliché.

"Have you seen your GP about it? Ruled out any kind of medical condition, like sleep apnea?"

Lucy nods. "I had a blood test a while ago. It came back normal."

"I'd have a repeat done, just in case. To rule out something like anemia, diabetes, or—" I hesitate.

"Or what?"

It's an awkward question, only because it's her. "Could you be pregnant?"

She smiles. "No."

I nod, not wanting to pry further. "But it could be something else. You should get checked out."

"I suppose I could. Would anemia or diabetes explain the sleepwalking?"

"No, but it could explain the fatigue, the rash. Have you had heart palpitations at all?"

"Yes."

"Headaches?"

"Yes."

"Give me your hands," I say, reaching for hers. When she puts them in mine, they're as cold as ice.

"I think you might be anemic, Luce. I'd get another blood test as soon as possible."

"I suppose I could phone to book an appointment this afternoon." She looks happy, so relieved. "Could it really be that simple?"

I hesitate. The loss of time, the sleepwalking…none of that is explained by anemia.

"It's a start," I say, and her face falls. It feels like there's something she's not telling me.

"I just wish I could remember what I've forgotten, if anything." She scrunches her eyes as if trying, and more tears scatter over her cheeks. "I…" She hesitates. "I don't remember emailing you."

"That's okay. We'll work through this slowly. I'll see how I can help."

"You'll stay?"

She looks so like her old self with black mascara smudged across her face that a second image of her at seventeen flashes, transposed over this one. The seventeen-year-old Lucy says, *You'll come with me?* Her eyes just as wide and hopeful.

Unlike twelve years ago, this time I say, "Yes."

<u>Blood Rites: True Spiritualism and Folklore of Wales</u> (1837)
by Garthewin Helig Jones

Beware and do not tempt the attentions of the evil one, master of death, nor his stygian lord, the Arglwydd Gwaed, who roams the midnight paths, seeking out heedless travelers. Beneath the roar of wind and ocean, the grotesque howl of the Gwyllgi, the black hound, with its baleful breath, or the pwcas, wicked-minded beings, which oft carry the form of a wild colt, are telltale signs he is near. Carry rowan berries in your pocket and braided hawthorn about your neck, and should you hear the disembodied moaning of one of his Cyhyraeth, or see the luminous corpse candle, by wood, and field and mountain, keep to walking and do not turn back, no matter how it bays or cries, lest your eye fall upon him and take breath no more. Should you meet a crossroad, hold your breath until you have passed—the Arglwydd Gwaed craves living blood above all.

6

When I wake up in the morning, I feel lighter than I have in years, despite being in my childhood bedroom, which hasn't changed since I skipped town at seventeen. At least Mum kept it. I stretch luxuriously, watching sun motes through the crack in the curtains. When I got back to the house last night, I found a curt note from Mum telling she had "given up waiting" and gone to bed.

I'd stayed up and scrubbed her bathroom from floor to ceiling, which took four hours, but was worth it. Now I know I can get up, complete my ablutions, go for my run, and re-shower with peace of mind before I scrub everything again. The second time will be much faster, maybe even faster than it is in my shower at home, since this one is over the bathtub and won't involve me scrubbing hundreds of individual tiles.

Mum isn't awake when I reach the kitchen, but she's left me another note on the fridge. I guess this is our new form of communication.

Mina,
Was up late for the Full Moon ritual cleanse and then
waiting for you.

Don't wake me.
Please pop to the village and get some bread, milk, and
eggs.
Money on table.

Fantastic. I'm twelve again. It all comes rushing back in a horrible wave.

I was going to go for a run anyway, I reason. I don't see why I can't run all the way to the village for her supplies and back. Eggs for breakfast would be good, and what better way to break this icy veneer she's wearing than French toast?

So, I head out, locking the door behind me even though I know Mum never does.

The morning air is cool on my face and in my lungs, the frost heavy and white on the hedges. This is my favorite time of day, the hours before the crisp fades into the bustle of another Monday. Halfway to the village, I see a pair of vaguely familiar faces. The old ladies stop and scowl at me as I pass, their dogs yapping and straining at taut leashes.

"Isn't that...?" one of them says.

The other makes a sign to ward off the devil. I jog faster. This village. This fucking village. Nothing has changed.

The run is longer than the ones I'm used to, and by the time I reach the newsagent on Market Street, I'm a sweating mess. I wonder, dimly, if Mr. Wynn still owns the shop when I head inside.

And yes, he does. Hugely aged, Mr. Wynn sits behind the counter reading the morning paper. He doesn't look up when the little gold bell over the door announces my entrance. I wonder if he remembers the summers I worked here, stacking the shelves for a bit of pocket money.

I hastily grab a loaf of bread and see that the same Tylluan village logo is stuck onto the side. Nothing here ever seems to change. The milk bottles are still the old-fashioned glass kind,

the ones you only see on London doorsteps from the households
getting milk delivered. I add half a dozen eggs to my haul and
head for the till.

Mr. Wynn doesn't look up when I place the items down, and
I note a newspaper clipping pasted to the ancient till he sits behind: "Local Girl Missing."

Below it, a photo of the girl beside another of a familiar face.
I squint and lean forward to read.

"'We are doing everything we can to find Seren Evans,' local
police inspector Quincey Morris said in a statement."

Lucy's ex-girlfriend, Quincey, looks calm and confident in
the photo, and I shake my head, astonished. Quincey, usually
the first to join the lads when they'd ripped off the corner shop
for a beer or two, is a *copper*. Mad.

"Good morning, Mr. Wynn," I say, when he still hasn't ac-
knowledged me.

He harrumphs in surprise and looks up. "Well, well."

"Just the basics today."

"The prodigal daughter returns," he croaks, staring at me,
his eyes rheumy and full of judgment.

"I suppose so."

"And I suppose the great big world didn't meet your lofty
expectations?"

I suppress a sigh. "Not at all. I live in London. I'm just visiting."

He huffs, punching the prices into the till manually. No up-
grades for this little corner shop, then. Of course not.

"Snooty."

"Pardon?"

"Four-fifty," he says without pause.

I dump the coins Mum gave me, exactly four pounds fifty,
onto the counter.

"Could I have a carrier bag, please?"

"Five pence."

I don't have it, and I suspect he knows that, given my Lycra joggers and lack of pockets.

"Never mind."

I grab the groceries, annoyed at him and this village and at myself for not thinking about a stupid bag. Now I'll have to run home holding these to my chest.

I'm a psychiatrist, a professional of the mind, and I let that grumpy old man get to me, just like I always did when I was a kid. *Put the milk in straight, girl. Stack the chocolate alphabetically, girl. You're doing it wrong, girl.* I'm so distracted that I pull open the door and step out onto the street without looking up, slamming hard into a broad chest as I do.

I drop everything and watch with a horrible sense of inevitability as the eggs and milk bottle shatter on the pavement. The bread rolls under a van parked nearby.

"Shit!"

I glare at the fleece-covered wall of muscle in front of me, only to meet familiar gray eyes.

All sensation leaves me in a whoosh. *"Jonathan?"*

Jonathan Harker's eyes are the only thing that hasn't changed in twelve years. The rest of him...his face... I try not to stare at the grisly scars that have split his once-lovely visage from left temple to right-side chin, pulling his mouth down into a perpetual grimace. Some are livid and red, others twisted, a shiny silver.

Those eyes widen for a fraction of a second, and then narrow, his heavy brows descending like shutters.

"Hi," I add feebly.

He doesn't reply, but he doesn't move out of my way either.

"Mina," he says at last, his voice graveled.

My throat closes. What's happened to him? Something terrible, and painful. I almost loose a sob but catch it at the last moment by focusing on the other ways he's changed.

Like how he's grown up. His neck is broader, his shoulders

wider, and a layer of tempting stubble spatters his cheeks in the patches of skin that aren't knotted or shiny with scars. There aren't many of those... A wave of horror descends again when I process how beautiful he used to be, how perfect I always found his face, but I focus on how tall he is now instead, forcing my lips not to tremble.

I open my mouth to say something, not quite sure what that something is, when he edges past me and into the store, deliberately stepping over the eggy, milky mess on the pavement.

"H-how are you?" I manage, my voice breaking.

He stops, considering, then turns back to me. "Well. You?"

I nod dumbly. "I'm back in the village for a visit with Mum."

"Are you staying at the old house?"

"Yes. It's like nothing's changed."

But of course it has...and seeing Jonathan proves that. I stare for a beat too long. He clocks my eyes scattering over his mauled features and stiffens.

Jonathan and I had been in school together, him a couple of years above me, and I'd liked him a lot. Lucy had known it, of course, so one particular night, during one of the regular beach parties, she'd pointed him out to me across the fire. "Nice face," she'd said, which just seems cruel now. I'd gone scarlet, but hadn't disagreed. I suppose it had been confirmation for her. Mina Murray fancied Jonathan Harker.

I'd been fifteen at the time. Jonathan, at seventeen, was loud, confident, the leader of the lads. He was rich off the farmland his *tad* owned, but didn't rub it in anyone's face. Instead, he'd forked out for hot chips from the beach café, bringing cones of them over to us where we'd loitered near the skip in which the bonfire blazed. One of his mates, Lee, carried a bag of Cokes, and the two of them had doled them out casually like it was nothing. On a frigid beach night, though, it was what made the gathering feel safe and prosperous. *He'd* made the gatherings feel safe and prosperous. In a village of nothing and nowhere, he'd made Tylluan beach feel like our secret. Our clubhouse, sans house.

The lads had brought alcohol with them, a bottle of cheap vodka pilfered from a parent's stash, and we were getting loose and lightheaded, sitting in clumps near the skip-fire and passing it around. We'd been toasty warm, outside and in, full bellied, hopped up on carbs and booze.

It was Lucy that suggested Truth or Dare.

When Jonathan's turn came, he'd picked truth.

"Tell me who you fancy," Lucy had said, and I was horrified.

Until, of course, Jonathan answered, with perfect equanimity, "She's sitting right next to you."

The lads had whooped and fell about laughing, but Jonathan just stared at me, his gaze solid and unflinching, a half smile on his lips.

"Cocky," Quincey had muttered, but I couldn't help but grin when Lucy whispered, "It's destiny" in my ear. Jonathan didn't care what anyone thought. He was his own man, even at seventeen.

We were together for two perfect years. I still remember the way his lips felt on mine, the smell of him, the taste of him—

"Jonathan—"

"I have to go."

I frown and watch as this familiar yet unrecognizable man turns back into the shop.

I shake my head, getting down on my knees to try to fish the only grocery I have left unharmed—my bread—from under the van. I snag it between my index and middle finger and scoot it out, still befuddled and thrown by Jonathan.

The shop door opens and closes again, tinkling as it does, and Jonathan strides past without a word. I want to reach out to him, to beg him to understand, but the man striding away is a stranger.

II.

The invisible weight of the business card feels heavy in her clutch, the call of the void. Magnetic. An opportunity. A job. A new life.

She had gone back to the grimy flat she shared with three others and dialed the number on the card, hugging the phone to her face like a lifeline.

You'll be picked up tonight from your flat.

The voice had been deep. Alluring.

When the other girls asked what she was getting dolled up for, she lied and said she wanted to go out again. Two nights in a row? Alone? "Party animal," they said. "You'll get into trouble," they said. "She's worse than we were," they said.

Confidence leaked from every one of her glittering pores as she pulled on her dress and carefully applied fake lashes. Confidence. She was drunk on it. Until she was standing on the pavement outside her flat realizing that she never gave the man on the phone her address.

Her disappointment was crushing.

It was a joke. A hoax. A prank.

But now a black 4X4 with tinted windows pulls up beside her just as she is turning away. She frowns, uncertain.

The door opens on a dark interior. "Jennifer."

She nods, dumbfounded. Blindsided. How did they know where she lives?

"Get in."

She hesitates, glancing back. But what was all this for if not to take a chance, a leap of faith?

When she gets into the car, she can no longer see the street. The back of the vehicle isn't just tinted; it's been entirely blocked out, giving her no indication of where they are going. The front of the car is closed off from the back seat, and it feels like a coffin.

The darkness is complete, but she knows there is someone sitting beside her. Is it the same man from the pub?

She is dropped in front of a narrow alley.

"That way," the man's voice says, and a gloved hand points her on.

She doesn't know where she is. There are only two choices. Go where he says, or get back into the car.

She walks on.

At the end of the alley she comes to a pair of black doors bearing the same symbol that was on the business card. There's not a soul in sight. Now she's feeling less certain. A chill creeps along her spine, some inbuilt sense that all girls have, that she shouldn't be here. That she should run. That she's come too far. The door opens before she can turn away, and she's ushered into a dark corridor. A side room.

A woman in a mask that does little to hide her middle years strips the girl out of her best dress, one she got from ASOS at a reasonable price, tossing it aside like a piece of rubbish. And it is, the girl thinks. She is getting the beginning of a sense of things. This is the tip of the iceberg.

Her fake lashes are peeled off, her face scrubbed clean. She no longer looks the way she intended, but bare. Fresh. Young.

She is put into a silk dress that feels like air, sliding over her skin like a soft water spring. She is oiled, perfumed, fed things she couldn't name, watered with champagne and what she is told is Dalmore 62. It means nothing to her, beyond that it is whiskey, and bitter. She asks for more champagne instead, and receives it, golden bubbles bursting on her eager tongue. It goes to her head quickly, so that by the time she is escorted from the tiny book-lined changing room, through labyrinthine corridors and twisting teak staircases, she couldn't find her way out if she wanted to.

This is reckless. She knows it. She loves it.

Men in masks stare as she passes, and she feels that intoxicating thing again, that thing she has never had before: power. Every man here has his eyes on her. Wanting. She is floating among the clouds, taking drinks and canapés and strange substances whenever offered. She is touched, gently on the hand, the cheek, the shoulder, fingers brushing her skin chastely, with reverence, passed around like a rare piece of art for admiration.

She wanders over to an ornate bar where men whisper into the ears of beautiful women. They glance at her, every one of them, and she wonders: *Why am I here? What is the job? To look beautiful?*

A young woman leans against the bar to her left. "Another," she says, placing a glass on the gleaming surface.

She turns to Jennifer. "Isn't this wild?" she says, a conspiratorial smile lifting her lips. "Paying us to *flirt?*"

Jennifer arches a brow. "Is that what they pay for? Only that?"

"Yeah. And I'll do it gladly." She grins. "I'm Chloe by the way."

"Jennifer." It's getting easier to lie.

Shadows grow in the corners of things, turning the world muggy and soft, and she laughs and dances and feels her immense beauty, Chloe beside her just as lovely.

A minute or an eternity later, a man comes for Chloe.

She kisses Jennifer on the cheek. "See you later."

She watches as Chloe is led away.

Some time later, she is escorted from the winding, twisting rooms, away from the glittering splendor, into cold night air. She has no sense of time or place, but the sky is open above her. There is the black 4X4, and she is bustled inside.

He is sitting across from her on the seat. His face is a mask, hiding something terrible and beautiful beneath. When he smiles, she wants to scream even as a warmth spreads between her legs. Terror and arousal commingled into one aroma that is inescapable.

She cannot speak. But he can.

"Good evening," he says.

7

I drive over to Lucy's house again, a box of wine sloshing on the seat next to me. I chuckle mirthlessly. Lucy used to think they were the height of sophistication. I remember one summer when she begged me to try to steal one from a Tesco by putting it under my hoodie and faking pregnancy. Her argument had been that my face was the most trustworthy, and that no one would dare bothering a pregnant girl.

Jonathan had been with us, and he'd refused to let that particular shenanigan happen, saving me, I suspect, from having to refuse Lucy, who had a temper on the best of days. Instead, he'd gone into the shop, spoken to one of the girls who worked there, and led us around the back where, not five minutes later, she appeared with the boxed wine under her arm.

"Careful not to get caught," she said, winking at Jonathan, and we had dutifully and somewhat embarrassedly said we wouldn't.

We got sloshed on the beach that day and watched the sun go down, laughing and dancing, our mouths tasting of cheap wine and vinegar.

This time when I knock on Lucy's door, I'm greeted by the young woman who brought us tea the last time I visited.

"Mrs. Holmswood will be with you shortly," she says, her voice sweet and high.

Mrs. Holmswood. So strange for her not to be Lucy Westenra anymore. I've always been and will always be Mina Murray.

I'm led to a smaller sitting room and left to my own devices. I wander the space for a while, taking in the photos: Lucy standing next to a larger, slightly red-faced man. There again, the two of them in their wedding attire. Lucy looks beautiful, her hair pulled up and back, dotted with what appears to be diamond pins that glint in the light. Her dress is elegantly formfitting with long lace sleeves and a sweetheart neckline. She is turned to smile at a very proud, younger Arthur, in three-quarter profile, revealing the drop back of her gown. She looks radiantly happy.

And I wasn't there to see it.

An uncomfortable prick in the corner of my eye tells me it's time for the viewing to stop. I take a seat by the tall window and stare out at the manicured grounds. They're a lush green, even now in the fading September light.

The peculiar sensation of me being the patient awaiting therapy comes over me, and I firmly remind myself that *I* am the therapist. Still…it's been a while since I had any kind of personal life, and I'm out of practice at not having barriers between my patients and myself.

This is not a social call. I eye the wine and wonder if I should take it back to the car before Lucy arrives, but get caught up in this strange feeling of…something. A warmth at the idea of having my own person to talk to.

"Mina! I'm so sorry. Cariad only just told me you were here!" She walks into the room laughing, still radiant, her arms open.

I freeze for a moment, not knowing if I should stand or not, but she is over at my chair in three long strides and has bent over me for an intimate hug.

The box of wine at my feet sloshes in its box-locked bladder.

"Oh—" Lucy spots it. And then her face splits open and she

laughs. "Oh God! I remember! You didn't bring that in under your top, did you?"

"But of course I did. Beware Greeks?" I offer, grinning.

That familiar *something* inside clicks into place again, comfortable, and I remember what this feels like. Laughing over something stupid with a friend, but once again it's undercut with a pang of sadness. I never made another friend after Lucy. Not a single one. My life at Oxford was lonely, caught up in studies, most of my time spent in the library and lectures. Early bedtimes, early-morning starts. I had taken on three work placements—anything to *not think*. The cleaning tic had started there. Others had followed later.

"Wait right there," Lucy says, hurrying from the room.

I stare at the carpet, at the fading spots her heels have left behind, and try to swallow down these rising emotions. They're all taking me by surprise, but I don't have time for them. I'm here to assess her, not bring up past feelings that I clearly have no ability to cope with.

Lucy returns with two mugs, waggling her eyebrows at me.

It's my turn to laugh. "God, I forgot that we always drank out of mugs, pretending they were fancy wineglasses."

"Except the day at the beach with the box wine, remember? We had turns holding it up for each other and turning the pourer."

A bubble of laughter ripples between us.

"It was like we were gurgling it," I say, giggling.

"Gllullullullu!" Lucy says, miming the movement.

"Jonathan had more wine on him than in him at the end, I think," I say, remembering the easy way he had laughed back then.

"God, I was so worried when I woke up the next morning because I was convinced the wine I spilled would turn my hair purple."

"Not the hair." I laugh, my eyes wide. "Anything but the hair!"

I crack open the spout at the edge of the box like an old pro, while Lucy nudges a sitting chair closer to mine. She sits down with a long sigh and holds out the cups expectantly.

Once we both have a mugful in hand, we turn to stare at the grounds almost at the same time.

Lucy takes a sip and sputters.

"Jesus! That's revolting."

I sniff mine and pull a face.

"No, no way," Lucy says. "You brought the stuff—you have to drink some too!"

I take a tiny sip and watery vinegar pricks at my throat. "Oh God."

"How did we drink this crap?" She gets up and takes my mug from me, then walks over to the window, opens it, and throws it out.

"Let's call our younger selves idiots and have a real drink."

She dumps the cups on a radiator cover by the door and heads over to a minibar on the adjacent table.

"What'll it be?"

I had intended to stay sober, even with the kiddie wine, but... *bugger it.*

"Whiskey, if you have it."

"In buckets."

She pours a healthy measure into two tumblers and brings them over. She hands me mine, then kicks off her shoes and folds herself into the armchair.

I try not to be too conspicuous as I check the glass for cleanliness and, satisfied, take a sip. It goes down smooth.

"Better," Lucy agrees.

We sit in companionable silence for a few moments. My eye drifts once more to Lucy's wedding photo, their shining faces.

"You look so happy in that photo… You know, you've not told me much about him."

"Arthur? Haven't I?"

I run my finger along the edge of the glass, wondering if I'm prying.

"He's away on business, but he'll be back—" she checks the gold watch on her wrist "—in about four hours, I should think."

"What does he do for work?"

Lucy gets up to refill her drink. She nods to the decanter in question, and I show her my still fairly full glass.

"He's got his own logistics company," she says, coming to sit down on the sofa again.

"How did you meet? At some swanky club in Conwy?"

She laughs, her gaze turning inward. "Yeah. I was eighteen or nineteen and I heard about the club from a mate of mine. I got dressed up, threw caution to the wind, and walked in like I belonged."

I smile. "You were always good at that."

"Thank you. I only wanted to dance, to drink some champagne, and have a few canapés before I left to go back to my hovel. Arty found me by the piano. I'd lost some of my nerve and was hiding."

My brain stutters on his nickname. *Arty?* "That's hard to believe. You? Losing confidence?"

She glances at me sideways, then away. "It's been known to happen over the years. He asked me to dance. I was terrified because I thought it was so obvious I didn't belong. My idea of elegance back then had some refining to do. But Art…he made me feel welcome."

"Did he find out you weren't supposed to be there?"

"Of course. He knew the whole time. It was *his* birthday party. His twenty-fifth. I suppose that's why he came up to me. When the dance was over, we talked for a while. I knew I had to get out of there, so I slipped away while he was making his birthday toast."

"How did he find you again?"

"He ran after me. Caught me near the exit and asked me to come to his house, *this* house, that weekend for lunch. So I did. I confessed that I'd gate-crashed and he confessed he'd known it the whole time."

She laughs again, blushing prettily at the memory. I wish I had been here to experience it with her.

I sip my drink without comment, glancing at the plethora of portraits on the mantel and then the oil painting of the two of them above the fireplace.

"I know," she says, grinning. "We're completely nauseating."

"Oh, just a little. And…no children."

She flicks the comment away with her hand. "Who the hell has time?"

"And you always hated children?" I offer.

"That too." She is silent for a moment, and then she shudders. "Ugh. Ew."

That gets a bark from me. It's just so…so *Lucy*. I put down my empty tumbler, noting how my head is becoming warm and loose. Time to rein it in.

"Did you end up going to university?"

Lucy shakes her head. A curl, gleaming, falls free of her clip. "Nope. I stayed here. Didn't get the grades. Just as well, or I wouldn't have met Arthur." Her voice turns soft and warm. "And he's the best thing that's ever happened to me."

I smile. "I can tell. You look happy. Really happy."

She bows her head, as though abashed. "Thank you."

"You know, we both got out of the village, in our own way."

She smiles. "Like we always said. You with uni and me with Arthur."

"Well, Arthur certainly beats Mark Rhuddlan," I say, deadpan, naming Lucy's Year Two boyfriend, who was ugly as a toad and who once drew her a crayon love-note signed with his snot.

Lucy freezes in her seat and then howls with laughter, snorting through her nostrils. "Mark Rhuddlan! That was a low blow, you cow!"

We scream with laughter, both of us convulsing on the sofas. The door opens and a worried-looking Cariad dashes in.

"Ma'am, are you—"

We both stop when we spot her, frozen like rabbits in headlights. And then we're crying with laughter again because she looks so appalled, more so when Lucy slips off the sofa, landing hard on her arse and rolling onto her back, legs in the air.

"I'll just leave you to it," Cariad says, withdrawing.

I decide I might as well join her down there and slide onto the carpet as well. Lucy sits up, leaning against the base of the sofa, kicks off her shoes, and puts her stockinged legs in my lap like she used to. Like nothing has changed, and I feel...safe.

"I haven't had a drink in years," she says, chuckling. "And now I wonder why."

"Because we both become giggling idiots when we're drunk."

"There are three types of drunk," she recites, as she always did as a teen. "The weepy drunk, the prankster drunk, and—"

"The giggly drunk!" we cry in unison.

"Two of a kind, you and me," she says, grinning. She reaches out with her hand. "I can live with that."

I take it in my own. "So can I."

"But I want to know about your love life, Mina Murray. I want to know every sordid detail, ever—"

Lucy stops talking and goes very still, eerily, slowly, like time winding down.

"Luce?"

Her lips tremble—she looks terrified, staring over my shoulder. A shock of fear pulses through me and I spin to look behind, but the room is empty. I'm suddenly feeling very sober.

When I turn back, she's shivering. I remember vividly what I'm here for.

I take her hands in mine and squeeze. "Lucy, it's Mina. Can you hear me?"

Nothing.

She stares at me, wiping at her face repeatedly, as though she's trying to brush away a hair, and then her mouth opens very slowly and keeps opening in a silent scream. Her eyes widen and a tear slips down her cheek before she collapses, muscles violently contracting. Awful, guttural, straining grunts spill from her mouth.

I drop to my knees and turn her onto her side, noting the time on my watch. She froths pink and I curse that I didn't react sooner. Hopefully she won't bite through her tongue. I soothe her by stroking her hair and shushing. She's likely not aware of me or anything else, but, like my reaction, it's instinctive.

A minute passes.

Two.

At three, I begin to worry. More than five minutes and it's a medical emergency. I reach for my phone, ready to dial 999, but her convulsions slow and then cease. She sighs and her breathing falls into a normal rhythm. Her skin regains some color.

This is not the first time I've witnessed a seizure. I'm certain it won't be the last. But it's different, isn't it, when it's your friend, someone you know and care about, when it's unexpected…

I check her pulse and use the throw on the sofa to wipe away the saliva around her mouth, checking while I'm at it that she's not hurt her tongue too badly. I put her into recovery position, and I wait. This postictal period could last several minutes.

How long has she been having seizures? There's a chance she's not aware of them. Her report of confusion and loss of time—how she didn't remember sending me that email—could simply be this: epileptic episodes. I try to remember if she'd mentioned a fall or head injury, but nothing rings a bell. I make a note to ask her. I try to recall our youth, of her ever having had a tonic-clonic, but no...there was nothing. We were almost always together, and she was the picture of perfect, effervescent health.

After a while, she moans, her eyes flicker open, and she tries to sit up. I let her, checking her palms. They are cold and clammy. She lifts a hand to tug weakly at her shirt and I see the rash she mentioned—and a horrified cry ripples up from my stomach. I almost scramble away, wanting to get as far from it as possible.

The rash, if that's what it is, is grotesque.

It is as though the scaffolding of her skin has collapsed beneath her pores. Dozens and dozens of minuscule black holes like ant-heads are scattered like gnarled confetti over her pink-and-purple skin. I can't look away, even as my skin crawls and my throat closes. It is utterly trypophobic. Horrifying.

I can't look away.

Lucy's breaths are shallow and rapid, and she is swaying a little as she sits. She lets out a sigh and my alarm bells go off again.

"Okay, it's all right," I murmur, laying the throw over her, ignoring the truth of why I'm doing it. "We're going to lie back down again, okay?"

"Mmm..." Lucy murmurs, trying to get up.

I push her gently down and check her pulse. It's fast, but strong.

"No," she groans, pushing me away. "Master—"

I try to hold on to her, but she rises swiftly once again with surprising strength. I clamber to my feet after her. She stares me dead in the face, leers perversely, then rips open her shirt in one swift movement, buttons flying, exposing two pale breasts and a smattering of a rash. I stand, frozen, as, with a horrifying grin, she begins to rake her manicured fingernails over her skin, leaving bloodied scratches in their wake. She laughs.

The blood shocks me back to myself, even as gorge rises in my throat. "Lucy!" I grab her hands, trying to stop her, but she wrenches free, holds my face, and runs her tongue up my cheek.

"Sweet," she whispers in my ear.

I yank back, staring with horror as she wanders toward the window, stumbling over her own feet. I hurry after her, but she collapses in a heap, convulsing for the second time.

"Shit, Lucy."

"Mas...please...please... M...na... Mina!"

And then another cry rends the air. *"Lucy!"*

The red-faced man—her husband, Arthur—is running across the room, a wild gleam in his eye. He's of medium height and build, his ginger hair thinning atop his head, with kind eyes that right now are filled only with concern.

"Lucy! Are you okay?"

"Mina," Lucy moans again, as Arthur almost collides with me.

"Is she okay? What's happened?"

"We need to get her to a hospital—now."

I'm about to try to lift her into my arms, make some gallant show of strength, or to yell at Arthur to phone an ambulance already, when her eyes snap open and, through a juddering nystagmus, she looks at me and sits up.

"I'm going to fucking kill you."

His breath plumes on the icy window.

Beyond the glass: two women.

Blood pumps, warm, tempting, through fragile veins and thin membranes. They sip from crystal glasses, moist tongues running over plump lips, fine hands running through silken hair. Their heat radiates through the glass like a homing beacon, driving him wild with a silent frenzy.

The urge to claim them is strong; their flesh, youthful and unmarred, smells sweet even from this distance. Follicles from their hair fall like crystals in the rising moonlight as they move and dance, their breath pulsing like ripples in the surface of reality.

He wants to collect their screams.

He swallows, and lingers, and watches.

And waits.

17 Fifield Road, Peckham, London, United Kingdom
02:43 am GMT

Anemic light flickers along the walls of a basement London
apartment complex, the echo of somnolent drips of water bounc-
ing over the gray drywall like death knells. The flats are the
shitty kind, boxy and damp, bedsits for those too poor to care
or too desperate to mind.

In 2B, a woman stares at the wall in front of her; her shrewd
eyes—rimmed with fine lines borne of scowls, not laughter—
search for patterns in the chaos. The dingy plaster is littered with
magazine articles, newspaper clippings, photos, forum printouts, hurriedly scribbled notes, maps by continent and city, and
Post-its of various colors, all connected by threads of red wool
that spider out from a single question-marked silhouette in the
middle.

Who are you?

She whispers that question over and over, like a mantra, her
own private obsession. *Who the fuck are you?* Sometimes it's: *I'm
going to find you.* And most important of all: *I'm going to kill you.*

Her husband thought her crazy, manic, obsessive...so she left.

She doesn't need much. A cot. A toilet. A single hob cooker
plugged into a blackened socket. Her computers. An external
hard drive wired to blow its fuse if she doesn't enter the pass-
word daily.

Fail-safes.

Outside, the world continues on.

Inside, she continues hunting.

8

Swallows wheel and dip as I walk the once-familiar track up through the hills, the morning frost crunching beneath my borrowed wellies. Hemmed in on either side by towering hedges, I feel small again. Young again. I realize, as I trudge along, that Wales never leaves the blood. The sharpness of the frosty air, the loamy smell of the earth in my nostrils, the deep and ancient bones of the path beneath my feet... London has none of this primordial wildness.

As it drizzles, a mizzle of fine mist in the penumbral pre-dawn, my mind is swallowed up by Lucy. She's safe in the hospital now, a panicked Arthur by her side.

I'm going to fucking kill you.

I'm still a little shell-shocked by the severity of Lucy's episode. During our visits, she had seemed so lucid, so normal, that it was easy to forget why she'd called me here in the first place. Easy to convince myself that perhaps everything she was describing was in fact the result of stress, that perhaps she wanted me back in her life as her friend more than needing me as her therapist. I can only hope that the doctors here are able to get to the bottom of it and prescribe her the right anti-epileptic medication, so it never happens again.

And that rash… I haven't been able to get it out of my mind. I searched for a reference to a rash like it all night and came up with nothing. I'm haunted by it.

Shaking my head, I walk on. I find myself veering onto a familiar dirt track, barely there, boots squelching in the ever-thickening mud. The overhanging trees are the same as they were twelve years ago, and just as I did then, I stare, mesmerized by the dancing shadows on the ground as the day lightens into dawn, shive-light lancing through the branches like spears.

The trees whisper secrets I still wish I could decipher. The birds are in on the gossip, passed from tit to robin, dunnock to lapwing.

Eventually the trees open up onto a deep blue sky electrified with the beginnings of a coming storm and a waxing moon, but I don't stop. The echoes of bleating sheep paired with the crass call of carrion crows add to the symphony that is my past. And my present.

I spy Jonathan trudging along in the distance, a dark but recognizable silhouette, head bowed against the wind and hands in the pockets of his fleece as he nears Eithin Hill, named for the common yellow gorse that blankets it in spring. I know that I came here looking for him.

A sudden, all-encompassing feeling drops like a stone in my chest and a memory surfaces, sharp and focused.

"*Saudade.*" Professor Milton paced back and forth at the front of my Introductory Psychology class at Oxford, tapping a wooden ruler on his palm. I was counting the rhythm. Step, tap, step, tap, step, tap.

He spun abruptly and paced in the other direction. "*Saudade* is a Portuguese word that encapsulates the feeling of deep, profound melancholic nostalgia and longing for something or someone we love but might never have or see again."

Hiraeth, I remember thinking, the weight of grief on my chest.

I wipe my nose, flinching as the north wind fondles my hair, whispering down my neck. Jonathan pauses to survey the valley, spots me, and goes very still. I bow my head, hurrying to catch him where he stands at the crest of the final rise. The wind is picking up now, icy as a reprimand in my ears.

I'm breathless by the time I look up into his weather-beaten, ruined face. And now I can see that more than his eyes are the same. His hair still sticks up the same way, more on the left than the right. The dimple in his nose is still there, maybe even deeper, like the dips in the valley itself. He is still Jonathan, and I am still Mina. Yet nothing is the way it was before.

Please forgive me.

"Hi," I manage, controlling my voice.

"Didn't expect to see you on my hill again."

"I didn't expect to be here." I shove my hands into my jacket pockets. "So. Our corner shop encounter was…"

"Unexpected."

"Definitely unexpected."

He glances away and back again, tucking his hands in his armpits. I'm struck once again by how tall he is, and how broad in his fleece jacket, which looks soft enough to fall into. And how awful those scars are, how they mar one eye and contort his mouth into that terrible grimace. I yearn to reach out and wipe them away, restore what's been taken, not just on his skin, but deeper. Warmth radiates from him in waves, quickly whipped away by the wind, and I want to lean in like I used to, to tuck my head into his chest and feel his arms come around me, a safe place.

A sheep lets out a pitiful cry and Jonathan glances away and back.

"I'm sorry I was abrupt."

I laugh bitterly. "You weren't abrupt. You were cold. Aggressive, even."

He closes his eyes for a fraction of a second and when he opens them, they are the same unyielding gunmetal gray of the sky. "What did you expect?"

"I'm not sure," I admit.

"What are you doing out here?"

"I think I came to find you."

He frowns, squinting. "Why?"

He wants answers. I can see that in his hard edges. Above us, the clouds coil and twist, growing angry. At any moment, we'll be drenched. I tell myself it's nothing either of us haven't suffered before, but it feels ominous.

"I'm... You've been on my mind. Seeing you again was a little jarring."

His face darkens.

"Memories," I clarify. "I was just overcome with so many memories."

He grunts. "Mmm."

"What are *you* doing out here?"

"What does it look like?"

"Scouting for a good place to bury the body?" I offer, laughing awkwardly.

He says nothing.

"Did you forget how to laugh over the last few years?"

He sighs sharply and looks away. Again, he says nothing.

I bite my lip. "You're not giving me much to work with, Jonathan."

"Hard to know what to say."

I hesitate. "Do you...want me to go?"

"Not necessarily."

We stand in a silence that grows thick like mugwort.

"I hope you don't mind me trespassing."

"That's all right," he mutters in a low voice. "Look, I can't hang around. I've got a pregnant ewe waiting."

I release a long breath through pursed lips. "I'm trying to say something pertinent."

"You could start with the truth."

The truth. I can't go there. But, to be fair, he is owed an explanation for why I ran away without a word and never spoke to him again.

"Do you remember that night on the beach when Lucy suggested Truth or Dare?" I flinch and my cheeks flush. Why the fuck did I just bring that up?

"No."

I want to crawl under a rock. "Right."

I plow on recklessly, since I'm here anyway. "Yeah...you picked truth..."

Again, he says nothing.

"Did you know?"

"Know what?"

My cheeks are blazing. He's not making this easy. "You know, like...that I..."

I can't tell if I see the tiniest hint of amusement. Maybe I'm imagining it beneath his scowl.

He stares me down. "You what?"

"Surely you know."

"Fuck's sake, Murray, get on with it!"

"I'm trying!" I yell, nervous laughter bursting out of me. "I'd been *trying* to say that I'd been enamored with you for months by then."

"And? Long time ago."

Anger flares. "Is that why you told them all you fancied me? I was a sure thing?"

"Lovely," he snaps. "That's what you thought of me?"

"No... I mean, maybe. My self-esteem wasn't the highest back then."

"No," he agrees, eyeing me up and down. "You're the picture of confidence now."

My careful veneers, one upon the next.

I step closer, unable to catch my breath all of a sudden. "Back then you said what you thought."

His chest rises. Falls. His eyes search my face. "Look where it got me."

"Your scars," I blurt. "Whatever happened to you." I reach for him. "I'm so—"

He turns away, stepping out of my grasp. "Don't. Don't you fucking dare try to comfort me."

Thunder cracks across the sky.

"I—"

And then he turns to me, closing the distance between us, his lips inches from mine.

"You left. Without a word, Mina. You *left*. So you lost your right to do...whatever this is."

His eyes flash and his lips pull back from his teeth. I watch his walls rear up. So familiar. Akin to mine.

With the scars already pulling his mouth out of shape, his sneer looks fearsome, like the terrible gaping wound on an oak split by lightning. And yet, there's a wretched beauty in his face still. My heart pounds against my ribs, my breath matching his where it curls, white, into the morning. He leans closer, and my body follows like a magnet.

I swallow. "I could be your friend..."

I so badly want him to say yes.

But his walls are impenetrable. "Not when you broke my heart."

He walks away, leaving me staring after him as the sky opens, drenching me with the cold Welsh rain.

To: MinaMurray@Murray.net
From: RonaldWexler@StaffordPractice.co.uk
Subject: Your Jane Doe

Dear Dr. Murray,

This is Dr. Wexler, the Brookfields night registrar. I'm writing to keep you apprised of a situation. I was called to treat your Renée Doe intake this evening, and I have to confess I'm a little alarmed at the condition I found her in. Staff have informed me that after your initial assessment three days ago she was calm and lucid, but since then she has become destructive and has managed to injure herself. Inquiring after her current primary, I note it was a Dr. John Seward.

I'd be grateful if you could come in for a new consult, or will consider signing off as her primary therapist instead, if at all possible, since she seemed to respond well to you.

Sincerely,
Ron Wexler, MBChB

9

"Come out with me, Bambi."

Lucy's voice had been needling. She was used to getting what she wanted, and I was annoyed. It was almost the end of final term, and my maths exam was tomorrow at ten.

"Not a chance."

"Come on, it'll be quick. I promise."

Lucy, my incurable, fun-seeking bestie, was not known for quickie parties. That studies were fun to me she could never compute. I was exactly where I wanted, and needed, to be. But more than fun, my grades—a triple A was needed for my place at Oxford—were my ticket out of here.

Any and all parties I had attended were for Lucy's benefit when there were no exams looming on the horizon. I never enjoyed them.

I'd spent the night cramming the last chapter on integers, doing every equation I could find, and then tossing and turning in bed, worried that Lucy still hadn't messaged me. It had been a simple case of her phone battery dying and the party going too long, but I'd been panicked.

Now, driving back to London, that old familiar feeling is back, heavy on my chest like a sleep-paralysis gargoyle. Is she okay?

Should I be worried? Should I stay? But Arthur assured me that he had everything under control. He saw what happened to Lucy himself—he promised to take care of her. In the end, this knowledge, coupled with knowing that Seward interfered with Renée, makes the decision for me. I packed up my belongings this morning and left a note for my mother letting her know I'd been called home and that I'd phone her the following day, not wanting to wake her or disturb any ritual she might be performing. I doubt she'll be surprised. It might even be a relief. Knowing I won't have to suffer another fight with her, that I need not listen to her guilt-mongering lectures, makes me feel better about leaving. My only regret is Lucy. And Jonathan.

The drive is long and monotonous, with too much time to think about everything that's happened over the last few days, but I drown it out with Wagner. When I step into my flat, there is nothing waiting for me. It is familiar, of course, but uninviting and empty. It suddenly feels like a stranger's house, clinical and cold, full of straight gray lines, chrome pipes, and glass tabletops. There is no warmth, no color, no hint of personality—not even a houseplant. A machine lives here, not a woman.

Mum's house smelled wonderfully complex, sweet notes upon bitter, the scents of plants of various kinds, some in bloom, some not, rioting with the scent of freshly brewed coffee, verbena tea, bread, and bacon. Lucy's house smelled of the ocean somehow, of soft linens, clean bedrooms, and lilies. I close my eyes and try to detect a scent in my own home, but all I get is the faint tang of old bleach and self-control. There is no picture on any wall, nor a single photograph on any sideboard. I don't even have a bloody sideboard.

I think about all I gained back in Tylluan: a rekindled friendship with Lucy, seeing Jonathan again, and sharing a roof with Mum—even if it was grudgingly on her part. But Lucy's in hospital, Mum barely tolerates me, and Jonathan... Jonathan hates me. There is no lasting connection to my past, a fact that seems even starker now that I'm back here in my cold apartment, in my real life.

I rush into my bedroom and then the bathroom and turn the shower on full blast to the hottest setting I have. As the steam rises, I rip off my clothes and throw them into the wash basket in the corner. My thoughts roil and cluster, spin and congeal just like they did all those years ago when Lucy and I yelled at each other and said things we could never take back right before Jonathan and I—

"No," I murmur. "No, no, no."

The water, hot and sharp on my back, is not doing what I need it to do, and the feelings still rise without pause. Why did I do it? Why did I go back there?

Before I know it, I'm on my knees, bent over my thighs and hugging myself, the water a protective curtain. The sobs come, and I can't stop them. *Fool. Idiot. Weak. Breaking yourself open again, for what?*

After a long time, the water runs cold and I switch it off. Then I grab the special extra-strong bleach from the cupboard that I keep for bad days and return to my knees in the empty shower and begin scrubbing. I scrub harder than I ever have, and when my eyes tear up again, it's for a different reason, and that's okay. My nostrils burn, the tang of the bleach coats my tongue, and I feel poisoned but good. My knees are bruised and abused, and that's okay too.

All the while my thoughts go in one direction: *You deserve this.*

When the shower is gleaming, I wash my hands with the bleach too, over and over, counting, counting, always counting, until I have hypnotized myself enough to stop. My hands are red and dry, and I smell like chemicals, but my soul is numb and I have control.

I will always gain control.

In my room, I close the curtains, switching on the bedside lamp, then I unpack all the clothes from my bag—clothes that still smell of Wales, of long, precipitous walks through the hills, of spilled eggs and heated encounters, of passion, feeling, *life*. Never before had I missed my past. I always thought of it as a line I had crossed and moved far beyond. Now I know I built nothing real in its absence. A paper house, a card castle. How easily it almost crumbled.

I change into fresh pajamas, climb into my sterile bed, and wait for sleep to claim me. In the morning, I feel more like my old self, and I settle into my decade-long routine. Ablutions, brush my teeth, a hot shower, tile routine, nostrils burning with sodium hypochlorite, moisturizer.

I get the kettle going and switch on the gas fire in my small fireplace, allowing the creak of cold to melt from my bones. When the water is boiling, I reach for my container of Welsh verbena-and-nettle tea and hesitate.

I won't let Wales control me.

I make stale instant coffee instead and try to ignore the sensation of anxious hives breaking out on my chest and the itch, itch, *itch* on my neck. *It's in your mind*, I remind myself. *You are not weak.*

I dress for protection. My usual black ensemble, but this time I add a splash of red in the form of a pashmina scarf. It will soak up any remaining weakness in my system and allow me to face Renée. I have to expect that she may offer me a morsel of bug to share, and I must be prepared. As long as I wear this scarf, and as long as Renée does not touch it, I'll be safe. I will be strong. I can survive anything.

When I arrive at Brookfields, reception informs me that Renée has been moved to a permanent room in the western wing of the hospital and is still under the care of Dr. Seward. My hackles go up. He's a man interested in puzzles, not people. In curiosities—in the next bonkers psychological display for a medical paper or bestselling book.

I check in with the nurse's station, tension running like a live wire up and down the lines of my body.

"Dr. Murray for Renée Doe."

The nurse, a plump Asian lady, checks the system and nods. "Room five, down that way."

"What's the policy on free roaming on this ward?"

"Allowed depending on good behavior. But she's been confined for the last two days, and she won't let us turn on the lights or open the blinds."

I frown. "Okay, thank you."

The nurse shrugs. "It's a nightmare doing obs, but when we turn the light on she becomes violent."

"Yes, she's photosensitive. Do you have her file?"

The nurse rifles through a pile of manila folders on her desk, finally extracting a thin one from the middle and handing it to me.

I scan the contents. "Dr. Seward prescribed ketamine?"

The nurse shrugs again, looking unhappy, so I nod and head for Renée's room. All of the trust work I did with her may have to be rebuilt.

I knock on the door three times and step inside. It's so dark that I can only make out the vague shape of her bed, hospital table, and a smaller bundle in the corner. As the door closes behind me, the light fades away entirely.

"Renée? It's Dr. Murray. I've come to see you."

No response.

I take my phone out from my bag but hesitate. Even such a meager light could cause her distress. Instead, I light the screen so she can see my face, see that I am who I say I am.

All I can see is the rectangle of illumination in front of me, and vague dark shapes beyond.

"I'm sorry I've been away," I tell her, screen still in my face. "Someone was in trouble. But I came right back to see you when I heard you weren't feeling well."

While I'm talking, I have the strange sensation of subtle movement in the murk, as though there are shapes in the darkness
beyond my phone screen that I can't discern. My body goes cold
with horror as the peculiar certainty in me rises that Renée and
I are not alone.

I swivel my phone around out of instinct, and the meager
spread of light confirms that, yes, we are. Renée is curled up on
the floor in the corner, her face pressed to the wall.

"*Renée.*"

Her head snaps in my direction, as though she has only just
heard me, her face cracked in an eerie smile.

"Dr. Lady," she says through her teeth.

"Dr. Murray," I correct her.

"Dr. Murray," she echoes, not sounding wholly present, twisting her hands in her lap, pulling roughly at the skin of her fingers and picking at her stubby nails. She's unnerving in the
semidarkness.

"How are you, Renée?"

She doesn't answer, just keeps smiling at me in that awful way.

"Can I sit on your bed?"

"I like you," she says, which I take for confirmation.

I smile kindly after I'm sitting. "I'm very glad."

"But... I don't... This room."

She looks around with agitation, fidgeting nervously. The
hem of her hospital gown is frayed as though she has been wor-
rying at it with her nails or teeth. My phone light goes off and
I fumble to activate the screen once more.

"Tell me what's wrong."

"They clean here. Every day. Every night. All the time."

"You don't like that?"

"I have to feed my spiders so I can feed the mouse...when I
find the mouse..."

"The bugs."

Her eyes gleam in the penumbra. "I need their life."

"Don't you like the food here?"

She spits her disgust, saliva propelled from her mouth in an arching spray.

I grip my phone and I grip my scarf. "Bugs are dirty, Renée. We only want to keep you safe. Prevent you from getting sick."

"I *will* get sick!" she says with fear in her eyes. "Without the life force, I'll die!"

"Other than the cleaning, have you been treated well? Are they giving you orange juice?"

Renée looks almost forlorn as she confirms that they are, in fact, being very good to her.

"Too good to me," she mumbles.

"Don't you think you deserve to be treated well?"

"He won't like it."

"Who?"

"I'm...getting weaker," she mutters, her gaze sliding sideways and vacant. "But...but he will be pleased that the young woman is back. He likes her smell."

I realize she is talking about me and make a mental note that she has an affinity for scent. For now, I need to get into this "him" persona, construct, or memory.

"Who is 'he,' Renée?"

She ignores me, muttering to herself, eyes darting left and right as though reading from a book only she can see.

"Renée, is 'he' your brother? Father? Boyfriend?"

Renée moans, her eyes scrunching tight. "I *need* it!"

At that moment the lights blare to life and the door bangs open.

Dr. Seward is standing in the doorway. He pauses for half a second, then his face breaks into an easy, charming smile.

"Dr. Murray," he says. "Do I have the wrong room?"

He actually turns to check it, mocking me.

Before I can blink, Renée flies at him, her eyes wild, teeth bared. She is heavier than her slight frame implies, and Seward is knocked back several steps. Renée gnashes at his face, but he grips her wrists and holds her away with a grimace.

I rush forward to grip her around the waist, but she turns and screams in my face; her breath plumes in my mouth, potent and vile.

"Sedation!" I yell.

All I hear is my pulse in my ears and her growls by my face. Renée gives another tug with a surge of energy I don't expect, and she almost bites Seward's face, but I use my body weight to pull her back.

"Renée, no!"

She backtracks suddenly, throwing her weight away from Seward and into me. Did he push her? She lifts her arms to rip off my scarf, screaming like a cornered animal. Her head snaps around, her back pressed into my torso, and she bites down onto my neck where my scarf once sat.

His smell is overwhelming. He's a boulder pressing me down, crushing me into wet sand. His hands gripping me like vises...

My skin cracks under her teeth and there is a piercing pain. I cry out, but she's lifted off me by Seward a moment later, kicking and screaming. She must've bitten him too, because he swears.

Two orderlies rush into the room to help Seward, who is struggling to contain Renée alone. I zero in on her eyes, noticing something.

"Come now, Miss Renée," one of them booms as they wrestle her to the bed. They tie restraints I hadn't noticed to her wrists and ankles and then secure Velcro straps across her torso and thighs.

I scramble away from her, trying to compose myself, but the wound on my neck is pulsing and my mind is screaming. I can see my hands shaking but I don't feel them. The entire world is just the thump of my heart screaming, *Run, run, run!*

The nurse arrives with a needle and Seward takes it from her, injecting sedation into Renée's cannula.

"I feel funny," Renée says in a small voice, looking at me with big, betrayed eyes.

In the same moment, she kicks out her restrained leg one more time, her hospital gown sliding back to reveal something that steals my breath and makes me gag. A horrifying, trypophobic rash. The twin of Lucy's.

"You're bleeding," Seward says.

I blink. "What?"

"Blood, Murray," he says, pointing at my neck. Dazed, I touch the sting just above my rapidly bruising collarbone. He turns to the nurse. "Get a first aid kit."

She nods and hurries away. The orderlies leave as well.

On the bed, Renée is screaming. "Master!"

A distant niggle in my mind worries at me, but I can't think while that rash is staring at me. Those horrifying little black holes in her skin like tiny poppy seeds buried in puffy purple flesh.

The nurse returns with the first aid kit, and I follow her out of Renée's room and into a side one not in use. I don't really feel like I'm here and know I'm dissociating.

"Are you all right?" she asks me, her lips tight.

I hear myself say, "Fine."

"You're missing a shoe," she says.

I suddenly realize my left foot is touching cold tiles—
Infected. Soiled. Unclean.

Seward enters the new room with my shoe in his hand.

"What the hell was that?"

I snatch my shoe from him—*besmirched, begrimed, muddied*—and slip it onto my now-buzzing foot.

"*You* tell *me*. Renée has completely deteriorated since last week!"

The nurse makes herself diplomatically scarce with a nod to me.

"I suppose I'll be seeing this incident in your next book," I mutter.

"Beg pardon?"

"I *said*, I suppose that this 'fun' incident will make your next paper."

The corner of his mouth quirks up. "Maybe. It would certainly cause a few chuckles, I should think."

Wanker. I don't deign his comment with a response.

Instead, I say, "I'd like to know precisely what you've done with Renée since I've been gone. Why she's been so agitated."

It hasn't escaped me that Renée was in no way violent with me during our time together, and only became so after Seward presumably threw things off between us.

"*You* agitated her, Murray. And I'd sure as hell like to know why you're here."

My nostrils flare. "Ron emailed me. He was concerned that Renée was doing badly and asked me to come and check in with her."

"The registrar?"

"Yes, the registrar."

"Mmm. Maybe he didn't realize I'd signed off as primary. I'll have to send him a strongly worded reminder."

"I think he emailed me because I made good progress with Renée. She was lucid. We built trust."

"Yes, but you left," he quips.

"Clearly you've done an excellent job in the meantime," I snap. "I'm not the one prescribing ketamine, John."

His eyes flash and I know I've gotten to him. "It's cut-and-dry trauma-induced psychosis. She needs medicating. End of story."

"She's *my* patient."

"Actually, no, she's not. The board signed off with me as primary since you were—" an exquisitely timed pause "—unavailable. They clearly feel I'll do a better job of it. So stay out of my way."

My blood is boiling. "This is just a game to you, isn't it? This whole profession and what we do, it's all just one big sandbox in your playground."

"Now, now," he says. "Calm down."

"These patients are people. Living, breathing human beings with feelings, not *toys*, and this profession is a sacred charge, not a *joke*."

Seward cocks his head, looking down at me with amusement. "Jesus, Murray. You're so earnest."

My eyes narrow involuntarily. "Excuse me?"

"You're wound tighter than a guitar string."

"*I'm* a professional."

He laughs and claps me on the shoulder before walking into the hall, forcing me to trail behind like a puppy. "Lighten up, Murray. Or you'll have a heart attack before you're forty."

"You can't just lock her in a room and sedate her into oblivion."

Turning back, he says coldly, "You no longer have unsupervised access to *my* patient."

He saunters down the hall and I have to try very, *very* hard not to throw my shoe at the back of his head.

I hand over my visiting-doctor's badge at reception and walk as fast as I can without running until I'm back in my car. Once there I drown my hands in sanitizer, then rip the gauze from my neck and check the wound in the rearview mirror. Teeth marks on my skin, bloody but not too deep, overlap the old scars that sit there, a permanent reminder, from collarbone to just below my earlobe. I apply sanitizing alcohol to them as well, wincing at the sting, then rip off my heels and use the last of the sanitizer on my foot and offending shoe.

What a *tosser*.

The niggle in my mind returns, and with it the smell of a Welsh morning.

Lucy had the same rash. I'm sure of it. And something else... something less definite. Lucy had the same vague, dazed look as

Renée did in that hospital room. Both women had a temporary nystagmus, and Lucy too had murmured, "Master."

What are the chances of two women, hundreds of miles apart, demonstrating very similar, if not the same, symptoms? Perhaps they suffer with a common illness I've not yet seen. Perhaps they have the same mental health condition. Could they both have taken the same drug in the last week? Have they crossed paths before?

Renée hasn't had a seizure, as far as I remember. I make a mental note to double-check. Whatever the connection, it seems tenuous.

I know until I get to the bottom of who Renée is and what happened to her, I can't know for sure whether there is something connecting her to Lucy.

Still, I have to pull this thread and see where it leads.

Session Recording [Date Redacted]
Dr. John Seward (JS), Nurse Ann Roberts (AR), and
Patient Renée Doe (RD)
Reference Number [Redacted]

Dr. Seward: This is Dr. John Seward recording on the twenty-fifth of September, 2015. Session number three. Good morning, Renée. How are you feeling today? How is that rash of yours doing?

[Pause]

[Muffled sound]

Dr. Seward: Please refrain from spitting at me. We talked about this last time.

Renée: [Laughs] Where is the doctor lady?

Dr. Seward: As I've told you, she's no longer treating you. I am.

[Muffled noise]

Dr. Seward: Please stop that. If you need to blow your nose, you can have a tissue.

[Noise repeated over and over]

Dr. Seward: Why are you blowing snot all over your face?

Renée: To smell the lifeblood better!

[Noise repeated]

[Silence]

Renée: Orange juice! I want orange juice!

Dr. Seward: Let's talk first.

Renée: [Mumbling] She said I could have orange
juice.

Dr. Seward: Last time we spoke, you were very
insistent that I go and look at the moon.

Renée: The moon...the moon...

Dr. Seward: I went to look at the moon. Can you
tell me why the moon is important?

Renée: Moon...moon...moon...moon...

Dr. Seward: Can you tell me more about the moon?

Renée: [Mumbling] Need medicine to make me better.

Dr. Seward: We talked about this before. I can't
give you medication without your medical file.
And without your surname, I can't get your medical file.

Renée: I'm...Renée. I need medicine.

Dr. Seward: We're going around in circles now.

[Incoherent muttering]

Renée: Fields, fields, fields, fields.

Dr. Seward: [Muttering] A new word. How delightful for me. [Sigh] [Rustling of paper]

Renée: Fly...fly...fly...

Dr. Seward: You can't fly. We also spoke about this. Which is why you can't have a window.

Renée: WINDOW!

Dr. Seward: [Muttering] Fly, window, roof, blood, moon, and now fields. We're making progress, aren't we?

Renée: [Panting]

Dr. Seward: Now, we went over each word already. [Rustling] Fly, window, roof, moon, blood. We went over each. Fly—you can't fly. You're a human. Window—you can't have a window because you're light sensitive and started screaming when the sun came up. Moon—yes, the moon is lovely. But what does it mean to you? Blood—you can't hurt people and it's not good to hurt yourself either. [Pause] Do you remember, Renée?

Renée: He's going to rip you to pieces and I'll laugh.

[Spitting sound]

Dr. Seward: [Sigh] Spitting at me isn't going to help you.

[Moaning and rustling in the background]

Dr. Seward: Please remain calm. Everything's okay.

[Moaning grows louder]

Dr. Seward: Look, if you want to be taken seriously, you're going to have to get ahold of yourself.

[Noises of distress]

Renée: [Screams]

Dr. Seward: If you don't stop screaming and scratching yourself, I'm going to call the nurse.

Renée: [Screaming. Movement]

Dr. Seward: [Grunt] Renée, let go— [Bustling]

Renée: No…no! No, please—no! [Muffled screaming]

Dr. Seward: Renée— [Grunt]

[Steps, door opening, distant voices, screaming]

Dr. Seward: [Aside] Two mils lorazepam in water for IM. Get the AED and suction equipment in case.

[Grunting]

Dr. Seward: Renée, unless you calm down, I will have to inject you, do you understand? Renée. Do you want to take the sedative orally?

[Screaming. Bustling]

Dr. Seward: Keep her still.

Nurse AR: I've got her.

[Screaming]

Dr. Seward: There. Yes, okay. Good.

[Screaming continues for two minutes before receding into incoherent mumbling]

Post-Incident Report: Dr. John Seward
For the attention of the Health & Social Care Governance Support Team

Patient Renée Doe was compliant and calm when recording began. [what triggered her violence?]. I deemed that nonconsensual Rapid Tranquilization was necessary under Section 62 of the Mental Health Act following a violent outburst where Renée began clawing at her face and eyes, then attacked me, injuring my left cheek with her nails. No information was available to guide the choice of medication, including the age of the patient, therefore 2 mg of intramuscular lorazepam was administered on the assumption that Renée Doe is of greater than eighteen years of age. No contraindications as far as we can tell as the patient has been in sectioned care for a week, and has no evidence of cardiac issues following an earlier echocardiogram. However, the patient arrived severely anemic and is being treated with ferrous fumarate. The patient is not pregnant. Rapid Tranquilization administered to the vastus lateralis muscle was only partially effective and was readministered after thirty minutes for full sedation totaling 4 mg. Intramuscular olanzapine and haloperidol combined with intramuscular promethazine has been added to her authorized medication in case of noneffective administration of further IM lorazepam. Order of medication administration has been filed in her chart. Filing for MHA has been completed online and assessment will begin within the week. Patient is currently in isolation, monitored by Nurse Stevens, with obs taken at fifteen-minute intervals. Upon waking, she will be given the opportunity to offer her own written account of the incident. See attached Incident Form.

Signed

Dr. John Seward, MBBS, MRCPsych, MRCEM

10

By the time I'm done reading the transcripts of Seward's sessions with Renée, kindly provided to me by Ron, the registrar, her list of words have become a sort of anthem in my mind. *Fly, window, roof, moon, blood, fields.* I would have done things very differently; RT would have been a last resort. She and I built trust in our two sessions. Trust that Seward completely destroyed.

You left her, a voice reminds me.

And it's right. I did leave her. One session over which I gained her trust, made her an unspoken promise, and then left her in the cold. I was so focused on Lucy, I essentially handed her over to someone else.

A niggling in my throat warns me of an attack of anxiety on the way, like the first lapping of water on a beach before it withdraws into a tidal wave I can't stop. Unlike my normal method of stilling my mind, scribbling in my journal isn't helping.

I push away from my computer and pace back and forth, noting the sound of water from outside.

It's raining.

Without thinking, I do what I haven't done in years: I pull open the window leading to the rooftop terrace and climb out, fully dressed, gasping as the rain hits my face, icy pinpricks of wakefulness.

There's something cleansing about a cold rain. Like a bleached shower. Like thousands of tiny kisses. Almost as good as a hug from a friend. I lie down and let the rain soak me, distantly feeling my body's transition from rigid resistance to a loose and calm acceptance. Release. Surrender.

I close my eyes and let my mind wander.

Fly.

Window.

Roof.

Blood.

Moon.

Fields.

Fly, window, roof, blood, moon, fields.

Her words become a mantra as my mind searches for the connections, moving them around on the whiteboard of my brain, trying different orders and combinations. I picture myself in Renée's shoes, alone, confused, trapped. How would she feel? What would her sensations be?

And then I am Renée. My mind is broken; I'm desperately trying to convey information to someone unable or unwilling to see.

"Okay, Renée," I whisper, raindrops hitting my tongue, cold and sweet.

I consider each word in turn, mulling them over. By the time I'm pondering the word *moon*, I'm beginning to lose hope of seeing anything relevant. It all feels like such a stretch, as if I'm forcing a round peg into a square hole and calling it a good fit.

But *fields*... My mind has been catching on that word over and over. In all of the recordings, until the last, she had never said this word. It's new.

The spark of an idea flashes across my closed eyelids. I get up and climb back through my window, dripping all over the floor. I strip off my clinging clothes in the bathroom, put on my bathrobe, and head for my computer, pulling up Google Maps.

I find the location they picked her up from and scan the area, looking for football stadiums, fields, parks, or greens—anything to give me an idea of where she might come from. After twenty minutes of careful searching, I admit defeat.

I go back to the email Ron sent me and pull open the transcript for session three again, reading, reading, trying to find any pattern, any clue at all. It could be the tiniest thing; it could be—

And then I see it. Every word spoken had been a response to a question. She responded "moon" when asked about when she was found. After checking the date, I realize it was a full moon. She responded "fly" when asked why she wasn't eating. She didn't want to fly, she wanted to *eat* flies. "Roof" when she was asked about her new room, and "window" when asked about her room on a different occasion. Renée is in a kind of fugue state, not wholly present, but she *is* answering questions.

I can see the connection with most of the words. Including the most vital:

Seward needed her name...and Renée had told him.

Fields.

Renée Fields.

I snatch up my phone and dial the number for my favorite contact at the Met.

"George Baxter." As brisk as ever.

"George, it's Mina Murray."

"Hi, Mina. What can I do you for?"

"I have a Jane Doe over at Brookfields. I think her name is Renée Fields. Late teens or early twenties, blond hair. Do you have any missing persons reports matching that description?"

"Give me a sec. Renée... Fields... Docklands area?"

My shoulders sag with relief. *"Yes."*

I forgot what night tastes like, that salty, moon-licked rot of London after dark. As I lace on my running shoes, banishing the impulses shrieking that I'm breaking the pattern, that the back hand of fate is chomping at my heels, I chew on a diazepam. Maybe the lazy benzo tide will smother the compulsions, sweep me away from the broken glass of my thoughts and grind them into soft, fine sand.

Before we hung up, George gave me Renée's address when I told him I needed to follow up on some questions for her medical treatment. A stretch, technically and ethically, but one I was willing to make.

It's an easy ten-minute jog from Kensington to Notting Hill Gate, where I hop on the Central line to Bank. I watch the moonrise as my trainers pound the pavement, feeling my skin prickle as a low fog rolls in from the distant river.

Another short jog to the Princes Street stop, where I take the 141 Palmers Green bus five stops to Bevenden Street, Hoxton. I discreetly allow my maps app to lead me verbally, via my headphones, through a half-mile walk to Caliban Tower, where Renée's family lives. In the pocket of my hoodie, I grip my keys between firm fingers just in case.

The fog has risen higher, turning the shuttered, graffiti-riddled shops into mini *Cewri*. I can't read many of the neon spray tags, but one looks like Demon Lord, and another like Farce Princess.

The tang of kebab grease from the takeaway fifty paces away and the sour stench rising from endless clumps of rubbish bags awaiting the morning collection commingle into a unique aroma of carrion sweetness. I breathe through my mouth, avoiding the man sitting on the pavement devouring a doner, oily onions dripping into his beard. By his foot, a used condom sits in the gutter.

"All right, love?" calls a skinny man as he passes. He makes my skin crawl and I hurry past, but he turns and follows, a swagger in his step. I grip my keys harder.

"Great tits," he says so low I almost don't hear it.

I wish I had a Taser or pepper spray, but my keys will have to do.

"Oi, you, chat to me," he demands, walking too close now. "And give us a smile."

Something venomous rises in my chest and I stop and face him, meeting his gaze. "Fuck off."

"Oooh, very rude!" he says, mock offended. He reeks of nicotine and beer. "What? You think you're too good for me?"

I stare at him, not moving, not speaking. It takes everything I have not to scream and I clutch my keys so hard they dig into my skin. Eventually, after far, far too long, he glances from side to side, uncomfortable.

"You're not that good-looking anyway." He spits on the road and saunters away.

By the time I'm knocking on number forty-two, I'm still shaken. Somewhere in one of the flats, an infant screams a hungry protest and in the small concrete square below a bunch of lads kick a football about, yelling profanities at one another.

The door creaks open a few inches. A little boy, maybe two or three years old, stares up at me. He's in a nappy and nothing else, and a dribble of slime that reminds me very much of Renée glistens on his chin and chest.

"Hello. Is your mummy home?"

He shakes his head and closes the door.

I frown and knock again. There's a long wait, a yell from inside, and then the door is yanked open and a teenager with brown hair glares at me from the entrance.

"Yeah?" she spits, a hand on her hip.

"I'm looking for—" I check the name on my phone "—Janet Lucas?"

"Who's asking?"

"My name is Dr. Murray. I'm treating Renée Fields over at Brookfields. I really need to talk to Janet."

She looks me up and down.

I dig in my pocket and pull out my Brookfields ID. "Here."

She takes the card and scrutinizes both it and me, then finally nods tersely. "Janet's me mum. She's at work."

I frown, considering what to do.

"What you screwing at me for?" she snaps suddenly, her face pushed forward like a snapping turtle.

"I'm...sorry?"

She blinks, frowns, and considers me, eyes trailing up and down my body.

"You're Desiree, yes?" I ask. "Renée's cousin?"

She scowls. "How'd you know that?"

"The police gave me your information. Look, I really need to ask you a few questions about Renée, if you have the time."

She folds her arms. "Rude to rock up unannounced."

"No one was answering the phone, and Renée needs help."

Desiree pokes her head into the corridor and checks both directions. Then she looks me up and down again, sighs, rolls her eyes, and goes back inside, leaving the door open for me to follow. I step in and close the door behind me.

"Desiree—"

"Desi," she says over her shoulder.

I follow her into a narrow kitchen littered with dishes, plastic cups, and boxes of formula. I note that she's got baby bottles and a breast pump sitting on the counter too.

"Desi, look, I won't take long—"

A cry from the other room. "Fuck's sake, hang on."

She leaves and I cautiously follow her into a dim room where a newborn is wailing from a crib in the corner.

"You woke her," Desi says, accusing.

"I'm sorry—I'm... Do you need help?"

She glances at me, considering. "Nah, she's just fussy. Hungry more like."

I can't work out if she's the infant's sibling or mother. For that matter, I have the same confusion regarding the little boy in the living room.

Desi lifts the baby into her arms and just as deftly lifts her tank top, revealing a swollen, veiny breast.

"Shall I watch...?" I gesture vaguely at the living room we walked through where the TV is blaring cartoons.

"D'you mind?"

"No, not at all."

I hurry away from her, uncomfortable with such casual intimacy, and stand awkwardly in the lounge. The little boy is sitting in front of the TV staring at it with rapt fascination, so I take a moment to look around. The space is small and cluttered, but clean. Plastic toys litter a hoovered carpet, and a box of nappies has been knocked over by the sofa. I pick up the scattered white squares and replace them in the box before standing near the door.

Eventually, Desi returns, sans baby.

"She's changed and down again," she says, sighing as she sits. "You have kids?"

"Me? Oh, no."

She laughs. "Don't. Bloody nightmare."

"I need to ask you a few questions about Renée—about before she went missing. I'm trying to understand what's wrong with her."

"Is she off her rocker?"

"That's not quite accurate."

"You her doctor, you said?"

"Yes."

"But you don't know what's wrong with her?"

"Not yet. Can you tell me anything about the days before Renée went missing? How was she acting? Did she seem normal?"

Desi leans back, kicking off her slippers, and folds her legs under her.

"Ren," she says, half scoffing, half laughing. "She was annoying but, like, also amazing at the same time, you know what I mean? Like, she was pretty *and* talented *and* clever *and* friendly, like that, you know? But then also she was, like, massively in-

nocent. No boyfriends, not really." She rolls her eyes, an affec-
tionate smile on her lips. "Dead annoying."

"Did you notice anything strange in the weeks and days leading up to her disappearance?"

"She was acting a bit…mysterious. She'd be sleeping in late,
which she never used to do, and then if you asked her about it,
she'd get all jumpy. One night I heard something and looked
outside and saw her sneaking out and getting picked up by a
fancy black car."

"Like a limo? But she never told you where she was going or
who she was seeing?"

"Not my business, innit? She'd never really gone out much
before, which got my brows up. 'Cos, like, yeah, *Ren*? She's real
shy, like. But yeah, probably she met some rich bloke because,
like I said, she's well pretty, and let's be honest, that's all that's
going for us down here in the slums—pretty face and a good
pair of, well, you know."

Desi reminds me so fiercely of Lucy that for a split second
it's her sitting there, seventeen and strong. I blink and it's Desi
again, mirage-Lucy vanished into the void of memory.

"You think she fell in with a wealthy gentleman—that they
were dating?"

Desi shrugs. "No idea. Just assumed 'cos we don't get many
cars like that round here." She tamps down a clump of tobacco onto her paper and rolls the cigarette with a deft, practiced hand, her tongue darting out to wet the edges and seal it
shut. "Anyway, she went one night, and when she came back
she was weird."

"Weird how?"

"Sick. We thought it was the flu. She stayed in bed, didn't
eat, slept all the time. But then a week passed, and she didn't
get better. Then another week and she seemed worse. Sleepwalking, talking all kinds of mental stuff. She was probably on
something—"

"What did she say?"

"Fuck if I can remember. I was nine months pregnant by then and she was just doing me head in." She lights up and takes a long drag and exhales. "I do feel bad but, like, I had no idea she was off her rocker, you know what I mean?"

I nod.

"Then one day she was gone. We thought she felt better and went to college. But she didn't come home. Wouldn't answer her phone. We rang 999 but they said we had to wait twenty-four hours." She leans forward, spitting a speck of tobacco from her tongue. "Where did you find her?"

"The police found her wandering the docklands area. She wasn't wearing any clothes."

Desi exhales forcefully through her lips. Every woman knows what this implies, rich or poor, young or old. "Fuck."

"She was malnourished and anemic. Otherwise, she's physically fine. But her mental state is disordered and she was sectioned."

"Crickey. Mum's been in a state, thinking she's dead. I can't wait to see her face when I tell her Ren's safe with you."

"Can you look over this list and tell me if I've missed anything?" I hand Desi my iPhone, where I've made notes on everything she said in my Notes app.

"Is this the latest model?"

"Oh. Um, yeah."

"Nice." Desi reviews everything I've written carefully, but I flinch when a bit of ash falls onto the screen and she doesn't wipe it away.

"You forgot the nightmares."

I take back the phone and add nightmares to the list. It's all looking very familiar.

"Can she come home?" Desi asks. "Maybe that'll make her feel better."

"I can't promise anything. But I'll see what I can do."

Desi nods, then leans forward to stamp out her cig.

"I have to get back to it."

I'm not really sure what she's getting back to. "Do you think I could have a look in Renée's room?"

She eyes me up and down. "Why?"

"I'd like to get a sense of her character before she got sick."

A pause. "Yeah, all right. But if you take anything, I'll call the coppers."

"I would never—"

She bursts out laughing. "Your face! I'm just pulling your chain. I don't give a shit."

She slips a stray strand of hair behind her ear in a way I've seen Renée do and stands. "Through that way."

I head for Renée's room. It's simple and clean. No posters on the wall. No art. Just blank white walls and gray curtains. Even her bedspread tells me little besides the clear fact that she was neat and organized. Undemanding, I'd say. Shy, even.

A picture of Lucy in my memory again, slipping cigarettes and Quincey's bra under her mattress—her secret place, the one area her mother wouldn't check.

I look over my shoulder to make sure that Desi isn't watching, then I bend down and slide my hand beneath Renée's mattress. The cool softness of cotton is broken by the sharp edge of cardboard.

I grip the small rectangle and pull it out.

It's a black business card with a strange logo on the front, a telephone number on the back.

My skin crawls at the sight of it.

"What are you?" I whisper.

III.

She's back at the club, and glad to be here. She got two hundred quid to throw back a few cocktails, wear fancy dresses, and flirt. It's just like Chloe said: easy money. If rich men wanted to pay to talk to her, why refuse? It's the way the world works. And another couple of hundred will help with next month's rent.

The man at the door recognizes her and shows her in without preamble. The routine is the same as before—except this time she came without makeup, so they don't need to scrub her clean. Once she's dressed and plied with another few drinks, she is shown into the same room as before, a glitzy bar with well-dressed men in masks. She is more confident now, and soon she'll be an old pro.

She looks for Chloe, wanting the comfort of a familiar face. Wanting to tell her, *You were right. This is fun.* Wanting someone to confirm in her the knowledge of her allure. Screw university. Screw slaving away at a job she hates to bring home a pittance. Here, she can rake in the money while draped in silk, while brushing up against a whole new world.

She circles the room, eyes sliding over the men without interest, analyzing the women, searching. But Chloe isn't among the girls. She remembers that she was taken to a side room—right through that door in the corner, the one with the red architrave.

A tap on her shoulder; a firm hand on her arm. A man in a suit tugging her closer.

"Come with me to the other room." It isn't a request.

He's handsome enough, but she has an innate and indescribable sense that he is *less than*. Less than some of the other men in the room, the ones who linger in the shadows, who hang back, who have an air of power.

He nods toward the door with the red trim—the one Chloe was taken through last time. He tugs again, fingers tightening, and his smile is less indulgent.

She arches her brow at his hand on her flesh and wants to spit at him. Instead, she smiles. "If you want to touch me like that, you might have to buy me dinner first."

His grip tightens even more, and she raises her chin and tosses her hair, using the motion to yank herself free. She laughs, like he made a joke, but her eyes say it all: *Hands off.*

He reaches for her again, shifting from foot to foot, and she steps back, a finger raised. "Dinner first," she teases, feeling that surge of power again. *This is my game.*

A tall man with an earpiece approaches. "Not this one," he says, and Mr. Handsy scowls and saunters away.

"My apologies, miss," he says with a small bow. "If you would accompany me, the owner of the club would like to apologize."

She smiles. "No need. It's all in good fun."

"He insists."

Mr. Earpiece—security for the girls, she assumes—turns and heads in the opposite direction. She follows, and the other girls look on, jealous. She notices a small security camera in the corner of the room. Its angle subtly shifts as she passes, as though watching her. Perhaps whoever is behind the camera is the owner. A few of the men in shadowy corners grin as she passes, so she smiles back and raises her chin.

She is led past the room where they dressed her, along several winding wood-paneled corridors that smell of secrets, down two flights of stairs, and into a long hallway full of identical metal doors. It's incongruous, the stern metal at odds with the plush wood everywhere else. She counts them as she passes. Supply rooms? Storage?

At door number six, he pauses and nods for her to enter.

"An apology isn't necessary," she says again, stepping inside. She knows how it is when people imbibe too much. "I'm not upset—"

It's only as the door closes firmly behind her that it occurs to her to be terrified.

SONGBIRD:
@Revenant34 Found another possible hit with UKPREDATOR—Bessy Klein, missing since 2007. Nineteen, blonde, was reportedly sick before she "ran away." Any hits?

REVENANT34:
@Songbird No go. Her body was found in the Thames after decay. No evidence to be logged.

SONGBIRD:
@Revenant34 She could have been a vic of UKPREDATOR even if her body was found. Maybe he made a mistake. As for the other evidence, it could have been disguised by decay. Also check out missing person Leslie Folk 2010. Family said she was displaying strange symptoms before she vanished. Could be a link.

REVENANT34:
@Songbird Agreed about Leslie, will add her to file. Seems like a girl goes missing every seven months.

SONGBIRD:
@Revenant34 That we know of. I suspect more.

DRMUK:
Looking for info on girls with mysterious symptoms as detailed in your list in Symptoms.doc after contact with a very secretive club. Both alive but unwell. Can anyone help me?

11

It's three in the morning when the message pings into my inbox on the forum, which I've been periodically refreshing since I decided sleep was a lost cause several hours ago.

After leaving Desi's house, I had phoned the number on the card from a pay phone several blocks away. It rang twice before someone picked up. I hesitated, perplexed by the silence, then asked to speak to the manager. Whoever it was hung up on me without a word or a breath. When I rang again, the line went dead immediately. On the journey back to Kensington, I googled the number but there were no results.

I was perplexed; I played around with different ways to search the logo, describing it, looking through message boards for any mention of it. I thought about what Desi said about Renée going out with a rich guy and wondered where he might be taking her. A club, surely—where else would a wealthy man take a beautiful, poor, young woman? Who else would have a card with a logo but no name? Where else would be so exclusive and secretive?

Googling "club with no name" turned up little, but under Image search there was a single result: the photo was pixelated, but it clearly showed a pair of black doors at the end of a narrow alleyway. The same symbol on the card was emblazoned on the wood in matte paint.

I clicked the link on the image, which took me to a forum focused on conspiracy theories. Amid the threads on aliens, lizard people, and Mandela effects was a brief mention of a club with no name. Attached to the post, the Google photo, and an address: 41 Cloth Fair. I screen-capped the post to review later, in case I couldn't find the forum again, and a good thing too. When I went back, the post had been deleted.

I googled "41 Cloth Fair and club with no name" and found several archived web results that I couldn't access, not even when I went in via the HMTL code—a trick I learned at uni.

This whole thing feels remarkably hidden. Like it's well protected by someone with influence—it must be if they have power enough to edit Google itself and keep prying eyes away from every corner. Secretive enough to not be listed anywhere I can find except a conspiracy theory forum that, by the looks of it, hosts more crazy lizard people theories than actual fact.

Still, my heart races when I get a message from someone on the forum.

Hello @DrMuk.
This is Songbird.

I'm busy typing a reply when a follow-up message appears.

Eloise Reid

Mandip Bhatta

Georgia Murphy

Laura C. Bradford

Olivia Helman

Diya Singh

All of these women were last seen
in Central London. Most of them
lived in the area between Limehouse
and Finsbury. Upon checking, the
symptoms that their family members
observed prior to the disappearances
match the ones listed in Symptoms.doc

Between Limehouse and Finsbury... I pull up Google Maps.
Renée and her family live a six-minute drive north of Finsbury,
in the Caliban. I lick my lips and type, my whole body buzzing
with this new information.

They all had the same symptoms?

How did you get this information?

How doesn't matter.

I take a breath and lean back in my chair. Whoever this Songbird is, they're the only other person I've come across who can
see a pattern like I can. Still, the skeptic in me needs more.

Tell me who you are.

There is a long stretch of time where I'm certain I've scared
whoever they are away. I sit up straight and type another message.

My name is

A text message jingles onto my phone, startling me before I can finish typing. When I read the message, my blood runs cold.

I know who you are, Mina Murray.

I have been looking into this for a very long time.

How did you get this number?

Anything and everything can be traced. That's something you should remember going forward if you're going to keep digging into this particular hole.

I don't appreciate the rebuke, if that's what it is. I decide to test them.

If you're the expert, then trace this number: 07929886726.

Give me a minute.

It takes them less than that to reply.

The phone associated with that number last placed a call about a mile out of Finsbury. What is it?

A business card one of the girls was
given before she got sick.

I sit back from my computer, my mind racing, taking it all
in. All these women, including Renée, going missing from the
same areas of London, displaying the same symptoms, and the
only link that I have—the phone number on the business card
handed to one of the girls directly—last placed a call from the
same area. A logo that turned up an image search of a door at
the end of a narrow alley and linked to a forum discussing the
same missing girls?

It can't be coincidence. It just can't. These things—all these
girls—are all connected.

And, somehow, so is the club with no name.

To: MinaMurray@Murray.net
From: RonaldWexler@StaffordPractice.co.uk
Subject: Renée Fields

Dear Dr. Murray,

I thought you'd want to know that, unfortunately, Renée Fields was found deceased in her room early this morning. I have no further details.

Sincerely,
Ron Wexler, MBChB

12

Renée Fields was found deceased in her room early this morning.
There is no time to scream. No time to yell, to beat my
pillow bruised, to demand some kind of answer from the uni-
verse. My pitiful, selfish grief says more about my ego than my
heart. Renée was mine, and I failed to keep her safe.

She was a person, not a project.

Every phone call I place to Seward goes unanswered. I don't
have his email address, but even if I did, I want to hear his voice
when I confront him, not read some carefully constructed written narrative. I want to hear what happened for myself.

The tenuous grip I have on my anger has frayed to nothing
by the time I'm marching into Brookfields. It pulses in my ears
like a siren. Renée Fields, dead. I left her with Seward, and
now she's *dead*.

"I want to speak to John Seward," I tell the receptionist.

It's a young man this time, someone I haven't seen before.

"Um, name?"

"Dr. Mina Murray."

He picks up the phone and mutters into the line, then hangs
up after less than three seconds. "I'm sorry but Dr. Seward is
busy at the moment."

"He can *un*busy himself," I snap. "Tell him I'm here to see him and I am not leaving."

He sighs and reaches under the counter for a guest pass, sliding it over lazily. "Just go up. I'm sure it's fine."

I head straight for Seward's office, bypassing the psych reception and nurses' stations. I pause at his door, listening. He's on the phone. *Laughing.*

When I step inside, I find him reclined in his chair, perfectly relaxed, tie flung over his left shoulder.

He throws a quick glance at me but carries on with his conversation, his mien, voice, and posture unaltered.

I wait for a full minute, each second an infuriating eternity, drilling him with my eyeballs to signal I want him to wind it up fast.

Dr. Seward persists in his telephonic conviviality without further glances in my direction. I might as well be an artificial plant.

"Dr. Seward," I say finally.

No effect. On the contrary, he cracks another joke, his trachea undulating with joviality.

My rage dilutes with a perverse satisfaction when I step forward and manually end the call. I press the switch hook. Seward sits up and stares at me with a frown of almost comical astonishment, as though he can't believe I have the audacity.

"Dr. Seward," I say, "I've been informed Renée Fields has died."

He points at the phone. "Did you just end my call?"

"I did. I'd like to know the particulars about Renée."

He holds my gaze for a moment, his face serious, until it breaks into a smile. His body once again relaxes. "Well, you're in a foul mood today."

"Never mind my mood."

He replaces the phone on the receiver. "I like this. A doctor who truly cares about her patient. We need more of that in the world."

I purse my lips. "I'm not going to ask again."

He sighs. The smile fades. "As you may well expect, the matter is currently under investigation. I'm afraid I can't disclose anything beyond that."

"So, there's been foul play."

He sighs again, as if suddenly exasperated. "Why do you assume there's been foul play?"

"Why an investigation otherwise?"

"Routine. You know that." He says it shrugging, showing his palms, as if he can't believe he has to state something so obvious.

I take a deep breath. "Renée was my patient."

"*Was*. Exactly."

I raise my voice slightly for emphasis. "As I was saying, there've been other girls involved—"

"Are these girls your patients?"

"No, but—"

"Then I'm afraid as far as you're concerned the matter is closed."

"Don't tell me how to do my job."

"Then do it. The patient's death is under investigation. I can't discuss the matter with you, so unless there's something else…"
He stands.

"Look." I press the air down with my palms, glancing at the edge of his desk for a moment before making eye contact again. "Renée fit a pattern that involves other girls, some of whom have gone missing without a trace and others who have been found dead."

"Unfortunately, there are many Renée Fieldses in the world. When she got to us, she was too far gone to be helped. It happens."

"I don't accept that. Especially when there may be more to the story."

He raises sardonic eyebrows. "More to the story."

"Renée had a certain set of symptoms. There are other girls

who have gone missing in the same area of London whose families reported similar symptoms. I have a friend in Wales with the symptoms as well. And then there seems to be a link with a club in London—a nightclub."

Seward squints at me like he's trying to understand whatever language I'm speaking, and I realize I'm not making much sense.

"Let me get this straight," he says slowly. "You think that Renée Fields and a list of other girls that you somehow magically stumbled across, plus your friend—in *Wales*, of all places—have contracted some, what, disease because of a *nightclub*?"

I purse my lips. "It's possible."

"And the reason that we don't have a pandemic on our hands, given that nightclubs see hundreds, if not thousands of visitors every week is because...?"

"I don't know that yet."

"And what are these symptoms, exactly?"

"Fatigue, anemia, insomnia, sleepwalking, nightmares—"

Seward barks a laugh, the tension in his body suddenly dissipating. "God, you're joking! I thought you were actually serious for a moment. You're pulling my leg."

"And a rash—"

"I shouldn't have to tell you that in our profession, we base our actions on *evidence*. Pegging a list of common symptoms that the entire population has most likely experienced at one time or another to a bunch of missing women is a bit of a leap, surely? As for Ms. Fields, until a report is produced, I have nothing for you. And since the patient was no longer under your care—"

"I'm telling you there's a pattern!" I say this more loudly than I intend, and inwardly curse myself. "Other girls may be in danger. These girls all had links to a club—"

"What club?" His hands are on his hips, his smirk expectant.

I hesitate for only a microsecond. "I don't know. It has no name. All I have is a logo—"

He chuckles. "So we're into conspiracy theories now."

My nostrils flare and I count the ticks on the wall clock.

"I'll tell you what," Seward says. "I'm going to pretend we never had this conversation. It's obvious you've been under a great deal of stress. And it was a cool case."

"A 'cool case'?"

"Patients sometimes die under our care. It's a reality in our profession."

"She was a human being, *Dr.* Seward." My tongue gets caught on the dry roof of my mouth at the word *doctor*. I swallow hard.

"There are any number of things that could have gone wrong. And sometimes it's nobody's fault. By the time these types of people reach our care, there's very little that can be done."

My anger is truly boiling now. I clench my teeth, my fists, my toes.

"These types? You're heartless."

"I'm a professional. Try to be one too, Mina. Go home, take a hot bath, have a glass of wine," he continues, with easy calm. "Give it a couple of days. I know it's upsetting when you get invested, but you'll get over it. There'll be new patients."

I want to say something, but I'm unexpectedly at a loss.

Does he have a point?

Did I get too invested?

Is it because I feel guilty at having left?

He starts toward the door. "Meanwhile, if there's nothing else…"

I inhale to say something, but he's opening the door already.

"And, Mina. Stop reading crazy stuff on the internet, okay? Next time you'll tell me September 11 was an inside job and the Earth is flat! And then it will be *you* under our care!" He laughs and gives me a wink. "Go home."

Outside Brookfields, I stand in the middle of the pavement, unmoving for a long time. Shit. What the hell just happened? How did I let myself get so twisted up in conjecture and conspiracy? And for John *Seward* to point it out, of all people? That charlatan?

I pull out my phone and compose a text message to Lucy.

> Hey Luce, how are you feeling?

> Quick question: have you ever been to a club in London without a name, just a logo?

I pace the pavement as I wait for her reply.

> I'm back home from hospital
> Feeling better I think
> They say I'm severely anemic, so I'm starting infusions
> Yay for me, I guess LOL!

> I've never been to a club in London before
> You thinking of taking me clubbing?!

Humiliation sinks into my bones at her reply. I realize now I've been caught up these last days and weeks in the very thing I so often try to cure my patients of: a delusion, a madness, an all-consuming desire to search for answers where there aren't any, to make heads or tails of a world that, all too often, simply doesn't make sense. Seward was right: I'm seeing ghosts where there are none.

IV.

The darkness is impenetrable.

She spent the first day exploring the room with her fingertips, reaching hesitantly out in the blackness. No windows. No picture frames. No cornices. The walls are a solid metal that is ice cold to the touch. She stopped being able to feel her buttocks hours (days?) ago. Outside of a toilet with no seat, there is nothing for her to fix her mind on or keep time with. She has been here for days; that much she knows. Maybe a week.

At regular intervals, the door opens in the dark and a tray slides in. The first time it happens she is unprepared, and she yelps and backs against the opposite wall, later cursing her weakness and inaction. The second time, she's more ready. She rushes for the sound as fast as she can, knowing that it might be her only chance to get away. Hands grab her in the dark; a blow is delivered so hard that she can't breathe for long, agonizing seconds. An electrical zap, something clipped around her neck, then more pain—excruciating, endless pain that liquifies her eyeballs. Eventually the pain is gone, leaving behind a buzzing warmth, a haze of disorientation. The thing around her neck zaps in warning and she knows that she doesn't want to feel it come to life again. She'll do anything and everything to avoid it.

She eats what her fingers find, first tentatively feeling the contents, but now scarfing it down without thought or hesitation.
The food is good quality—that she knows—but by the third (or
fourth or fifth) day, it no longer matters. They give her water
that tastes stale, or medicated, and she sleeps for hours—or days,
or weeks, or months. Time means nothing.

She doesn't know who is doing this.

She doesn't know why they are doing this.

No one has touched her. Surely, that's the usual reason?

Nothing makes sense. But, slowly, a pattern does emerge.

The food comes three times a day. It is brought in by someone
with squeaky shoes. It is the same person, she knows, because
they have a certain scent. Something clean, like pine and mint.

She tries to ask questions—

What do you want with me?

How long will you keep me here?

Where am I?

Who are you?

What's happening?

What day is it?

—but they never answer.

After a long time, the pattern changes. One day, the lights
come on. The pain is so intense that her ears scream with it.
Her eyes weep, even as they're clamped shut.

A man's voice. A new man—he smells different, and his shoes
don't squeak. "Stand up."

She is hauled to her feet, still blinded.

"Up. Step up."

She is pulled onto a cold surface. She forces an eye open and looks down through the tears swimming over her vision. She's standing on scales. They're *weighing* her. She looks around the room, scared she won't have another chance. She was right: No defining features. No furniture.

Three men in the room. Two in black uniforms and a third—a doctor. She notes his badge and the insignia on it, but he's moving again before she can concentrate on discerning the letters.

"Good. Bring the chair in."

The two men in black wheel in a recliner-type chair. It looks medical, and she shivers and shrinks away.

"What do you want?" Her voice is so weak she realizes she hasn't spoken in…how long?

The men bolt the chair to the floor, each of four large screws turned into holes she hadn't noticed in the metal. They've done this before. She is "helped" onto the chair and strapped down.

"Hold still, unless you want to be sedated," the man in the white coat says, giving her a smile that makes her skin crawl. "It won't take a moment."

A tourniquet, a butterfly syringe. He takes six vials of blood with a deft hand. She complies with being still, reasoning that it will be less painful for her if she's not impaled more than needed or, as was threatened: sedated. Instead, she looks at everything while she can. She looks at his face, at every line and pore. She looks at the men who seem to be the muscle, who never glance at her or seem much bothered by anything. She looks at the door, trying to work out how she can fiddle the handle to escape.

They are obviously priming her for something. Fattening her up, as it were. But for what?

Eventually she is released, sans blood, and the chair unbolted from the floor. She wishes they'd leave it. She's almost forgotten what it feels like to sleep on something soft, and even the stiff vinyl of that contraption would be an improvement.

They lock the door behind them, and nothing she does can get it to open again.

The lights linger for a few precious seconds before she is plunged into darkness once more. With the night comes the thoughts:

Why did they bring me here?

                             Why are they taking my blood?

          Who is the man in the lab coat and what does he want?

                             Are they planning to sell me to the highest bidder in some far-away country where I'll never escape?

One thought persists above all:
I'm not getting out of this alive.

13

I am churning thought held back by practical sensation. The forgiving rubber on the bottom of trainers pounding the rain-slicked pavement. Breath hot in my ears. Lungs tight with adrenaline, stomach swimming in cortisol.

Seward's voice in my head. *I'm a professional. Try to be one too.*

I flinch and jog faster.

How could I have let myself get so carried away? So helplessly and determinedly wrapped up in fantasy? Conjecture. Conspiracy theories. Humiliation drives me harder, and I sprint the last half mile to my flat. Inside I strip off my running gear in the bathroom and turn the shower on as hot as it'll go, biting back my scream as the water hits my frigid skin. Forty-five minutes later—four-and-five-is-nine is three, three, three—I'm pink and raw and on my knees, shivering as I scrub the tiles with bleach. Back to the old routine.

I am a fool for thinking Renée was somehow connected to Lucy, for chasing theories and ghosts. I can't believe I fell down a rabbit hole of mysterious clubs, internet forums, and dozens of connected cases... And all for Lucy. This is the reason emotions are dangerous. I threw logic a decade and a half in the making out the window for the chance to save her. But where were the facts? Where was the evidence? Why did I ignore the glaring holes?

In the kitchen I make verbena tea with swollen fingers cracked at the knuckles and two perfect eggs that I eat without pleasure, left to right, right to left, ignoring the hollow space I live in.

Merino wool jumper.

Cotton blend trousers.

Sensible boots.

French twist.

Back to the life I worked so bloody hard for.

My nine-o'clock appointment is with a woman whose husband was arrested six months ago for domestic assault. She's dealing with the guilt of it. She ruined his life. What a worthless wretch. What a goddamn waste. If only she hadn't said anything. Now her son hates her.

At ten fifteen I see a mother whose daughter won't speak and hasn't for close to a year. I explain about selective mutism and suggest I work with her daughter alone. The mother is agitated and anxious. Her daughter is failing school. What future will she have if she won't talk? What will everyone else think? The embarrassment is unbearable.

Eleven thirty: a sexual assault case. I almost don't go. My own thoughts and feelings have slipped out of my chest like a lewd pair of breasts, no longer contained in the corset that worked just fine for years. Another mug of verbena tea and I zipper them back into place, thinking, *Renée, Lucy, Renée, Lucy*. I arrive thirty minutes late. The social worker is kind, but out of her depth. I run the show and provide a supplementary report to the police. I leave after having assured the terrified victim that I will see her soon. She looks at me like I have the answer. Like I can mend the thing that has been broken in her, and I feel like a charlatan.

I eat an apple for lunch in my car, staring ahead.

I shouldn't have to tell you that in our profession, we base our actions on evidence.

Patients sometimes die under our care. It's a reality in our profession.

I close my eyes and pinch the papery skin on my knuckles.

My days roll over one another like a formless blob, an endless cycle of trauma wrapped up in my new insecurity.

On Thursday morning, I wake with a sense of palpable gloom. I stare at the ceiling and try to mindfully focus on my senses. I see a white ceiling so perfectly plastered that I can't even form images out of the imperfections in the work. The dull smell of yesterday's bleach swims toward me from the bathroom. My flat is silent—empty—but the roar of the city behind these flimsy walls and flimsier glass is so loud I can't think straight. How have I never noticed?

I sit up and take a sip of the stale verbena tea on my bedside table and head for the bathroom (one, two, three, four, five, six, seven, eight, nine steps), pausing in the doorway. What is Mum doing right now? Harvesting squash in the garden, maybe? Off to town for an early book club meeting? And Lucy? Still in the hospital? Or back at home, recovering from her infusions? And Jonathan...what might he be doing now? Asleep in his bed? Alone? With someone?

I hit my forehead against the architrave, my head singing when the already paper-thin skin splits. I press my fingers to the wound and close my eyes, imagining Jonathan's lips in their place. Hot. Soft. I swallow.

Stupid...so stupid.

Later, in the kitchen, I've mostly got a handle on my roaming mind, but a niggling tug of curiosity draws me to the online Tylluan newspaper. Just a look, I promise myself. A peek, and then I'll forget it all.

The top story is a report on the Tylluan rural show. The pig racing was the highlight of the day. The photograph makes me smile and roll my eyes. A row of pigs in numbered tunics race toward a tiny jump, the blurred faces of the people watching open-mouthed, cheers and screams for the victor.

I scroll down to the next story, my shoulders beginning to unknit, and my eyes catch on the headline.

It's an update on the story I saw in Mr. Wynn's corner shop.

SEARCH WIDENS FOR MISSING LOCAL GIRL

Sixteen-year-old Seren Evans, who went missing from Tylluan over a month ago, is still missing after a nearly fifty-day search. Local authorities and volunteers have combed the surrounding area and trails, showing no trace of the missing person. Police are now working with other law enforcement in several adjacent counties to widen the search. According to family, Evans showed no signs of distress in the days leading up to her disappearance. "It's like she just vanished," Mrs. Catrin Evans told reporters. "One day my baby girl was knocking about with her friends, and the next day she's gone."

More updates will follow as the situation develops.

Beneath the article, there's an embedded video clip. I click Play and watch as a broad, rough-looking girl with square features scowls at the reporter somewhere off camera. The ticker tape below the screen reads: "Rhiannon Jones, friend."

"With me now," a fresh-faced reporter says, "is Rhiannon Jones, a local of Tylluan and best friend of Seren Evans. Can you shed any light on the situation with Seren? Was there anything unusual about her the night before she disappeared?"

Rhiannon tosses a roll-up away and spits a flick of tobacco from her lip. "How should I know?" She shrugs. "I mean, yeah. She'd been poorly a few days before, but that's about it. Hives. Shivers, like. I reckoned too many piss-ups. Lightweight."

I frown and watch the video clip again, paying close attention to Rhiannon's face. The tension around her mouth is ingrained—years of hard living and tough talking. But the twitch in the corner of one eye...that's stress. She's not saying something.

Stop it.

I shut my laptop and dump my cold tea in the sink, reminding myself to stop looking for connections where there are none. I'm leaping to conclusions. I'm making stretches. Maybe she didn't like being on camera—simple as that.

It's nothing. *Nothing.*

Yet...the niggle in my brain is still there. What harm would it do if I went back to Wales for a few days? What harm could there possibly be in going to see my mother and my friend?

Rationalizations are still running through my mind as I pack my bag once again and ask Kerry to postpone all my meetings.

14

I push back my shoulders and take a deep breath, steeling myself for what I know is coming. *She's just a woman.* I grit my teeth and let myself in my mother's front door.

"Mum?"

I find her in the conservatory, picking cherry tomatoes and cucumbers from plants that rise to the ceiling, putting them into a wicker basket that she holds against her hip like a toddler. She looks up when I approach.

"Back so soon?" Her eyebrows shoot up dramatically before she turns back to her plants. "Certainly not for my company."

"I'm sorry I left without saying goodbye, but there was a work emergency and I had to get back. It couldn't be helped."

"You practiced that how many times?"

I swallow down my retort and put my small bag by the door. *It's nice to see you too.* Forget pleasantries. They're meaningless here anyway. I doubt that anything less than falling on my knees and begging for her merciful forgiveness would do any good. Maybe not even that.

"You know Lucy's ill?"

"Of course I do. She's like my—" She swallows. "She's my friend, Mina."

I know what she was going to say. *She's like my daughter.* What she feels inside; what she never felt with me. I don't care, I remind myself. Our relationship was always complicated—I don't allow personal feelings to get in the way of my work, of my patients. And for better or worse, Lucy *is* my patient. She asked me to be her doctor, to come and help her, drunk or no, and so I will. London reminded me that inside, I'm steel.

"So, I'm here to treat her."

She sniffs. "So I'm to be a hotel again?"

"Would you rather I stay in one?"

The truth is, I still need to stay with my mother. As much as it galls me, fills me with a rage I clamp an iron fist over, my mother and Lucy have a unique bond. Lucy always confided in her, not having a mother of her own to do that with—at least, not a mother who cared—and so she told mine things that I would learn days or even weeks later. It was the one thing I never liked, but couldn't deny her. I could never deny Lucy anything. Still can't, it seems. So, I need to question my mother subtly, try to find out what Lucy is hiding. Because she *is* hiding something. A lover, a drug habit—something. It might be small. Something seemingly inconsequential. And if she won't tell me, then she'd tell my mother.

My mother.

The child inside me, the one aching over the hurt my mum has caused, of her blame and hatred toward me, yearns for the years when she would hold me and tell me everything was going to be okay, that I could shine a light on any shadows and make them vanish like an extinguished flame.

Lucy and I have a lot in common, the least of which is this: we both have mothers who don't want us.

"Well, what do you think you can do about it?" Mum asks, turning away like she doesn't care.

"Everything I can."

I imagine her lips pinch, the slight raise in her eyebrows that begs to differ. She glances at me like she wants to say something else—to confide in me—but then she purses her lips again.

"Your room's not changed location since you left," she says, nodding toward the stairs. "Off with you, then."

At Ifori, Cariad leads me up the curving staircase and along a white-carpeted corridor to Lucy's bedroom. It's an open space, and would usually be bright, I think, but now the curtains are drawn over what I assume are floor-to-ceiling windows, casting the room in muggy shadows. Lucy is propped up on pillows, smiling wanly at me. Now I am sure she and Arthur don't share a room. There isn't a lick of masculinity anywhere in this place. No telltale male lived-in-ness. All I see is Lucy when I look around.

Lucy lies pale against her white sheets, propped up with pillows so fluffy they make her look even more gaunt than she is. I try not to let my shock show. In only a week, she's deteriorated so quickly. Her cheekbones protrude below shadowed, sunken eyes. Her lips are chapped and pale.

I realize she's been putting on a brave face in her texts, pretending everything is normal when it clearly is anything but. The infusions aren't working. Lucy is getting sicker.

"Lucy…"

She looks worse. Why does she look worse? I put the plastic bag I brought with me on the floor and take her hand, papery on the bedspread and just as sallow. "How are you doing, Goose?"

"Bambi," she whispers, her lips parting like sandpaper, a trail of white gunk stretching between them before popping, a depressing balloon. "You're back."

My stomach jolts to see her so pale and weak. Only last week she was laughing raucously as we drank cheap boxed wine and fine whiskey, chatting about the old days.

"You're not doing what you're told and getting better," I say, mock accusing.

"I'm a rebel."

I squeeze her hand. "I know. What have they told you?"

"Nothing much. The infusions help, for a while. Then I just get bad again. And the ferrous... Those pills?"

"Ferrous fumarate. Iron tablets."

She grins, her teeth large in her skinny face. "You know they make your poop black, don't you? This was all an elaborate prank, wasn't it?"

I force a smile. "You got me. It has been my quest all along to give you black cack."

A breathy laugh, a weak cough. "Knew it. At least it isn't vaginal leeches."

A surprised laugh pisses out of me. *"What?"*

"Oh come on, you don't remember the vaginal leeches?"

"Should I?"

Lucy chuckles. "We used to have a fact battle about leeches. I can't believe you don't remember."

A memory rises from the mire. "Amazonian leeches can grow to be as long as eighteen inches..."

"Most medical leeches are Welsh! And even though life sucked as teens..." Lucy prompts, eyebrows raised.

"At least we didn't have—"

"Vaginal leeches!" we scream, together.

We fall about laughing, but Lucy has a coughing fit and can't get enough air and the levity falls dead, fast. I fix her pillows. Eventually, she lies back again, panting.

"I really am feeling better," she says. "The sleepwalking hardly ever happens now. I'm just a little tired. They gave Arthur a copy of the bloodwork results. There, in that folder."

She points to the dressing table at the other end of the room where a blue folder sits on top.

"Mind if I look?"

My mind goes to all the darkest places. Has she had a stroke? Is she suffering from early-onset dementia? Did she have a traumatic brain injury that no one remembers? Could it be a brain tumor?

She shakes her head. "You're the doctor."

I get up and flip through the pages, running my finger down the list of blood results. They don't look great. The repeated FBCs are odd. They improve and then get worse, then improve and then get worse.

"They told me to rest as much as I could," she says. "So, I'm doing it. But it's boring." She pats the bed, calling me over again. "Enough of Dr. Mina. I want to know how my Bambi is. What was it like seeing your mum again? I bet she was glad to see you."

"Seeing Mum was…interesting. She's the same as ever."

"Batty?"

"Very. She loves leaning into her reputation. I'm convinced of it."

"'Course she does," Lucy says, grinning. "And when I'm older I fully intend to take on the mantle of batty after her. I'll cultivate it like a fine wine. People will smell me before they see me."

I pull a face.

"Because of all the herbs and incense!" Lucy clarifies, laughing, her lips stretching so wide I worry they'll split.

I wince at the smell of her breath. Sweet. Fruity. Her liver isn't doing well. Even if I hadn't seen her LFTs, I'd know it because of this scent.

"And Jonathan?" she asks after a moment, watching me closely.

I take a breath and pick lint off my jumper. "What about him?"

"Did you see him again? Did you talk?"

"We sort of talked. I'm not sure you could call it a conversation. He's very different."

"How?"

I gesture vaguely. I don't really want to get into it, but I blurt it out anyway. "Something took the light away. He's more…"

"Like you?"

I think about this. "Yes. I suppose that's one way to put it. He's more like me."

"Mistress of mystery," Lucy intones importantly. "Cone of silence."

"Just more… I don't know. Like me."

Lucy smiles with her eyes. "Well, that can only be a good thing."

"You're too good to me. Now, tell me when your next trans-fusion is."

She rolls her eyes and I see a tinge of yellow. Damn.

"Next week. Monday. *So. Boring.*"

"You'll let me know how you feel afterward?"

She scoffs. "I can see this is what you're going to take for juicy gossip now."

"Only when it's about you."

"I'm flattered."

"Oh, and I brought you something," I say, reaching down to grab the plastic bag. "But I suspect you won't be able to enjoy it until you're feeling a little better."

I lift out the gift bag inside so she can see.

"What is it?" she asks, perking up.

A pang of nostalgia; she always did have a penchant for gifts. She hasn't changed. Which means that in some ways, I still know her very well.

I lift the pink teddy bear I picked up from a tiny shop when I passed through Birmingham. It has a patched-on ear in a checked pattern that makes it look like it's scowling. Lucy gives a girlish squeal of delight.

"Oh, Mina! I love her!"

She makes grabby hands, the pantomime of a child, and I hand the ball of fluff over. She hugs it to her and kisses the top of its head.

"I shall name her Ellie-belly," she declares, rubbing the bear's stomach, which is a circular area made of the same checked material.

"She reminded me of—"

"*Shauna-Sore-foot!*" she finishes my sentence.

Shauna-Sore-foot was a teddy that Lucy had since she was a toddler. One day my mother had found Lucy screaming in the middle of the kitchen. The bear's foot was on the floor surrounded by the carnage of its own cotton fluff. My mother had sewn the thing back together—sans foot, which Lucy declared was full of "the *green gang*"—while Lucy hiccup-sobbed and I watched with wide, fearful eyes. She had been known as Shauna-Sore-foot thereafter.

Lucy and I sigh in unison.

"I'd forgotten about that ratty old thing," she says wistfully. "She started out pink like this and ended up being a muggy sort of beige."

"I thought Ellie-belly might be a good companion to help you feel better."

"As long as her feet don't fall off, I'm good."

"No, we can't have any of those *green gangs* turning up."

She snorts a laugh and I grin. This is us. Being goofy and ridiculous.

"Now let me get some rest, you vagabond," she says, leaning across her bed to put Ellie-belly next to her beneath the duvet. As she does, the shoulder of her nightdress slides off.

The rash is worse.

"Lucy, have you had this looked at?"

She blinks and looks down at her shoulder. "Oh this? It's a bit of contact dermatitis from the hospital sheets. I refuse to believe they cleaned up after the last person died in that thing."

"You had this rash before you went in. I saw it when you had that seizure."

"Oh." She shrugs. "I don't know. I'll have a doctor look at it."

"I have to go," I manage, forcing a smile. "I'll text you."

"Only if it's about Jonathan or your mam or anything else that's juicy. I refuse to allow you to bore me with my own mortality."

A sliver of cold cuts through me at that word and the sight of that rash in such close proximity.

"I love you, Bambi," she whispers, and closes her eyes. There's a peaceful moment and then a cough ripples through her. Before I've blinked, she's vomited up bile and blood on the bedspread. Her eyes roll into the back of her head and her body goes stiff, her hands and feet rigid.

In one horrible motion, a convulsion throws her from the bed onto the floor, where she vomits up more blood. It smears over her face, slimy with bile, and sticks in her hair like blood on snow.

"Lucy—shit. Help! We need help in here!"

How many seizures has she been having? This one is so much worse than the one she had before. I can almost feel her bones creaking. She's turning blue, the blood frothing at her lips.

I call again, for Arthur, Cariad, whoever is closest—but it seems I'm too far away for anyone to hear.

I ease her onto her side and drag one of her fallen pillows across and put it under her head. She fell on the floor pretty hard and could have a concussion, but I can keep it from getting worse. A spreading warmth across my knees where I kneel, and I realize she's lost control of her bladder, her white nightdress soaked with dark urine.

I call her name to see if she's conscious, but her eyes are still rolling in her head and there's no response.

Suddenly, Arthur bursts into the room, panting. "Oh my God!" he says, racing toward us.

"She's having another seizure," I say weakly.

"I'm so glad you were here—again." Arthur's voice cracks as he strokes Lucy's hair.

I glance at my watch. It's been three minutes. "Can you get me a phone? I need to ring an ambulance."

Arthur scrambles to his feet and grabs the phone, which sits on the wall by the door, all the while I curse my negligence in leaving my sodding mobile in the car. He hands it to me, almost dropping it, and I call 999. I go through the motions, and she's put on priority 1.

My hands shake as I give the phone back to Arthur. Unbidden, tears spring into my eyes and I turn back to Lucy.

The tonic-clonic lasts for another harrowing minute, during which she turns a deeper shade of blue.

When it finally ends, Arthur and I adjust her recovery position and she gasps in a rattling breath. I can't believe this. Why did they discharge her when she's clearly not well?

The sound of sirens echoes through the windows. A sigh escapes my lips and Arthur's entire body begins to shiver uncontrollably. When our eyes meet, his expression is a mirror to my own. Love. Despair. Worry. Relief.

Cariad bursts into the room with the EMTs, and in a cacophonous flurry, they lift Lucy onto a stretcher. Since I'm not family, they won't let me ride in the ambulance. Arthur casts one last glance toward me as he trails behind them, a silent *thank-you* on his thin lips. Within moments, the room is nearly empty.

The sudden silence is deafening. The grandfather clock ticks in the corner, and a draft blows through the room as Cariad lifts a window to air out the putrid smells. For the first time I notice my hands. Covered in bile and blood. I feel the icy wetness on my knees where I knelt in Lucy's urine. My neck begins a furious itch, and soon my hands are burning.

"Take me to the bathroom," I manage.

Cariad hurries me into the bathroom next door, where I blast the water until it's scalding and wash my hands over and over and over and over. My mind is screaming.

I am in control.

I am in control.

IamincontrolIamincontrolIamincontrolIamincontrolIamincontrolIamin-
controlIamincontrolIamincontrolIamincontrolIamincontrolIamincontrolI-
amincontrolIamincontrolIamincontrolIamincontrolIamincontrolIamincon-
trolIamincontrolIamincontrolIamincontrolIamincontrolIamincontrolIamin-
controlIamincontrolIamincontrolIamincontrolIamincontrolIamincontrolI-
amincontrolIamincontrolIamincontrolIamincontrolIamincontrolIamincon-
trolIamincontrolIamincontrolIamincontrolIamincontrolIamincontrolIamin-
controlIamincontrolIamincontrolIamincontrolIamincontrolIamincontrolI-
amincontrolIamincontrolIamincontrolIamincontrolIamincontrolIamincon-
trolIamincontrolIamincontrolIamincontrolIamincontrolIamincontrolIamin-
controlIamincontrolIamincontrolIamincontrolIamincontrolIamincontrolI-
amincontrolIamincontrolIamincontrolIamincontrol—

The next thing I know I am rushing out of the house and throwing up on the gravel drive.

I hear someone behind me and hold out my hand to tell Cariad I'm okay. I hear a tread on the gravel as she draws closer so I turn to tell her to go back inside, but when I look up, I see nothing. No one.

I spin in a circle, sure I heard someone following me. The wind whistles in the trees, and for a moment, I swear I can hear a voice whisper my name. But I'm all alone—with my thoughts, with my despair.

"Lucy," I murmur. "How am I going to save you?"

15

I head to the beach. The skip is burning again, and a handful of kids mill about, sneaking booze from water bottles. The ones sitting closest on the pebbly sand eye me warily as I approach.

I pull free the pack of cigarettes I just bought and open it slowly, looking at the waves. I remove one and place it between my lips, despite the fact that I haven't smoked since Lucy and I were kids.

Lucy is still in hospital, still being poked and prodded as the doctors try to determine once more what is wrong with her. I visited her yesterday, but there was nothing for me to say or do. Sitting in the hospital waiting room, awash in the antiseptic smell and harsh overhead lighting, I reminded myself what had driven me back to Tylluan in the first place: the tenuous but possible connection between Lucy and the missing girl. And so, feeling helpless there, I decided to come here.

"I'm looking for someone," I say, not looking at the group of teens.

They ignore me.

"A cig for pointing me in the right direction."

Now I do look at them and am gratified to find them staring at me, considering.

"I'm not a snitch," one of the boys says, but he looks at my cigarette uncertainly.

"I'm not police."

"Who are you, then?"

"I grew up here."

They scoff. "Bollocks."

"My mam's Vanessa Murray."

They drop into a stunned silence for half a second and then fall about themselves laughing.

"Your mam's the batty witch up on the hill?"

At that I do light the cigarette and take a drag. "Yep."

Some things never change.

One of the lads offers his friend a broken crisp from a packet pulled from a pocket.

"What the fuck are that?" his mate gripes. "It wouldn't feed a bastard mouse!"

His friend snickers, shrugs, and eats the potato shard himself.

"Well? Want it or not?" I ask.

"I'll take the whole pack," the same kid says, leaning back and smirking.

"Only if you point at the person I want to talk to directly."

"And if I don't know them?"

"Then no cigarettes. I grew up here, remember? I know you kids know everyone and everything there is worth knowing."

He chews on his lips, glancing uncertainly at his mates. One of the girls nudges him and hisses, "Go on, Ig."

"Yeah, all right."

"Rhiannon Jones."

"Rhiannon?" One of the girls scoffs, sitting straighter. "What d'you want Rhiannon for?"

"My business."

"You said you weren't police."

"I'm not."

"Well, Ig?" I ask, holding the cigarettes out to him just beyond reach.

He sighs and points toward the skip where a group of boys and a large girl are mucking about.

"There. In the red anorak."

I toss the pack over and stroll away, hands in pockets, ostensibly to appear casual, but in reality I don't want them to see that I'm shaking. Behind me, they whoop and begin fighting over who gets the first one. My own cigarette falls to the sand to burn to ash—if they don't make a grab for that one too.

Rhiannon clocks me before the lads do and she's immediately on her guard. She looks rough. Like nothing fazes her and nothing gets through her exterior. She looks, for the most part, like most of the clients I had in my early days of work as a psychologist and I find that surprisingly reassuring.

"Rhiannon," I say calmly. "I need a word."

"Fuck off, lady."

"Unless you want your mates to hear what I have to say," I warn, sounding to my own ears like a teacher and hating it.

She glances at them and then back at me. "I ain't done nothing."

"No one said you did. I still need a word."

"Got any cigs? Saw you give Ignatius a bunch."

I eye her, then nod. "Only if you talk to me."

She scoffs and saunters away from the boys, who stare after her in bewilderment, like they never do anything without her say-so and without direct instructions are utterly stumped.

We walk in the opposite direction. I take the lead.

"Yeah?" she asks, when we're out of earshot.

"Where were you and Seren the night she went missing?"

"I wasn't with Seren the night she went missing," she claps back, a little too quickly.

"Look, I know you were. You were interviewed about it. I

saw the clip online. If you're going to lie, then I'll take the cigarettes and leave. Maybe I'll go chat to your parents instead."

"No!"

I turn to face her. "I don't give two shits about what you
were doing. I just need to know where you were and how Seren
seemed."

"Seemed?"

"Yeah. Was she acting normal? Was anything wrong with
her?"

"You're police?"

"Do I really give you a copper impression?" I snap.

She considers, eyeing me. "Not really."

"So? Out with it."

She sighs and pulls a stick of gum from her pocket, unwrap-
ping it and folding it into her mouth, chewing obnoxiously as
she talks. I try my best to ignore her saliva and my rising miso-
phonia.

"She was normal. Same as always, 'cept for some hives she
had, but you know that, and anyway, it weren't nothing too
unusual. We were bowling in Wrexham. She went to the loo
and never came back. I figured she went home. I was wiping
the floor with her and she was being a total baby." She shakes
her head. "Daft twat."

"That's all?"

"Yeah, that's all."

"Was she on drugs?"

Rhiannon snorts. "Seren? Fuck, no. Chinless wonder that
one, more like."

"Pardon?"

She shunts her chin forward, widening her eyes. "You know, a
mug? A ninny. A fucking baby—learn English, why don't you?"

"Did you notice her talking to anyone?"

She sighs, bored. "No. Can I go now?"

"Are you *sure*?"

"*Yes!* God."

"Nothing unusual at all about that night?"

She spits out her gum, missing my coat by a centimeter. "Nothing. Same as always. Now give me my cigs and leave me alone."

I frown and hand over the second box of cigarettes I bought, but I don't let go. She tugs and gives me a filthy stare.

"Your friend is *missing*, and you're acting like it's all a bore."

She swallows and for just a moment, I think I reached her. Then she scoffs again and rips the box from my hand and saunters away.

I'm about to leave when I hear her mutter, "Cunt."

V.

Something different finally happens.

They bring a young woman into her room.

She is pretty and dressed in the same sort of clothes they'd put her in when she first arrived. A chintzy dress that is more sparkly napkin than actual garment.

"Fuckers!" the young woman yells. "Fucking dick-swabs!"

She is feral. Pacing and scrabbling at the walls. Jennifer watches her for a long time, knowing they'll turn out the lights soon. This is the most interesting thing that's happened since she was doomed to this dungeon.

Eventually the girl calms down enough to sit on her haunches in the corner, looking everywhere but at the other person in her cell.

"Here," Jennifer says, handing her a jumper to sit on. She knows it will only be minutes before the bone-chilling cold of the floor sets in. The woman eyes her, then snatches it and pulls it on over her head.

She'll learn soon enough, Jennifer thinks with a sick sort of amusement.

"I'm Tiff," the woman says minutes later.

"Jennifer," she returns. Jennifer is like a coat she wears, a warm protection that keeps the real person safe inside. She doubts this girl's name is Tiff either.

"They can't do this," Tiff says. "This is totally illegal. This stuff doesn't happen in real life. Not *here*."

And who's to say she's wrong? Who's to say that this, here, right now, is real life?

She is angry. But indignation soon melts into fear. Into panic. Into terror.

Tiff scoots closer and closer, until eventually they are huddled together. Jennifer doesn't pull back. When Tiff cries, Jennifer wipes her tears away until they run dry.

"Best not waste the water, I suppose," she says.

"Oh, they feed and water us. It's actually sort of strange."

"I know," Tiff replies. "I've been here a long, long time. They take me out every now and then for a party. I haven't found a way out yet."

"Have they...?" Jennifer's sentence trails off.

She doesn't need to finish it. Every girl knows that almost-question.

Have they touched you? Have they hurt you?

Her silence is enough of an answer.

"They haul me upstairs for parties, and I always think, *This is it. This is my chance.*"

But they blindfold her and there are so many of them, all in on it. They dress her and parade around a room and then give her to one of the men. She fights and kicks and scratches, but he only hands her back with a laugh after he has his way with her. They bring her back down.

"'Still feisty,' one of them said tonight," Tiff says, spitting out the words in disgust. "Not broken yet. Good sign."

"Good sign for what?" I ask.

"For their creepy sex cult," Tiff says, kicking at the wall point-lessly. "Some of the girls are kept at the club, like me. Others are kept in the cellar until it's time for the big event." Her lips curl up in a smirk.

"What happens there?"

Tiff moves close to Jennifer and lowers her voice. "The first girl I ever met down here was named Laura. Laura had been told she was special. That she was invited to an exclusive party. She was never taken upstairs. Months passed. One day, she was taken away and never returned."

There's a wildness in her eyes now, a fear.

"I bet you're 'invited' too," she says, laughing. Scream-laughing. She sounds mad. Like a wolf. Not even human.

Jennifer knows what Tiff is implying. This event isn't something you come back from alive. Jennifer always knew death would come for her one day, but it's not something you can prepare for or think too closely about. She never would've imagined this.

"My nails are sharp," Jennifer says. "So there's that. None of the doctors they've sent in, or the lackeys who bring the food and drinks, have thought to cut them. And I have my teeth. I can at least do some damage."

Tiff responds with a grim smile and nods, pondering her own fingers.

"Do what you can," she says, but her eyes are dull when she says it.

Hours pass, and then days, and then weeks.

The women make a plan to escape. They scrap it and make it simpler. They go over it and over it, poking holes in it and looking for second-, third-, fourth-case scenarios.

It's enough to make Jennifer hope they actually have a chance at making it out of this place.

The day finally comes when the metal door swings open. Guards step forward and grab Tiff by the arms. She screams, and Jennifer knows it's now or never. She grabs on to one of the guards and quickly fixes him in a chokehold. For a moment, he's distracted, and Tiff tries to wriggle free. But a sudden flash of pain shoots through Jennifer's entire body—a bolt of electricity that sends her crumpling to the floor. Her limbs twitch involuntarily and her vision blurs. She can just make out the swing of the door as light evaporates from the room.

She is shut in. Alone.

The plan disappears on a breath. They weren't ready. The men were too strong.

Tiff is gone for hours. Jennifer paces the cell four hundred times and wonders dimly how many steps her pedometer would have tracked.

When they bring Tiff back, something has changed. They throw her in, and she doesn't get up off the floor.

"What happened?" Jennifer asks. "What did they do?"

She gets down and pulls Tiff onto her lap. Her head lolls and her eyes roll back before lazily meeting Jennifer's gaze.

"Who are you?" she says. "Geddoffme." Her voice slurs, and Tiff pushes weakly against her. The jumper Jennifer lent her is gone.

Jennifer leaves her on the floor, groaning and rolling about like gravity can't make up its mind. "Tiff," she says, a jolt of panic bursting inside as her eyes roll toward her.

"Who?" she asks.

16

The high street is a different world, which isn't a surprise. Businesses came and went during my childhood like changing lightbulbs, a procession of hope and dismay. One constant was the hairdressers, Cuts and Curls for Boys and Girls, which every parent in the surrounding villages used and every kid dreaded. Bowl cuts, anyone? Now I see it's under new management and has new branding: Curl Up and Dye. I smirk. Clever.

Roe's Plaice, the only restaurant outside of the local pub, is still here too, but I asked Jonathan for drinks, not dinner. Anything more would be presumptuous, especially after the way we left things. I'm surprised he was willing to meet me at all. There's still an hour and a half until he arrives, so I place an order for a fish and chips to go and then walk to the promenade, leaning into the wind. It's weirdly deserted, even though this beach is lined with arcades that stay open well into the night, preprogrammed voices calling *Candy floss! Popcorn!* And *Take your chances!* There's something depressing about a deserted beach arcade on a stormy evening.

I'm still not sure exactly what this drink is for...but I had to try to get him to talk to me, one more time. I know he has things he needs to say to me—he *must* have things to say. And he'll expect things said in return. Explanations, maybe, which I can't give. But maybe we'll dance around the issue, talk about the present, chitchat and bullshit our way through a pint or two, which would suit me fine. Who am I to therapize myself? Or him?

Tomorrow is October 1, the day I always insisted we change the autumnal décor my mother put up at the end of August in favor of dedicated Halloween fare. She would grin and help me, all the while telling me legends surrounding Nos Galan Gaeaf, the Welsh version of Samhain; Ysbrydnos, the spirit night.

As I left the house this evening, I passed by my mother silently. This year there are no decorations. No stories. No cheer. Not even her shrewd warnings to avoid churchyards, crossroads, and stiles, for the spirits gather there, making their communion. No tickles as she cried, *"Adref, adref, am y cyntaf, Hwch Ddu Gwta a gipio'rola!"* Home, home, at once, the tailless black sow shall snatch the last!

All the cheer, all the ridiculous tales, replaced with silent reproach, and I have never felt so unwelcome.

I wondered, as I walked down the garden path, when she'd stopped decorating…then realized I knew. I almost turned and said something. *Sorry*, maybe, but her back was to me, and I hurried away like a coward. The walls between us are so high I can no longer even see her, so thick, I don't think she can hear me calling her name.

I open my newspaper-wrapped parcel and pluck out a soggy chip. It's still warm, salty and tangy on my tongue. This used to be the best thing ever, a chippy on the beach.

Ever since I've been back, things I had suppressed keep rising to the surface of my memory, and he's in a lot of them. Jonathan. It was easier to forget him when I was two hundred and fifty miles away, in another world, occupied with work and research. But here, every street, every beach, every hill…all of it has some association with him. His image rises like a chimera at all hours. Lying in bed this morning, the Jonathan I knew and the Jonathan that is lay interposed in my mind, battling for space, and I kept wondering... How much of what he is, is because of what I did to him? The same self-involved question over and over.

When I'm done with my food, I throw it in one of the bins and begin the long, cold walk back to the pub. Once inside, I get a pint of Magners and find one of the tables huddled by the fireplace and sit down.

Ten minutes after eight, it occurs to me that he might not show. By twenty past, I'm certain he won't. I should have expected this... If I'd been in his place, I might have done the same, but it pangs nonetheless.

Then the doorbell chimes, and he's here. He looks uncertainly around, his eyes darkening when he doesn't find me. I panic, stand, and wave awkwardly, and he visibly relaxes.

"Thought you'd stood me up," I say when he reaches me.

"Thought about it," he admits.

There is a long silence.

"I was surprised to get your text," he says at last.

"As surprised as I was to send it, I'll wager."

We stare at each other for a second too long and then he mutters, "Well," and takes the armchair across from mine.

"I'm glad you didn't. Stand me up, I mean."

His face is undecipherable, but if I were to take a stab at a read, it would be: *Yeah, we'll see about that.*

"Pint?" I ask after a moment.

"Got an early start."

I nod. "Okay. Coke?"

"Yeah, cheers."

"Want any food?" I ask, but he shakes his head and pulls off his gloves, tucking them under his arm like he's not planning to stay long.

"Make it a Guinness, actually."

I smile. "Same old. Thought you had an early start?"

He looks at me.

I nod. "Back in a bit."

I return with his drink and sit down, then realize I've had more than half of mine and get up to fetch another.

"Remember that time we tried to go mussel picking?" I ask when I get back the second time, having thought of it at the bar.

He has all the power here; he can rebuff me or engage, can reminisce or brood, and I find myself yearning for an actual conversation with someone that doesn't revolve around the possibility of death.

He gives me a probing look. "You thought you were so damn clever."

"I *was* so damn clever. We got a free meal if you recall."

"I *recall* chewing on sand for half an hour and pretending to love it."

I laugh, rubbing at my hands, which feel hot and itchy now that they've defrosted. "Yeah, yeah. So, it wasn't my finest moment."

He returns his attention to the fire.

"What do you remember?" I ask at last.

He goes very still, raising his eyes to my face. I can't read his expression.

"Don't," he says quietly.

I nod. "Okay."

"Tell me about your life now," he says, leaning back in his chair and watching me.

I feel like I'm at a job interview, and I'm suddenly nervous. He's scrutinizing me. Testing me, maybe.

"Well…it's…life. Ordinary. Boring."

"Your ordinary and mine are different."

Fair.

"Well, each day begins the same. I wake early, go for a run, then get back and shower." I pause here, swallowing down my almost-blunder, nearly telling him about my rituals with the bleach and counting steps. "Then I go to work. It might be a session with a private client. It might be a consult—anything, really. I spend most of the day with patients or writing up notes. Listening to them, observing. Trying to figure out how to help people more broken than me," I say with an effort at a laugh.

He takes a swig from his Guinness, thoughtful.

"What about you? What does a normal day look like for you?"

"Farm work."

"Are you— I mean…you're not married, then?"

He narrows his eyes. "No. You?"

I shake my head, my throat tightening. "Nope. Work, you know."

"Yep."

Suddenly this all seems very funny to me. "God, this is…"

He manages a smile, which might look grotesque to others, with his face half pulled down by the scars, but to me it looks glorious. All of a sudden, that shiny, ruined skin is the most beautiful thing I've seen in a long while.

"Weird, yeah."

"You know," I hedge, "being home, everything reminds me of you. Of back then. The hills, the hedges along the lanes, the beaches—all of it."

He watches me warily, but I plow on.

"Remember how Mum wouldn't let you come round the house because Dad had always said no boys were allowed, besides himself?"

A nod.

"So, I snuck you round the back onto the hill behind the cottage and we'd climb up to the forest on the crest?"

Another nod.

"When the silage was stored there," I add, "we'd climb to the top, sitting on those black bales like kings of the land."

He heaves a sigh.

"Even the trees remind me of you."

"Mina—"

"Here we are, then." The waitress from the bar places a basket of bread on the table. "On the house," she says, eyeing Jonathan in a way I don't much care for.

"Thanks, Gina."

Gina hovers for a moment, grinning, then prances back to the bar, where she picks up a glass and begins polishing it, never taking her eyes off us.

"She's friendly," I mutter, gulping down the last of my first beer.

"She's just a kid with a crush."

I feel scolded somehow. Humiliated.

After a long, awkward silence, I ask, "You never went to uni?"

The muscles in his face twitch, distorting his scar. "No."

"It's just...you always spoke about it with such passion. You were going to Reading to study archaeology. Everyone knew that."

"Yeah, well. Things change."

"Yeah. They really do."

He sighs. "This chitchat—"

"Chitchat?" I can't help but grin.

"It's... I thought it would be..."

A silence stretches between us as wide as the English Channel. It's like we're both painfully holding our breath.

"Why are you really here?" he asks. "And don't lie to me again about visiting your mam. We both know that's not the reason."

I look down, wiping the sweat off my Magners. "It's because of Lucy. She's ill, Jonathan. And she asked for my help."

Jonathan frowns. "And why would you do that? After all the years she needed you. You didn't seem to care then."

"I never stopped caring about her. About all of you." The pitch of my voice begins to rise as my throat tightens. I purse my lips and swallow, regaining control.

He sighs. "You know...we thought you'd been taken. Kidnapped. Before your mother saw your empty wardrobe and the letter shoved inside the microwave. We went to the police. Me, Quincey, Lucy, and your mam, all of us marching up to the station like idiots."

I swallow. So, we're doing this now. Here.

"I'm sorry."

"You're fucking sorry?" He laughs derisively. He's so angry he's shaking with it. "That fixes everything, then, yeah?"

"I don't know what else to say."

"How about some honesty? What happened?"

My pulse quickens and my mind begins to race. Telling him should be so easy; I've now confessed to Lucy, or at least got close enough to the truth that she could infer the rest. I've also shared with a handful of clients over the years, in order to build trust, to let them know that someone understands. I've said the words before: *I was attacked.* And yet, telling Jonathan feels impossible, the words trapped in my throat. I'm afraid that if I tell him what happened, he will never look at me the same. Worse, I know that, because of when and how it happened, he will blame himself.

"I want to tell you," I say quietly. "I just can't."

He stands and puts on his gloves, then walks out of the pub without another word. I pause, my face red with humiliation, then get up and follow, angry now.

"Jonathan!" I yell, running after him. He's headed for the beach.

"Twelve years, Mina," he growls when I reach him. "I've waited twelve years."

"I know. But...you seem like you understand that the past is sometimes best left where it is."

He stops and considers me, the fury still there. "Sometimes, yes."

"Because it would cause too much pain to wrench it into

the here and now." I pause, choosing my words carefully. "Can we agree that mistakes were made—terrible mistakes?" I take a breath, resolved. "And that I won't ask about your pain if you don't ask about mine?"

There is something happening in his face as he unpicks the words I've carefully chosen. Some understanding that only people who own deep trauma have. The sky opens, drenching us both in bitter Welsh rain.

He steps closer to me, his breath coming fast. He's about to say something cutting, I know it—I can see it in the way he's bared his teeth. Instead, he takes a breath, searching my eyes, and then his lips are on mine.

We meet each other in a hungry kiss.

He holds me so tightly to his body that I can feel him trembling, and I grip him back harder. My stomach leaps up to join my racing heart. I moan, low in my throat.

He lets me go. Too sudden. Cold.

"I was addicted to you," he says, his lips almost touching mine.

"Jonathan, please—"

He closes his eyes. "Took me a long time to realize that you were bad for me." He looks up, his eyes bright. "You still are."

He turns and leaves and there is nothing I can do to bring him back to me.

17

Days pass, and I feel stalled, at a loss.

I talk to Lucy, who is once more back at home, having been discharged from the hospital without any more answers than she had before. She tries to be cheerful, but I can tell how exhausted she is, and I wonder for the millionth time what is happening to her—and what I can do to help. What am I doing here, if not making progress on Lucy's condition? Certainly not making any progress with Jonathan, who I haven't spoken to since our drinks date, if you can call it that. Not making any progress on my medical mystery, which plagues my nights, as I toss and turn, wondering what is happening to these women. Renée Fields, dead... Will Lucy be next?

Mum and I continue to circle each other carefully, trying not to get in each other's way as we go about our day-to-day. When she leaves the local paper out one morning, I read it with my coffee, and pause on a detail that makes me both frustrated and hopeful.

Explaining it to Mum, I ask her for a favor, and she grudgingly obliges. Maybe things aren't completely stalled, after all.

★ ★ ★

Rhiannon arrives at the house looking as sullen as ever, bundled in the same dingy red anorak she wore that day at the beach.

I meet her at the back gate and indicate the track leading up into the hills. Yes, Mum helped with getting Rhiannon here today—guilting her into talking to me again—but no need for her to overhear this conversation.

"Didn't know you were one of us," Rhiannon says accusingly when we're well away from the house, eyeing me sideways and fidgeting with her nose piercing. It seems she also wants to get away from prying ears.

"You never asked."

She scoffs, and the half smile changes her face into something less batrachian. It's drizzling, but she doesn't seem to mind.

"You lied to me—"

"I never," she snaps, cutting me off.

"The bowling alley closed down six months ago. I saw something about the new shop going into that space in the paper."

She scowls at the heather and gorse, purple and yellow against the dying bracken, but offers me no explanation.

"So maybe you'd like to tell me the truth? About where you and Seren really were that night?"

"Maybe you'd like to bog off."

"You realize I know your mother, don't you?"

A half-truth. My *mother* knows her mother.

"Yeah and…? Is that meant to scare me?"

I sigh and come to a stop. She's here, after all, which means I'll get her to talk to me eventually. I just have to be patient. "You know, I worked really hard to get away from this town, and here I am, right back where I started."

"Sucks to be you."

"Sucks to be *us*, actually. Some of us never leave places like this, but some of us don't survive it either. Seren is *missing*. Your supposed friend? Do you even give a toss about that?"

A flicker of uncertainty flits across her face, but then the shutters go down again. For all her bravado, she's still only a kid,
and I'd rather help keep her hale and full of that bastard attitude
than turning into a victim, like Seren. Like Lucy.

"Look, I'm no grasser. Not for a posh mouse like you."

"You can't snitch on the kidnapped," I point out. "But it's
not honor keeping you quiet. You're scared. I can see it all over
you. You're the mouse."

She opens her mouth to clap back, but I go on before she can
say anything.

"I'm a therapist, and I lost a patient recently—a girl a little
bit like your Seren," I say, resting my arms against the wooden
stile, looking out at the fields beyond. I glance at Rhiannon.
Note her penetrating gaze. "She was young, vulnerable. Went
missing, just like your friend. Nobody looked for her, not even
her family. They barely noticed she was gone. And now she's
dead. She died friendless, alone. Probably scared and in pain."

She gazes off into the distance beside me, thinking. Weighing my words, and her options.

"Someone is messing with young, poor women, thinking
they can get away with it because no one misses girls like you.
Like *Seren*." I turn to her. "And they're right. Girls from here are
the perfect victims because no one gives a shit, not even you."

She bites her lip, for the first time unsure. "If I tell you, you're
just going to go to the coppers."

I laugh, tired. "Honestly, Rhi? I don't care about what you
were doing. I just need to know where you were."

Rhiannon pulls on her bottom lip with two fingers. "We had
a row. Seren and me. Like a proper row. It happened because…
Well, she's usually such a mouse. Then she got this invitation
from a rich bloke to go to Cysgod to discuss some job. She had
his fancy business card—she was so proud, she showed it to me,
even though he told her not to bandy it about. I warned her not
to go. Said it was dodgy, but she said I was jealous that it was *her*

chosen to go on a date to Cysgod and not me, like I even give a monkey's. That was the last time we spoke. I saw her after that, but I was still raging. She looked sick though, I remember that, and I thought *Yeah, good. Serves her right.* And when I saw those disgusting hives I knew she'd got an STD or something. I knew it was a sex thing. How stupid can you get?"

All of my alarm bells are going off. "Why didn't you tell the police any of this?"

"I thought it was illegal. Didn't want to get Seren into trouble, even if she is a knob-head. I guess that might've been stupid."

"This business card, what did it look like?"

"Black, I think, with some symbol on it. Otherwise, fuck all."

"Is there anything else you can think of?"

"No."

I nod. "Okay. Thank you for telling me."

I turn to leave, but she grabs my sleeve. "I didn't mean for her to get taken."

"I know."

There's fire in Rhiannon's eyes. "I hope whoever did it dies."

"Me too," I admit, hating who I'm becoming. Knowing this is only just the beginning.

18

With Rhiannon's revised testimony and my information about Lucy and Renée, I head for the police station.

I was able to get an appointment with Detective Inspector Seb Davies for nine this morning, so I stayed up most of the night organizing my thoughts and going over what I was going to say to present my case. I googled everything I could think of regarding Cysgod Castle, but came up empty. Even the Land Registry and Cadw were like brick walls, unwilling to give up any information.

I need to know who owns it, what goes on there. The details of Rhiannon's story—the rash, the business card—and the fact that Cysgod Castle is somehow involved… It's my first tangible evidence linking Wales to London, linking Seren and Lucy to whatever happened to Renée, and the club with no name, and the girls I read about on the message boards, all experiencing the same symptoms before they disappear or turn up dead.

I know I'm coming to this meeting with next to nothing, but I'm also at a dead end without more help, and the clock is ticking for Lucy.

The local police headquarters occupy what looks like a large family home one village over, and when I ring the bronze buzzer in the redbrick wall, I almost expect a kindly old man to open the door and invite me in for tea and cake. Instead, a grainy voice asks for my name and whether I have an appointment.

"Dr. Mina Murray for DI Seb Davies, nine a.m."

I'm buzzed in and head to the small reception area where I'm asked to wait. At nine thirty, a burly man comes to collect me and shows me to DI Davies's office.

"Come in, come in," he calls in a friendly tone, rising from his desk and gesturing widely with his hands.

He's a short man, balding, with bright eyes and a warm smile.

"When I heard we had a London doctor in town with a theory about our missing girl case, it piqued my curiosity," he says, sitting back down.

"Thank you for your time."

He rubs his hands on the worn vinyl armrests. "Now, what can I help you with?"

He's expectant. A good start.

"I've located a pattern. Numerous instances of missing girls across the country, Seren Evans being the most recent. They all seem to be linked by a series of physiological symptoms and a location in London. Possibly one here in Tylluan too." I riffle through my papers.

He leans back in his chair, his smile fading. "I see. Tell me more."

"This place," I say, sliding a photograph of the doors to the club with no name across his desk. "They're recruited by men offering 'job opportunities' of some kind, sharing the same mysterious business card. After working there or perhaps attending an event there, they'd present with odd symptoms. Many of the girls simply vanish from their lives like Seren, only to be found weeks or months later, dead. I believe these cases are all connected. The illness lasts for variable amounts of time, but eventually leads to their deaths. These are the common symptoms."

I slide a stack of paper across to him and he flips through it, frowning. He nods slowly as he turns pages over, while I go through the history of my involvement up until the moment Rhiannon told me the truth.

"Seren's best friend, Rhiannon Jones, said that Seren had received an invitation to Cysgod Castle before she went missing—a job offer, a business card—and was sick shortly after that. Rhiannon claims she saw the same rash, and then Seren vanished. So, I'd like to see if there are closer links between the Cloth Fair club and Cysgod. I've looked into their ownership online, but there's not much that's publicly available.

"It might be a type of STI," I continue. "Or maybe a new designer drug circulating. Something we haven't seen before."

DI Davies slides the pages back toward me. "I can see you've thought a lot about this."

"Yes. And I'd like for you to open an investigation into the owner of Cysgod Castle."

DI Davies exhales and leans back in his chair. "You must know I can't do that."

I purse my lips. "Excuse me?"

"You're suggesting targeting a well-established, high-profile property with nothing more than hearsay from a...a known troublemaker."

I squeeze my knees together to keep myself from standing. "With testimony that the missing girl was there only days prior to her disappearance," I clarify.

He holds up his hands in a shrug. "To begin an investigation, *you need evidence.*"

He is the second man to say this to me and I could scream.

"The same principle applies in the beginning, middle, end. Evidence. Otherwise any Tom, Dick, and Harry can waltz into a police station with a file of rumors and speculation, alleging all sorts, and start a witch hunt. I could lose my job."

I lean forward. "I understand you can't *press charges* on the owner of Cysgod simply from what I've told you. I'm not naive, and I'm not asking you for that. I'm simply suggesting that, given this new information and the possible links to an active case in London, there's something to be looked into here."

"We're up to our ears in cases," he says, rubbing the bald spot on his head. "To allocate resources to this we'd need something compelling, and it just isn't there. I don't mean to be rude, but for all I know, you could be a jilted ex looking for revenge."

I blink several times. This man has just received a report of a possible predator in his sleepy Welsh town, and he doesn't think it's *compelling*? I knew I didn't have much coming in, but I was at least expecting him to take down some notes, make a few calls, look for a paper trail, any link between Cloth Fair and Cysgod.

"So you're going to do nothing? Not even see if there's a connection between the club and Cysgod? Not even if women are turning up dead?"

DI Davies raises his eyebrows and shakes his head. "Look, what you've told me isn't sufficient to pursue. However, I'll keep an eye out and if something more presents itself, we'll follow it up." He stands, releasing a long sigh.

This man is not going to pull his finger out; that much is clear. Not without overwhelming evidence—and maybe not even then. I'm angry with myself for thinking I might find an ally here. I need more. I need to find Seren, if she's still alive.

"Is there anything else I can help you with?"

I get to my feet, sliding the pages back into my file and picking it up. "No. *Thank* you."

He ushers me to the door. When I'm standing outside, he says, "I'm sorry you had to come all this way for nothing."

"It might not be nothing," I say firmly. "I could be seeing you again."

He laughs. "Let's hope not."

And he closes the door in my face.

I've counted thirteen steps toward the exit when I hear a voice.

"Mina *Murray*?"

I turn to see a female officer leaving one of the side rooms. She's a tall, imposing woman with cropped blond hair—beautiful, and vaguely familiar. Her face breaks into a smile.

"My God, it *is* you!"

I blink, the puzzle of her sliding into place. *"Quincey?"*

Quincey Morris, Lucy's ex-girlfriend, towers in front of me. "I can't believe you're back."

"For a while, yes."

Quincey glances behind me. "Is everything okay?"

"Yeah," I say sourly. "I had an appointment with DI Davies."

"Did you get everything you needed?"

I grimace. "It didn't go as well as I'd hoped."

Quincey shifts her weight to her heels and regards my expression for a moment before saying, "Listen, I've got to head out now, but can you swing by my house later? Around seven? It'd be nice to catch up."

"Sure. Where is it?"

"Remember my parents' house?"

I nod.

She digs into her duty belt and pulls a business card from one of the pockets. "That's my number if you get lost. See you at seven."

Quincey's house is off Cefn Close, just past the mountain zoo. It's a small, detached bungalow with a loft conversion and dormer window, an ugly beige pebbledash monstrosity with an exterior garage. A tiny BMW i3 is parked outside.

I hesitate in my own car, wondering if I'm doing the right thing. The file of printouts is sitting on my passenger seat. I know Quincey probably meant this as a social call, but I can't help it... I'm tempted to bring her in, tell her everything I know, and hope she's more open to hearing what I have to say than DI Davies.

I grit my teeth and get out of the car.

Before I know it, I'm knocking on the door.

"Mina fucking Murray," Quincey says when she opens it, as though we didn't just see each other at the station. I almost laugh at how different she is in a tartan robe and slippers.

"Quincey fucking Morris," I reply, laughing.

"How the hell do you look exactly the same?" She pretends to block her eyes. "It's revolting how young you look!"

"You bugger," I say, her arms wrapping around me for a tight hug. She lifts me off my feet, her arms like a vise. When she releases me, she pulls my shoulders back and takes a long look. We grin like schoolgirls at one another.

"Come inside and tell me what you've been doing with yourself. Sorry I was a little formal at the station."

We go into the front room, which is still decorated like a little old lady lives here instead of a hardened copper. I suppose she hasn't felt the need to update it since her parents... I realize I don't know what happened. Did they move? Die? She catches my expression.

"Mum's old stuff. She passed last year and I couldn't bring myself to chuck it."

"Oh, shit. I'm sorry. I think I only ever saw the outside of your house when we were kids."

She spreads her arms. "Well, this is it. Been here ever since. Considering selling it to move closer to the station, but it's early days yet. What can I get for you?"

"A cup of tea would be lovely."

"Perfect. Back in a tick."

I use the time alone to gather myself, memories of our childhood flooding my mind.

Quincey Morris came into the picture when she moved here with her family from Texas in the middle of the spring term Year Eleven. She was an army brat who had lived everywhere, from Saudi Arabia, to New York, to Turkey. Everyone at school was fascinated by the new *American*, Lucy most of all. She seemed so glamorous and worldly to us. Quincey and Lucy became fast friends, which I resented until I realized that it wasn't friendship blossoming between them; it was romance. They were an item within the year and were still a couple when I left. Whatever happened between them during the intervening time, I have no idea. As far as I'm aware, they don't speak. Certainly, Lucy hasn't ever mentioned Quince to me.

"There we are," she says, coming back into the room with two huge bucket mugs full of builder's tea.

I take mine and sit on the sofa with a sigh. It envelops me like a bear hug.

"I don't have any sugar in the house. Hope that's okay."

"It's fine, thanks."

Her house is frilly, sure, but I can also see that it is spotless, and my nerves ease immediately.

"I'm guessing that's what the meeting was about?" Quincey says, glancing at my manila folder.

"Yes. I know you invited me here to catch up, but I'm hoping you can help me."

She nods, and her frown lines are deep. I wonder if that comes with the job, or just with time.

She ponders me, head tilted to the side. "Where did you run off to at the end of Sixth Form?"

"Oxford."

She nods. "Right, I remember that now."

She looks like she wants to ask more, but reads my face and leaves it alone.

I touch the folder once more and take a deep breath. "I need help because of Lucy."

She flinches. "Because of Lucy?"

"I think she's the victim of something…something big, bigger than just Tylluan. It's hard to explain. Will you just listen until I'm finished?"

Her eyes dart between my own, searching, but she nods and sits back to listen.

I explain everything. I tell her about Renée and Rhiannon's story about Seren, as well as the forum discussing a conspiracy theory about a predator under the alias @UKPREDATOR. How more missing girls turned up in the search, all of them matching the symptoms, if the database is to be believed, and all of them within a small radius of London. I tell her how I stumbled upon the club with no name and discovered that Renée had links to it. About Rhiannon's mention of Cysgod and a potential connection there, a "job opportunity" and a mysterious business card matching the one I found in Renée's room. About how Lucy is now showing similar symptoms.

"I think this club is spreading an unseen STI among these girls, something that eventually kills them. Either that or a designer drug—something we've not seen before. Something that's allowing this predator to kill girls slowly, methodically, quietly, without getting caught."

When I'm finished, I've laid out all my evidence across her coffee table and she's examining it closely.

"Who is the owner of Cysgod?" she asks. "Do you have a name?"

"I couldn't find anything. I've tried every kind of search I could think of, but there's no record of the owner. Same story with the club. It's why I went to the station today. I knew it was a long shot, but I was hoping they'd take me seriously enough to look up the deeds, or other information I don't have access to."

"Mina…" She sighs. "This could be something…or it could be nothing. It's all circumstantial."

"You could take it to your CO?"

"And get laughed out of the station?" She sighs again when she notices my face fall. "Look, I think you might be onto something here. But if I take this in, I'd need more. DNA linking the girls, eyewitnesses—firsthand—who are willing to go on record. Hard evidence. I know it's not what you were hoping to hear, but this just wouldn't stand up in court. It has to be beyond all reasonable doubt." She clasps her hands across her knees. "With powerful people like this...they have resources, lawyers, and much more aggressive means to defend themselves and scupper an investigation."

I close my eyes, feeling the weight of all this falling heavily on my shoulders. DI Davies was right. I'm not surprised, just disappointed.

"But listen," Quincey says, "don't let this drop if you think something's there. It wouldn't be the first time respectable-looking men turned out to be creeps." She stands up and walks to the window by the table. "I've seen women come in two, three days after an assault, when they've finally got brave enough to do it, but they've showered more thoroughly than they ever have in their lives, for obvious reasons. But they washed away the DNA and there's nothing we can do because all it amounts to is he-said, she-said."

I'm all too familiar with this. I see the other end of it, when the women are broken, enraged, desperate to repair their shattered dreams. People are liars at the end of the day, and without proof, how can anyone be certain of anything?

We're silent for a while, sipping cold tea.

"Outside of amateur investigations," Quincey says. "How are you?"

"I'm...okay. I'm worried about all of this, and it's hard to think of anything else."

She hesitates. "And Lucy?"

I told her that Lucy might be a victim, but neglected to mention that she's also very sick. "She's not doing well." I force the words out. "She's sick, and whatever this illness is...it's hit her hard."

Quincey's jaw tightens. "I'm sorry to hear that."

I want to ask what happened between them, why Quincey

isn't the one with the Mrs. Westenra ring, but I suspect that's a sore topic. I back off like she did for me.

"I should get back," I say, getting to my feet. "Thanks for listening."

"Hey, look, don't be a stranger. And I meant what I said. You're smart, meticulous, and you've got good instincts. If you've got a feeling about this whole thing, don't just let it drop. When you've got something definitive, bring it to me."

"Thanks, Quince."

"See you around, Murray."

I'm halfway down the street to my car when I hear footsteps behind me and turn. Quincey is jogging over, fluffy slippers and all.

"God, Mina. You're a pain in the ass. Ugh!" She shakes her head. "I am one hundred percent going to regret this, but I'll help you. We just need to keep it under the radar until there's concrete proof, okay?"

Something in my chest lifts. A weight I didn't know I'd been holding. "On my word of honor."

"Stay out of trouble," she says, rolling her eyes as she turns away.

19

The sun casts shades of marigold, tangerine, and grapefruit over the quaking ocean, and the wind whips my hair out of its French twist. It was a lifetime ago that I walked along this beach, looking at the painted sky as the sun died on the horizon. It should be beautiful. I should be able to see this, objectively. But I don't. All I can focus on is the roiling gray sea, churning like my insides. On the eastern end of the promenade a group of kids whoop and scream, chasing each other and smoking stolen cigarettes. The smell of tobacco in the briny air hits me like blunt force trauma to my chest, reeking of nostalgia so potent I have to turn and walk in the opposite direction, toward the cliffs and Cysgod Castle.

The past whispers at my shoulder—in particular, that last evening with Jonathan. I knew it would be then, on that night, when we finally went all the way. We had been together two years, had done other things, touched in secret, kissed forbidden places, but we hadn't crossed that final line. Jonathan had been with a girl before me and he didn't want to rush things, even though I burned for him so desperately that at night I woke tangled in my sheets, sweaty and breathless. When he was near me, I was hyperaware of his body, his scent, yearning for his hands on me. I thought I'd go crazy with longing.

And then, two weeks prior, it occurred to me that maybe he didn't like me in *that way*. After all, guys were supposed to be crazy for it, while we girls deflected. That was the natural order, Lucy said. It wasn't meant to be the other way around. When Jonathan and I met up to go to the cinema a week later, I was quiet and withdrawn. He noticed, because of course he did. He noticed everything. It all came spilling out, my frustration, my hurt, my perplexity at his distance—I burst into tears and suggested we end it. It was his turn to panic then. He grabbed my hands and squeezed tight.

"No."

"You don't want me, not really."

"Mina, you couldn't be more wrong."

"Then *why*?"

He made a guttural noise in his throat and tried to find the words to explain. "I... I've been with girls... I mean, with one girl. And it ruined things. It became all about that and nothing else."

"So your plan is to just *never*...?"

"Of course not." He laughed. "I do want to...but at the right time. I want it to be special."

I laughed, the tension unclenching in my chest. "I just want it to happen. I'm going crazy over here."

"I don't want things to get weird and distant. I want you to be sure."

It was my turn to squeeze his hands. "I *am* sure. I want you, Jonathan Harker."

And a week later we met on the beach after sunset, on a night just like tonight, with the plan to give ourselves to each other fully. I was scared, excited, *ready*. But it had all gone so horribly wrong.

Now, the sun melts into the ocean, fading to sad blues and

blacks, and the stars venture out. I rub my arms, shivering. A
different group of kids is huddled in the shadow of the cliffs
near the skip. A few lads work at lighting the kindling inside
and eventually a tentative glow radiates in the distance. By the
time I reach them, the fire is ablaze.

I see him through the flames.

He's watching me, hands in pockets in that familiar hunch,
his brows drawn together, gaze direct and unwavering. I have a
complicated response to seeing him like this, so similar to that
other night, fourteen years ago, when we also gazed across the
fire. The scars that pull the right side of his face down look like
terrible mirages in the dancing flames, and I feel that if I only
step closer, around the fire that separates us, they'll fade away
and he'll be whole again. Himself again. Maybe the bitterness
that lurks beneath the scars, which turns his lips down just as
much as the ruined flesh, will melt away with the fire too. I
find myself yearning for it; my sadness is sickness. Did I cause
all his pain?

Stop giving yourself so much bloody credit.

Not everything is about me.

He waits for me to join him on the other side of the skip and
we turn and walk together like it's still an old habit. We don't
talk for a long time, not until the fire is far behind us and the
wet rock face is within arm's reach, the yells of the kids just
background noise beneath the roar of angry waves crashing
over ancient rock.

I glance at him. "Thank you for coming."

He doesn't say anything. Doesn't look at me. He just stares
out at the Irish Sea like a silent watchman.

He smells of freshly turned grass and wheat fields at dusk; he
did back then too. Only now his boyish odor, hidden by cheap
cologne, has matured into something alluring and dangerous.
I still want, very badly, to touch him. To feel his lips on mine
once more.

He nods and we turn and walk up the sandbank together. We never had much use for words, and we seem to have preserved our trait of favoring silence. We watch the seagulls hover, dip, and wheel, listening to their piercing cries. Soon they'll huddle down on the rocks until dawn.

He was beautiful as a teen, but especially that night. He brought an inflatable mattress, a blanket, and pillows. A picnic basket with cheap (stolen) wine, cheesy breadsticks, and croissants. We ate and watched the sun bleed away, and when it got dark I inched closer to him.

"Don't be afraid," he said, his lips close to my ear. "There's nothing to be scared of in the dark."

He was right, I knew, but I was still happy to have the fire nearby, a lighthouse in the storm.

When he kissed me, it was electric. My heart jumped into my throat and my stomach twisted with butterflies.

"Are you sure?" he whispered.

"Yes. *Yes.*"

Were we afraid that we'd be caught? That someone would see? I don't remember. All I know is that I wanted him more than anything else.

"So?" he asks at last when we're at the top of the rise, scowling.

I smirk. "Pauciloquent as ever."

He glares at me and my smile fades. I can almost hear his thoughts. *Don't be a tosser, Mina. Drop the act. You're as plain as me.*

"So... I'm going to be around for a little while longer."

He turns to me and stares me down. "So?"

I swallow. This is harder than I thought. "I'd...like to spend some time together."

He frowns, looking for the catch.

"As friends," I add quickly.

"I see."

His eyes scatter over me, looking for something, and I feel naked, and it throws me back into memory.

He pulled my shirt over my head and unclasped my bra. His lips found my breasts and I gasped, leaning my head back. His shirt came off then, and I pressed my torso against his, the best sensation in the world. His skin on mine, warm. Safe.

He laid me back and pulled off my trainers and jeans, his following soon after. I tried to cover my pale thighs, suddenly embarrassed, when he whispered, "So beautiful." I let my hands fall away, smiling shyly at him. When he went to pull off my underwear, he looked up and said again, "Are you sure?" and I loved him for making absolutely certain.

I hesitated, and he stopped, sitting back.

"I'm sure," I said firmly. "I want this."

When we were both naked, I looked with wonder and fear over his body. It would hurt. Lucy said it would hurt, the first time. But I was ready, and I wanted this, and I had waited long enough.

The pain was beautiful and brief, and it didn't diminish my awe at having him inside me. By the expression on his face, I thought he felt the same. I watched him with wonder; his desire was exquisite, and *I* was the cause. I felt powerful. In control. Beautiful. Changed.

He made sounds that I wanted to bottle and remember, to trap in a conch shell and revisit at a moment's notice, pressing his sighs, his moans, to my ear in the secret midnight hours beneath my bedcovers. And then it was over. We had a few, precious minutes together before his phone rang. It was his father. Something had happened and Jonathan had to leave.

"Will you be okay?" he asked as I pulled on my underwear and clothes.

"Of course. Go. Call me later."

He kissed me, long and tender, and then he left. I was happier than I thought possible. It had been a perfect night. Miraculous.

I couldn't wait to tell Lucy everything. She had insisted on details when it was "done and dusted." She was waiting for my call.

"Don't skimp on details," she'd added, grinning.

And then everything changed.

Had he been watching us from the shadows? Waiting, and hoping, for Jonathan to leave? Had he been watching me for longer than that? Following secretly behind as I walked the streets and then the prom?

I should have sensed something, but I was too caught up in the haze of love and lust and wonder, and when he struck, it blindsided me.

Now, on the sandbar, Jonathan nods and again he regards me, expression guarded, and I *still* want to touch him. And I always knew I was coming here to tell him.

I pull two bottles of beer from the deep pockets of Mam's coat and offer him one. He takes it, still watching me, and unscrews the lid, pocketing it. Same as always with the litter. I have never wanted to hold him more.

Please be gentle, I think.

"I'm ready to tell you," I say.

He nods once, and sits down in the sand. I hesitate, then sit beside him, and we look out over the inky sea. I fiddle with my bottle of beer, never quite getting around to taking my first sip. He lets me talk, never interrupting, except once when I mention the man in the shadows. At that part, he opens his mouth with a sudden intake of breath, but holds himself back and lets me finish without interruption.

"I didn't stick around for anything. I ran away from everything that reminded me of that moment, including you. What happened existed in me like a fire at my core—too painful to touch or look at too closely, but always, always present. It's informed every decision I've made since I left. It's why I went from medicine into psychiatry. It's why I'm committed to helping women through their trauma—as a sort of patch on my own."

I swallow. Jonathan lets the silence sit for a moment.

I'm doing okay, holding it together—until he touches me. Until his arms come up and around me, and he presses me into his chest, his eyes haunted with something I can't decipher.

"Shit," he says. *"Shit."*

His arms are warm and strong, and I break. My entire body trembles uncontrollably, as though it has needed this all these years. As though it can finally stop holding up the weight alone.

I love you, I want to say.

What comes out is different. "Is that a yes to spending more time together?"

He pulls back to look at me, his eyes scattering thirstily over my face. Beneath the burns, a war wages. Emotions flicker in quick succession, none that I can catch.

"Okay, Mina Murray."

I smile. "Okay, Jonathan Harker."

TODAY 7:54 A.M.
UNKNOWN

Hello @DrMuk.
This is Songbird.

UNKNOWN

I told you to be careful about leaving digital trails.

TODAY 7:54 A.M.
MINA MURRAY

I'm being careful.

UNKNOWN

The government keeps records of searches.
Whoever owns that castle you're looking into
will know you're digging if they care to check.
But you won't find anything there anyway.
These people have ways of covering their tracks.

MINA MURRAY

How the hell did you know
I was looking into that?

UNKNOWN

I'm sorry for my silence.
I was checking a few things before I got
in touch again. We need to meet.

MINA MURRAY

Who are you?

UNKNOWN

Thursday, 6:00 p.m.
You will receive instructions.

20

On Thursday at 6:00 p.m, a set of coordinates arrives on my phone by text from the same mysterious number. When I plug it into Google, the pin drops in a remote location at Llyn Idwal, the national park.

I text back.

> You're not going to make this easy, are you?

I get no reply.

I borrow mum's old hiking boots and pack a few supplies. The last time I did the Llyn Idwal circular I was a lot younger, with far more stamina. The message this stranger is sending is crystal clear: this is a meeting they don't want anyone to overhear. Which means they have information. But the whole thing is ridiculous. Ludicrous. Am I really going to meet up with a stranger who somehow has my phone number, can read my computer, and might be, for all I know, one of the same people linked to this whole thing trying to silence me? Once again, I wish I had a weapon. A police baton. A machete. A mace. Anything.

Still, the allure of this being a real lead is too tempting to ignore.

I park in the National Trust's Carneddau and Glyderau parking area, which is deserted this time of year. I pause and wonder if I'm about to be hacked into little pieces by some crazy axe murderer, but force myself to go on anyway. Lucy's life is on the line—of that I'm absolutely certain. And then there's Seren, who might still be alive somewhere.

I take the path left of the toilets, a path I last took on a school field trip when I was fourteen. I clamber over heather-draped stone slabs, heading uphill until I reach a wooden gate and go through, coming to the Afon Idwal River and the wooden sessile oak bridge. Y Garn looms high in the distance, hidden in dancing mists that blanket it like a tablecloth of fine lace. Despite the cold, wet day, I'm warm. As the rocky path grows steeper, I have to stop and drink the first of my bottles of water. The path grows more treacherous the higher I go, and I almost twist my ankle several times. Eventually I pass through Clogwyn Y Tarw and Bochlwyd Buttress, at last coming to Nant Bochlwyd, a raging white peaked river. I check my map app to make sure I'm on the right path, and I am. Ahead of me lies Llyn Idwal, the waters calm and gray.

I sit down on the grassy bank and wait.

After fifteen minutes, the cold has set into my bones, and I'm beginning to wonder if I've been sent on a wild-goose chase. Then I get another text message: instructions to continue following the main trail. My amygdala screams for me to turn around, but I ignore it.

I dial the number, frustrated, but the line is cut off after two rings. I reason that at least someone's on the other end of the line.

I climb a series of steps along the cascade, counting each one, which grow harder and harder to get over, until at last the terrain flattens onto a boulder-strewn field with tufts of grass and braided waterways.

Ahead lies Llyn Bochlwyd, a placid lake well off the tourist path to Llyn Idwal below, where the first set of coordinates led me. The Glyderau Mountains, which my teacher pointed out to us with wonder in her eyes, are now hidden by churning mists that look more like ominous storm clouds gathering a furious tempest.

I shoot off a text.

> What now?

"Now, we talk."

I spin to see a middle-aged woman emerging from the gunmetal rocks behind me. She has a weathered, no-nonsense face and cropped gray hair only slightly lighter than the rocks behind her, but her eyes are sharp and shrewd.

Despite myself, I'm relieved that the person standing in front of me is a woman. Could she still murder me and hide my body? Sure. She looks strong. But somehow her sex makes her less threatening, out here, alone.

"Why the theatrics?"

"I had to make sure you were who you said you were."

"Who else would I be?"

She cocks her head to one side. "You don't spend much time on the internet, do you?"

"I have a life, so no. But I'm guessing you do." We eye each other warily. "What was with the train station?"

I had received a set of instructions to go to Conwy train station the previous evening, only to get another text ten minutes after I arrived that said, False alarm. More soon.

"I needed to watch you. Make sure you weren't followed."

"Your paranoia is verging on pathological."

"When you know as much as I do, *little girl*, prudence is my least precaution."

I'm tempted to leave. To trudge out of this national park and all the way back to London. I even turn away.

"Is she still alive? Your friend Lucy?"

My left eye spasms and it takes all my willpower not to rub it. I look back to her. "How did you know about Lucy?"

She answers my question with one of her own. "Why are you looking into UKPREDATOR and Cloth Fair?"

I could ask her the same question; I could badger her about how she found out about Lucy—but we'll get nowhere unless one of us is willing to make the first demonstration of trust.

"Women keep getting sick. One is dead, and at least one other is heading in the same direction."

"Lucy is one of them." It isn't a question.

I nod. "Yes."

"How far along is she?"

"I'm... I don't know."

"Symptoms?"

"Hallucinations, losing time, sleepwalking, anemia, petechiae-like rash."

"Seizures?"

I nod.

She turns to walk along the stone path, nodding that I should follow.

"It's only women being targeted," she says. "Usually young, innocent types. I've been tracking their disappearances for a long time."

I shake my head. "Lucy's older. Established."

"She's an outlier, then. Or she's not part of the pattern."

"What pattern? What links them?"

She glances sideways at me again, assessing. "You're not what I expected."

"Well, you're not either. How did you get my phone number?"

"The subreddit."

"What about it?"

"You downloaded a file."

I remember. "Symptoms.doc. It's on my phone."

"I wrote a backdoor into the program. For security."

I purse my lips, stopping to face her. "You're a hacker."

"I'm many things."

I grit my teeth and speak through them. "So you've seen everything on my laptop."

"Like I said. I had to make sure you were who you said you were."

"Confidentiality be damned, then?"

She scoffs. "Do you really think that confidentiality matters to the people doing this? There are people in this world who hold *all* the cards, Sweet Pea. Unless we find ways to fight back, we're just crops for the picking."

"So fatalistic," I mutter, turning back to the track and walking, shoulders hunched against a light drizzle. It's getting colder, the smell of cold earth and storm clouds commingling into unease in my bones. "So what's the link?" I ask when she's walking beside me again.

She's built solidly. I doubt she ever feels the cold.

The path winds to the left between two towering buttresses and we slow to a halt. She looks left and right and up to make sure we're not overheard and stops.

Overkill.

Pages of textbook diagnoses pop into my head, falling over each other as I watch her. *Pervasive, persistent, and enduring mistrust of others...profoundly cynical view of the world...hypervigilance... aloof, cold, distant, argumentative...guarded and secretive...* A diagnosis jumps to the fore: Paranoid Personality Disorder.

"The girls have similar characteristics," she says. "They're almost always from poor communities up and down the country. Mostly up north, but London, Portsmouth, and Falmouth have been hit too. Late teens and twenties. A few even underage." At this, the woman shakes her head quickly, as though clearing a memory, the skin under her jaw following suit.

An alarm bell pings in my head. "How many more do you know about aside from the list you sent me?"

"About one a month go missing, on average, though it's by no means clockwork. I've been tracking the pattern for as long as I've been doing this, so…fifteen years."

"But…but that's astronomical. That's over a *hundred* women!"

Her nod is somber. "Yes."

"That's impossible. Someone would know something."

"I'm sure many people know *something*. But connecting the dots, finding evidence, and proving it—that's another story."

"How do you know all of this when the police seem oblivious? You could be wrong."

She turns to walk again, and I have no choice but to follow.

"You ask a lot of questions," she says. I've been told this before and it's getting old. "That's a good thing," she adds, and I side-eye her to see if she's mocking me. She isn't. "Don't stop. The people who get jittery when you ask questions are the ones to look out for. They're the ones hiding something."

"So, what's your connection to all of this?"

She doesn't answer for a while, and I let her study the rocks like they're fascinating while she decides whether to unveil her answers. I expect more conspiracy theories and dire warnings.

"Fifteen years ago, when all this started, my daughter, Beatrice, ran away from home. We'd had a row the night before about some test results and she accused me of ruining her life. That night was the last time I saw her alive. We tried to find Bea, but she'd changed all her numbers. Police said they couldn't report her missing since she'd just turned eighteen and left home of her own accord. Months later, her body was found floating in the river."

"Oh…" I glance over at her to see if she's all right talking about this. The woman stares straight ahead, her expression impassive, unreadable.

"I've been searching for the reason ever since. It was ruled an accidental death because she'd been seen at a nightclub, then again on the street walking home looking less than sober. A witness gave a statement that she had hardly been able to walk."

"She was drunk?"

"No. She wasn't. Bea didn't drink very often—she complained about losing control."

"But in theory she *could* have been drinking?"

"That's what the police said, only I've checked the file. There's no record of her being at a nightclub that night. No CCTV footage of her walking home. I called on her supposed roommates and they hadn't seen her for *weeks*. They thought she'd moved out without telling them. Then there was the rash."

I nod slowly. "Always the rash."

"Still. Accidental drowning, they said, a mugging gone wrong maybe—the other symptoms were irrelevant. *She* was irrelevant."

"What did you do?"

The buttresses open up into moorland and we find a low mossy verge to sit on.

"I worked for *Instigator* paper at the time. An investigative reporter. I took the story to my editor, and he forcefully shut me down. Said I didn't have a story, only a conspiracy theory. Made a comment about keeping my nose out of business that wasn't mine, as if my daughter hadn't just fucking died.

"I quit that day. Handed in my notice, which I wasn't required to serve because I had mourning leave. I went home and I began scouring the net for everything I could find. I hacked my daughter's old phone records and found the last number she called."

"Let me guess," I cut in. "The club with no name."

"Hole in one."

I swallow and wait for her to carry on.

"I went there to get a meeting with the owner, talk to bar staff, anything. They wouldn't let me in. I became obsessed with figuring out everything I could about this place. My husband thought I was crazy, obsessive, mad. He left, and good riddance. I was on the trail of the truth—I knew it.

"And then, one day I went out for groceries. When I got home, something was off. I couldn't place it. It felt like something, or everything, in the room had been moved. I picked up the phone to call a friend and the line began ticking before it connected. I hung up. I left that night, under cover of darkness. I took one bag with me, that's it. I fled."

"You left everything behind?"

"Everything except a change of clothes, my bank cards, and Bea's diary and photos. I went into central London. Figured I could disappear there like she had. Closed my bank accounts and began using cash only. Untraceable. I moved from place to place, even went to Eastern Europe for a while. I made...friends. Learned how to work the internet."

"Learned how to hack?"

She eyes me. "Learned how to survive digitally. There are people out there, like me, who want answers."

"How can you trust them?"

"They've proven themselves."

"Tell me about the club with no name."

"Not much to tell. It's all a dead end. I stumbled upon other girls who had gone missing and who'd been found with one or more of the symptoms that Bea had, so instead of focusing on the wolf, I focused on the girls. Who they were, what they

did, their medical files, their schools, their hobbies—no detail
was too small. It was like looking at Bea all over again. Each of
them has a file as thick as my palm.

"Slowly, over the years, similarities began to emerge, and I
found patterns. Poor usually, young always. Each of them had
strange behaviors before they died, and most were ruled suicides
or accidental deaths. Every single one—discounted. To keep
these people hidden. To keep the girls forgotten."

This woman, this stranger…she sounds like a person in the
grip of hysteria. She's ticking all the boxes for PPD, and I should
keep my head on straight, should avoid getting caught up in
conspiracy theories. But…her thoughts follow the same tracks
my own have traveled these past weeks. Everything she's saying makes sense.

"And Cysgod?" I ask. "The castle I was looking into. Do you
know of any links there?"

"I haven't checked yet, but I wouldn't be surprised. Follow
the Money is my motto. And a space like that, it's owned by
someone wealthy, powerful—someone with resources, financial
and otherwise. Why do you think it's connected?"

"A local girl, Seren Evans, went missing a while back. I spoke
to a friend of hers who told me that she had been invited to some
sort of interview or party at the castle, and that she'd been acting strangely afterward. And that she'd seen a rash."

The woman nods. "Okay. I'll start digging there too."

I nod, rubbing at my hands. "We need proof. Solid evidence."

"That's why I came here. You're the first person outside of
the vagabond hackers I've met anonymously who brought new
information to the table. I knew I had to come and talk to you."

"Who are you, anyway?" I ask, realizing I have no idea who
the hell I'm talking to.

"Singer. My name is Helen Singer."

"You're on a hunt, aren't you?" We stare at each other for a long moment, and I feel something settle between us. Crystallize.

"Guilty as charged. I won't rest until I find what I'm looking for." The hatred in her eyes is the purest I've ever seen.

I nod. "I know it sounds mad, but I have a feeling that Cys-god is somehow at the heart of this."

At this, Helen barks a laugh. "I've been mad for fifteen years. Hasn't stopped me yet."

21

Singer calls me at 4:00 a.m.

"I'm going to stake out the castle, see what I find. You in?"

My brain doesn't compute, groggy with half-sleep. "Huh?"

"Are you coming with me to stake out Cysgod or not?"

I squint at my clock. "Now? It's four in the morning!"

"Yes or no, Murray."

Shit. My eye begins to twitch and a hot flush of itching rises up my neck. A near-epileptic stroboscopic sequence of images judders through my mind—twelve steps to the bathroom, scalding shower, sodium hypochlorite, glistening white tub, Lycra jogging suit, trainers hitting the pavement, two eggs on a white plate—

"How did you get access?" I ask, rubbing sleep from my eyes, buying time.

The silence is heavy.

I sigh. "You're going to break in, aren't you?"

"Pretty much."

"Singer, no." I pinch the bridge of my nose. "Absolutely not. We have to go through the proper channels and do this the right way, okay?"

"Do you think these people ask permission before they kid-
nap, rape, and murder girls?"

"We're better than them."

"I'm not. I have no scruples. Not for monsters. Not in a world
that is this cruel to women. I'll do whatever it takes to get Bea's
killer. *Whatever it takes.* Will you do the same for Lucy? If not,
then this ends now between us."

I love you, Bambi. I scratch phantom ants on my arm and fall
back into my pillows. "God, okay, fine. When?"

"Can you be at the beach in thirty minutes?"

Shit. Fuck. I squeeze my eyes shut.

"Yes or no, Murray."

"Fine."

"Wear black."

I hang up and push off my duvet, getting quietly out of bed.
No need to wake Mum. I hurry to my suitcase and grab a pair of
black trousers and a black top, *Fuck*, pushing them on to my un-
showered body. Itchy scalp—*shit*—greasy hands—*shit*—pounding
heart—*shit*—burning neck—*shit*—moist armpits—*shit*—twitching
eyeballs—

Shitshitshit.

This is all wrong.

For Lucy, I tell myself, gritting my teeth. *For Lucy.*

The beach is deserted, the sky charcoal black, the sea throwing a tantrum. The sun won't rise for another three hours. Even
so, Singer makes me move my car to a hidden patch of pebbles
on the other side of the promenade in case something happens.

"What might happen?" I ask, alarmed.

"Hopefully nothing. But it's better to be prepared."

To demonstrate that she's taking no chances, she stuffs her
vivid salt-and-pepper hair under a black beanie, hands me one,
and waits for me to do the same.

"It's pitch-black out," I protest, handing back the ridiculous thing.

"We don't want to be recognized."

I groan and pull it on, stuffing my hair under it.

"Do we really need to be dressed like cat burglars, though?"

"If we want to sneak onto Cysgod's grounds, we can't be seen. Shadows will cloak us, but only if we help it along."

"And you've done this before?" I mutter, pulling on the black gloves she hands to me.

"You'd be surprised the places I've snuck into," Singer says, eyeing the castle as she waits for me to finish. I find that I'm not the least bit surprised.

Her car is parked around the side of the train station, which runs along the back end at the other side of the beach, behind the hills. She walked the rest of the way here. Together we cross the sand and stand in the shadow of Cysgod hill, looking up at the castle above us. The ocean sucks away most of our sounds with a shuck and hiss, the water crashing noisily as the wind picks up. It is bitterly cold.

Singer leads the way, carrying a large black gym bag, gesturing for me to keep low. The hill rises steeply, and we keep off the dirt track that has tire prints embedded in the sand. Eventually we reach a towering iron gate twice our height. An expensive-looking digital pad with rubber keys that glow yellow like eerie ectoplasmic eyes sits in the center of the gate. It looks poisonous.

"Shit," Singer mutters under her breath.

"You weren't expecting a gate?" I ask, incredulous.

"I thought we could scale it and avoid doing it the hard way." Singer crouches down and opens her bag, rummaging inside. I spy a coil of black rope and scoff. She really was prepared to climb over like some vigilante.

"Scale it? Do I look like Catwoman?"

She considers me. "Actually, yeah."

"And what if they have security cameras?"

"I've already checked. They don't have Wi-Fi access on the property. Even if there are cameras that feed into a central video hub, I'll find it and delete the footage." She pulls out a weird iPad with several wires hanging out of it, then uses a tiny screwdriver to remove the face of the pin pad, revealing an array of coiled wires linked to a little monitor. She connects the ends of the wires on her device to those in the iPad and begins typing commands in code into her keyboard.

"Okay, then they'll definitely know we were here."

Singer rolls her eyes. "Trust me, they won't. I've gotten used to covering my tracks. But honestly, I doubt there'll be cameras at all. Too much evidence against them, if you ask me."

"That's assuming they bring the girls here."

"Didn't you say that Rhiannon girl said her friend was brought here?"

"Well, yeah."

Singer types something and then sighs. "This would be so much easier if it was linked to Wi-Fi," she mutters. "I guess whoever owns this place is as paranoid as I am."

It takes several minutes of furious typing on Singer's end and a string of coded commands several pages long before the gate clicks and swings open.

Singer smirks at me, packs up her things, and replaces the face on the pin pad like nothing ever happened. Then she saunters through, her previous mistrust and caution apparently gone.

A strange bubbling in my chest alerts me, with surprise, to the inescapable fact that I am enjoying myself. There's something alluring, almost intoxicating, about taking control after all these weeks of feeling helpless and alone.

Singer ends up being right about the cameras. We don't find any. But there are well-hidden signs of technology among the ancient stone and aged wood in every direction. A subtle alarm trip is visible at each diamond muntin in the sash windows. The same over all the doors and access points. Whoever owns this castle is careful about hiding their technology. Hiding their wealth. From afar, the castle looks like any impressive but un-assuming Welsh castle.

From here it's a fortress.

It also has a labyrinthine feeling. We take stone stairs up to closed doors, walk under arches, and go around corners that end in solid stone walls. The whole thing is dizzying. It's a farce of a castle.

"Nothing," Singer says, wiping her mouth aggressively when we're back in the courtyard. "No access. I can't hack any of this without tripping alarms."

"We should go. We're not getting anywhere."

"Let's check out the grounds first, then we'll go."

I nod, and Singer tucks her bag in a gap between the castle wall and the arch, which leads to a patch of dense woodland on the eastern edge of the hill. At first there's not much to see. Then I spot the copper finial on the main spire of what appears to be an open-air space built in limestone, an eroded shape with a hole in the center beneath a five-layer archivolt that towers only just above the tree line. I beckon Singer over. Four buttresses with pointed pinnacles rise into the trees, draped in greenery.

No wonder we couldn't see it from the beach.

For the first time since I was a child, I have a peculiar yearn-ing for my mother.

"An atrium," Singer whispers. "Strange."

We both seem to feel the need to be quiet.

Columns of limestone rise and curve to meet at pointed arches, open to the sky, covered in the detritus of autumn.

"What's the point?" Singer mutters, yanking a piece of ivy off one of the pillars and throwing it down distastefully.

"It's a mask," I say slowly, turning in a circle.

"Eh?"

"A cover for a hypogeum."

"Can you bloody translate?" Singer snaps.

"It's hiding an underground burial chamber," I explain.

Singer grimaces. "That's messed up."

"Look for a hidden door or a panel. Steps, anything."

We spread out, searching. After a few moments, Singer whistles at me.

"Grab my bag, will you?" she calls, some feet away. She is bent over a metal door, tugging at it. "This is a bitch to open and I don't want to let it go in case I can't get it up again."

I run back to the arch and pull Singer's bag free, then hurry back to her. Together, we open the door, letting it fall to the ground. There's a crumbling stone stairway into impenetrable darkness. As I shine my phone torch down the passageway, a draft of cool air hits my face. I shiver.

"Shall we?" Singer asks, arching a brow.

I grimace in response. We inch down uneven, crumbling steps until, feeling entombed, we enter a lone crypt in the center of a stone room. The air is like brackish water and, rather than feeling empty, the vibe is vaguely...haunted. Like I'm being watched by something invisible—a phantasmal voyeur.

Singer strides forward and looms over the crypt, sweeping the dust away from the carved inscription. "Maybe this will tell us something about the owner's lineage. A father perhaps?"

I nod, looking closely at the markings on the grave. They're indecipherable. My brows furrow. I've never come across this language before—the markings use a non-Roman alphabet. Another mystery.

Singer snaps several pictures, and I get the sudden urge to leave, as though staying any longer will swallow me whole, doom me to the crypt's digestive system. I practice steady breathing and envision my shower at home, counting 393 tiles, imagining the sting of sodium hypochlorite filling my nostrils.

"Done," Singer announces. It takes every ounce of my willpower not to sprint back up the stairs.

We exit into the cool night air. I am so ready to be out of here.

As I turn back toward the entrance gate, Singer calls out, "Wait a second, I want to check something."

"Check what?"

"I want to see if I can get into the grounds again that way," she says, nodding to the edge of the cliff where the back wall of the castle seems precariously balanced.

"And die too?"

She smirks and edges along the tiny lip of rocky mountain between the castle and the air. I swear and follow.

The back end of the castle is mostly solid stone, and we suffer the brunt of the ocean spray and frigid wind. I step wrong and lose my footing, slipping toward the raging sea; Singer grabs my arm and hauls me back onto level ground, but I lose my hat, watching with horror as it vanishes into the churning mass of shadows below.

Shit.

At the last bend of the wall, we grip roots that have grown through the mortar in the stone, praying they don't snap, and haul ourselves over a low, perpendicular dividing wall and onto flagstones on the other side, which have been laid right to the cliff edge.

We hop over it, Singer practically dragging me over, and we find that we are on the other side of the towering gates, having skirted the entire structure.

Singer is grinning like a giddy child. "That was fun."

"Great," I mutter. "So in future, if we come back, we have the exciting choice of hacking a high security system again or risk falling to our deaths. Wonderful."

She laughs. "It's great to have choices!"

Within minutes, we're in a forest, hiking in silence toward the car still parked at the train station at the opposite end of the beach. I'm anxious to return home to research what language those markings are written in—and if they'll reveal anything about the person who lives there.

I suspect Singer is equally eager, because her pace quickens with each step. Soon, I have to jog to keep up with her.

As I catch a glimpse of the first hint of dawn through the trees, my foot catches on something and I fall spectacularly to the ground, my ankle twinging. I taste dirt.

"Shit," Singer calls. "You okay?"

I groan and get to my hands and knees, ready to swear at whatever tree root caught me unawares.

But it's not a tree root. Not even close.

"I think you better get over here."

"What is it?"

I swallow, unable to tear my eyes away. "Get over here. Now."

"What is it? What did you…?" Her voice trails away as she reaches me. "Murray, what the bloody hell is that?"

"I believe they're finger bones."

Flesh clings to the bases of each digit like minced pork as they desperately reach for the sky. A couple of steps away I spot a tuft of light hair that I might have taken for weeds if not for the bones.

Was she alive when they put her in the ground? Did she try to claw her way out?

"Jesus," Singer mutters under her breath, rubbing her face. "We found that proof you were after, then."

"We have to call the police. They won't be able to ignore it now."

"Not yet," Singer says, getting down onto her knees and digging up the earth around the tuft of hair.

I lean forward to stop her, draping myself over the body as though to protect it.

"Mina," she says gently. "We have to see who it is. We should take photos at the very least. In case they brush it under the carpet. Then, if they don't do something, we can."

I nod slowly. I'm not as paranoid as Singer by a mile; the idea that something as big as a dead body being covered up wouldn't have occurred to me. But she's been doing this a lot longer than I have, and I can't help but remember how dismissive Detective Inspector Seb Davies was.

"Okay."

She carries on digging. "The earth is fairly fresh."

Could the person who did this be nearby? I stare around, heart thumping in my dry mouth.

Slowly, inch by torturous inch, the excavation reveals a face too young to be so waxy. Too young to be so…gone.

I recognize her from the photo in the local paper in Mr. Wynn's shop. I wasn't expecting anything else.

Seren Evans has been found at last.

22

I call Quincey from what is probably the last phone box in the country.

"Quince," I say when she answers. "It's Mina."

"What's happened?" She must hear it in my voice. In the background the morning news jingle plays. I check my watch. It's six thirty. After all that's happened, it's only been two and a half hours.

"I went snooping at Cysgod."

"Do not tell me anything else, Mina, so help me God."

"There's a body just outside the grounds."

The line is silent for way too long.

"It's Seren Evans," I continue. "She was buried in the patch of woodland there. I tripped over her hand."

"Mina, you need to come in."

"This is an anonymous tip."

"Mina…"

"She's just lying there, Quince. It's…pretty bad. She's got that rash I told you about and she looks…*used*, somehow. Please go get her. Please."

"Okay. Look, leave it with me. I'll sort it."

"I need to have access to her autopsy."

Quincey swears. "Not asking for much, are you?"

"I have credentials."

Quincey sighs, short and sharp, and mutters, "It's too early for this shit. We should meet up. I want to hear everything you saw. I'll ring you—are you staying at your mam's?"

"Yeah."

"Okay. Sit tight. I'll be in touch."

The medical examiner, Mr. Gruffydd Jones, does the general examination of the anterior aspect first, and I make notes to distract me from the fact that there is a child on the autopsy table. Several prominent marks are noted, including the telltale rash and some black veining on her neck.

"Jugular vein distension," Mr. Jones murmurs for the recorder, "with petechiae and purpura on the left side of the neck." He makes a *mmm* sound. "Not petechiae, exactly. More like…little pits. I've never seen anything like it. I recommend an investigation by a dermatologic specialist consultant."

"When will you hear back about the rash?" I ask.

He shrugs. "Not my job. I just record what I see."

He checks everything thoroughly, including her broken fingers. "No matter underneath fingernails."

The posterior check reveals nothing significant.

Mr. Jones is meticulous, careful, and impersonal. He also doesn't care about the whys. I, on the other hand, struggle to watch him make his first vertical incision from upper chest to pubis—a stark reminder of why I decided to go into psychiatry when I chose to specialize.

"Chest musculature unremarkable," he continues, cutting with quick strokes that splice muscle and yellow fat. "Fractures to fourth and fifth ribs on the right side." He pokes at the starkly white bone peeking through with a finger and she wobbles with each impact.

The rib cutter makes fairly quick work of her young bones, and my neck begins to itch in that telling way. When Mr. Jones and his assistant fold the flap of her ribs back onto her covered face and it fractures with a snap, I almost run from the room.

Keep it together, Murray.

"Abdominal and thoracic cavities exposed. Visual examination is unremarkable."

Things get worse as each organ is removed, weighed, and samples are taken. Seren's dead blood pools in what is left of her body, which looks more and more like a bucket the further along the autopsy progresses. Her organs are healthy, however, including her liver and kidneys. Samples of her blood have already told us she wasn't on any drug—at least any we can currently test for.

"Incision through the pericardium. No fluid changes."

He cuts the heart out and a volume of dark blood spills from it like ink.

"Blood volume is low," Mr. Jones notes, frowning down into her cavernous corpse.

"Three hundred grams," his assistant calls from the scales where he took the heart to be weighed.

"Within normal range," Mr. Jones says. He dissects and examines the small organ. "No congenital anomalies."

Lungs, liver, spleen, heart, stomach, intestines—I have to contain my tics for them all, convinced that there is some infection, some terrible misfortune or catastrophe that I've absorbed from microbes in the air or, worse, from airborne droplets of her low-volume blood.

When it's time for the brain examination, I excuse myself and leave, asking that he forward her autopsy report to my email, which I leave with the front desk.

Back in my car, I try not to hyperventilate, drinking from the flask of verbena I brought with me and drowning my hands and neck in alcohol gel while I ponder the very clear message I got inside. The "I don't care more than I need to" message. No one is going to investigate the rash on Seren Evans. No one is going to probe any deeper.

Which means it's up to me to get to the bottom of what—or who—killed her.

TODAY 10:54 A.M.
MINA MURRAY

Hey Quince, it's Mina. Think you can pull a warrant for Cysgod now there's been a body found?

QUINCEY MORRIS

Tried to get one yesterday. Boss says it's been handed over to another agency.

MINA MURRAY

What other agency?

QUINCEY MORRIS

I don't know.

MINA MURRAY

So we can't do anything?

Is this normal, a case being handed over to another agency like this?

What about who owns it?

Can we check that?

QUINCEY MORRIS

It's not normal, trust me.

I've been shut out.

MINA MURRAY

Do you believe me now?

This is all connected. It's much bigger than just Seren.

QUINCEY MORRIS

I believe you.

We need to think about next steps.

23

This is what happens to women.

It feels like a weight is pressing down on my shoulders, so heavy that I can barely get my feet to drag me along.

Back at my mother's house, I collapse onto the sofa and groan.

Being young and healthy, Seren didn't have much of a medical file to speak of. An ear infection when she was eight, tonsilitis at ten, a broken arm at twelve. Before she went missing, nothing out of the ordinary was noted.

The petechiae-like rash was scattered along her collarbone, neck, and breasts. Flashes of it rise without warning in my mind and I flinch with every unwelcome assault. There was something so...lurid about it. Something so depraved. And Mr. Jones hadn't cared to chase the answers. He had grudgingly speculated that it may have been trauma from blunt force or a fall from considerable height. An impression from some pattern. Other injuries to the body were consistent with a fall, including the broken ribs and clavicle. "Maybe she fell," he had murmured. "Maybe it was an accident." I had gently pointed out that someone had still buried her.

He'd shrugged and moved on. His casual lack of concern

had been striking. Had been almost as disturbing as the naked sixteen-year-old corpse on the table.

Yet there is something even more dangerous than the medical examiner's disinterest: the news from Quincey's texts that Seren's case has been handed over to another organization. The two things don't compute...a village teen "troublemaker" presumed to have played some role in her own untimely demise, and the case status having been escalated so high as to no longer warrant being in Tylluan PD's territory? Why should these same people, who didn't seem overly concerned about her fate or the cause, choose to hand her case over to a higher power?

This disconnect can only mean that Singer was right: there are powerful people involved, and they don't want anyone finding out what exactly happened.

The question now is who we are up against—and just how powerful they are.

My mother comes into the room bottom first, dragging an overgrown money tree into the living room.

"What are you doing?" I ask, leaning away before she knocks into me.

"It's outgrown its pot," she pants, as if this clarifies why she is bringing the thing into the living room.

"You're going to repot it in *here*?"

She turns and gives me a look like I'm the one dragging a giant jade plant into the middle of the house arse first.

"Never mind," I mutter. "I don't even want to know."

She squints at me. "What's wrong?"

"Nothing."

"You can tell me or not, but you'll not be moping around all evening. I won't have it."

"I'm not moping, Mum. I've had a hard day. They found that missing girl."

"Seren Evans. I heard."

My mother nods like it's sad, but not news. And of *course* she already knows. Of *course* someone's been chin-wagging all over the village about it. Seren's been dead a few days and already it's old news. Word travels faster than light in a village where "everyone respects each other's privacy."

"Seren was Bronwen's best friend's girl. She rang me not two hours ago."

"I was at her autopsy."

To my surprise, my mother sits down on the sofa next to me, abandoning the money tree, and puts a hand on my knee. She smells of home.

"I knew her since she was born, I did."

"I'm sorry, Mum. I didn't know."

"We're family in this village. All of us connected."

I swallow down the rebuke. The implication. They are family, and I'm not, as if I wasn't born and raised here too, as if this place isn't stamped on my makeup as much as it is hers.

My mother must sense me stiffen, because she goes on: "Must've been hard to be there, see her on the table like that. I know you're a doctor and all, but I couldn't bear to see the things you see."

I nod, grateful for the small olive branch, for her hand on my knee, warm and comforting. The fact that she has a stake in this loss too—it makes me want to share a little bit of what I'm doing, of why I'm really here.

"I think... I think she's connected to Lucy and my old patient in London. Something's going on with them—some common thread."

"Connected," Mum says in a strangely careful voice. "How?"

"I don't know," I admit, shaking my head. "But the symptoms are similar. The sleepwalking, hallucinating, delirium... Lucy and my patient—her name was Renée—they both displayed those. They were anemic too—Seren as well. And Rhiannon told me that before Seren disappeared, she was acting strange. Then there's the rash, which all three have." I swallow. "Had."

Two out of three are already dead. "It's the key to helping Lucy, I think—figuring out what was wrong with them, what happened to all these women."

My mother sighs, short and sharp. "Well, I can tell you what's wrong with Lucy."

I resist the urge to roll my eyes or to laugh. *Of course she can.* It's been months now and even though I, a highly educated, expertly trained doctor, have pored through all the medical research in the world, my mother thinks she can decode this case within minutes of hearing its most basic details. "Really."

Mum shrugs. *"Sugnwr Gwaed."*

"Mother, please—"

"Fampir."

I sigh explosively. "Here we go again."

"She's under attack from a blood drinker."

I stand up with a start, her hand falling from my knee, my frustration abrupt and almost instinctual. "Oh, Mother, stop it. Just stop it! I'm not ten anymore. I live in the real world, and I don't believe in giants or fairy goblins."

"Oh, the *real* world."

"Yes. So, no more talk of vampires and monsters, for the love of God."

She looks up at me and her lips grow dangerously thin, her voice waspish. "Just because you don't believe in something doesn't make it go away. Remember Mr. Swales?"

A dead, sagging body. The reek of putrefaction. Sponging the slime from his skin, holding down my vomit.

I'm shaking now, though whether from anger or the memory, I'm not sure. "What I know," I say slowly, "is that he was a sick man, and you had me—a *child*—bathe his corpse. Children get taken away from parents for things like that, you know, Mum."

"I expect that's what you wish happened," she mutters, and with that, the fragile peace between us is ruptured, broken.

"Mum…"

"It's all right, Mina. I believe what I believe, and I know what I know. Why do you think I'm bringing the money tree into the lounge?"

Frustration boils in my blood. I thought we were sharing a moment, that we had a chance to relate to one another over people we both care about. But of course, she had to twist it all to fit her narrative, to explain away life's complicated problems with her usual brand of mysticism and folklore.

"Exercise? I don't bloody know."

"We have a *Fampir*—"

"For goodness' sake!" I snap, getting to my feet. "Would you please just stop this? I need real answers to save Lucy, not some bloody bedtime story!"

I head to my bedroom, blood boiling. Everything is a folktale with her. It's like her mind is woven from the threads of mythos, the logic centers replaced with fantasy and fairy tales. But I live in reality, a world where the *Tylwyth Teg* are nothing but a pretty story, and killers walk free—human killers that have no other purpose than to satisfy the cravings of their own depravity. In a world like this one, there is no need for vampires and monsters.

Humans are bad enough.

By the time I come downstairs again, Mum has put cuttings of the money tree all over the house, hanging by yellow cooking string from every point of entry, even the chimney.

Protection against *Fampirs*.

Not a whisper of light peeks through the trees as he treads silently through the frost-covered forest. He is one with the creatures that claim the night, who hunt their prey under the cloak of darkness. They howl and scream with delight in concert with the crashing waves along the cliffside. The sounds soothe him, even as he senses prey of his own.

He knows they found the body, even before he reaches the grave. He can smell the earth that's been freshly overturned, can detect their scent commingled with the lingering stench of rot and death. Silken sheets, soiled.

His mouth moistens just from the thought of it. Of how she might've tasted, even as she pulled the girl's lifeless body from the earth. The salt of her sweat, briny like the sea. The heat of her body from the exercise. He purrs involuntarily.

Quickens his steps. He heads for the clearing just to be sure.

As expected, the body is gone.

They're circling now, closing in. Playing a dangerous game of cat and mouse that will certainly end with more than one body below the ground or burned in flame. He wonders, bemused, if they yet know the mouse is more monster than man.

And yet, their meeting feels inescapable now; he's certain of it. He will be ready.

Let the games begin.

24

I bring the blankets myself, spreading them over the sand between tufts of seaweed and stubborn pebbles, all the while asking myself what I'm doing, and what I expect.

I'm out of practice with the fire. A life of convenient gas fires in my flat has softened me to effort. It takes a good hour to light, my hands fumbling, first with paper, then cardboard, and finally kindling, and another thirty to really take. Soft sideways rain thwarts my attempts until the clouds part to reveal a dark sky dotted with gems. In the end, it's a cheeky breeze from the bluffs in the east that aids the flames.

Someone has even given the old skip a new lick of paint; she gleams yellow under an equally jaundiced moon. Despite Cysgod looming over me on the hill, a stark reminder of everything I'm up against, I feel a swell of hope and excitement when I spot Jonathan in the distance.

He's here. He's coming.

And he's on time. No more making me wait, wondering if he's going to show. No more taunting me with the possibility that I may be rejected, as he was. Maybe it's a sign of forgiveness. A gesture of goodwill, now that I've laid myself bare. He is the better person.

If you count to thirty before he speaks, you will be fine. My treacherous brain again. I reach twenty-five when he chuckles sardonically at the sight of the blankets, the picnic basket, the wine, bread and cheese, his eyes crinkling in a new and pleasant way.

Age suits him.

Twenty-nine...thirty.

"Fancy," he says, hands in his pockets.

"It's warm by the fire," I say, noting his hunched shoulders, the fine mist of water on his jacket.

He eyes me with a wary amusement that says more than he'd allow to pass his lips, and then he steps onto the blanket and sits down.

"Aperitif?" I ask.

He nods and I pour us both a good measure of the wine. I might need a little social lubrication for this one.

"Two meetings in one week," he muses. "One might think you had a hidden agenda."

"Maybe I do."

We cheers to the night, to the seagulls who are sleeping on the pebbles nearby, paying close attention to my spread with lidded eyes, and to the moonlight. Our glasses clink into the ocean like crystal whispers.

"I'm actually terrified of the dark," I admit, after we've been sitting and drinking for a while.

"I know."

"You do?"

"Yeah."

"I never told you."

"I know. Why not?"

I motion for him to have some bread and cheese, and he does so with fingers that are suddenly mesmerizing. What would they taste like if I pressed them to my mouth?

"We went on dates to the darkest part of the village," I say. "To the beach and the woods and the field by your dad's house.

I wasn't going to ruin it. Besides…the fire made me feel safe when we came here. So did you."

He doesn't acknowledge this, and I lose some of my nerve.

The firelight heightens the texture on the back of his hands. I watch carefully as he lifts bread and cheese to his mouth, chewing thoughtfully. Again, I wonder about small things—the taste of his sweat, the warmth of his skin, the way that he is so beautiful it hurts.

It takes me by surprise to realize I'm laughing. And that he is too.

"Hang on a minute," I say, trying to suppress my grin. "What happened to me being bad for you?"

He nods like a kid with a secret. "I've never been good at taking care of myself."

My stomach leaps when he takes my hand.

"And…after you explained what happened…" He pauses, checking that I'm okay. I nod for him to go on. "I felt that something had been laid to rest. I can finally stop grieving you as though you'd died."

"What do you say to a corpse?" I ask wryly.

There is a long pause. He is examining my hand, fiddling with my fingers, not meeting my eyes. "I'd say…don't leave again. Don't throw me away like a used wrapper."

Tears spring to the surface and I choke on them. "I'm so sorry I did that to you." It's my turn to take a breath. No stopping now. "You haven't…you haven't told me…" I let my sentence hang, but reach out to touch his face.

He doesn't flinch. He doesn't shy away. He looks me directly on, like the warrior he is, and he nods.

"You hadn't been gone long. I was planning to go looking for you. I had my bag packed, I had my money saved for a ticket to Oxford, I had the speech planned out." He laughs mirthlessly at the boy he used to be. "I was determined to bring you back, or…or at least to say my piece."

"But you never came?"

He shakes his head. "No. Dad needed help with the fencing on Eithin Hill. The sheep were getting out onto the road… It was a small job. Nothing, really. I said I'd take care of it, but then I was leaving. We'd had the notice by then of the land being in dispute… Dad was determined to make sure everyone knew it belonged to us."

"Everyone knows the land was Harker land."

"I wanted to help him. I wanted to do my part. I couldn't stand the thought of another damn thing taken away. The plan was to do it late, after dark. Just in case they had people watching during the day. Mad, eh? Hiding on your own bloody farmland. Dad wanted to be sure, so we waited. It was easier for me to do it alone, so I did. It was an easy job, just tightening the wire fencing. None of the posts were loose."

He's delaying the moment he says it. I know the feeling well. So I sit silently and let him finish, the same way he did for me.

"There was this…massive dog. It came out of nowhere."

He flinches and shuts his eyes.

"I'll never forget those teeth. I'll never forget the way my skin tore away…the pain of it. The wet shock of it. The sounds…"

A lump in my throat, tears on my cheek.

"I know it sounds mad, but…somehow I felt that whoever sent those papers claiming our land sent the dog. It wasn't a normal dog. It was huge…the size of a pony. It was…eerie. Wrong."

Trauma contorts everything, I think ruefully.

I reach out my hand, and there is no hesitation, no resistance this time: Jonathan takes it in his own. His calloused hands are warm with understanding, kindness, forgiveness. We sit beside each other in the stillness and I take in all that he's been through, and how closely his path mirrors my own: plans for a future, gone in an instant. A trauma that cleaves your life in two. A belief that you've moved on, that you're living fully, while really,

with your pain buried, a part of you remains stuck in the past—
a fly in amber. Being in motion is not the same as being alive.

Now, with nothing kept between us, I feel the promise of
something as fresh and clean as the sea breeze that tickles my
skin: a real future free from any expectations of the past, from
any what-ifs, had our lives remained on their predictable courses.
With the truth laid bare, we can get to know these versions of
each other that neither of us planned for, but are all that exist.

Together we can build something new.

My voice is barely a whisper. "Jonathan... I think I'm still in
love with you." I whisper it into his shirt.

I expect derision. I expect rejection. It's no more than I deserve.

Instead, he lowers his face and presses his lips to mine.

 **VI.**

Tiff is taken

    and returned

        and taken

            again.

                Over and over.

Each time returning

    less of a girl,

        more of a shell,

            until

                one day

she doesn't return at all.

Tiff's absence stirs a renewed rebellion in her. A panicked spring into action. When the door opens for the food tray, Jennifer sprints out past the man—she's thinner than ever now. She makes it halfway down the corridor before a man in a white coat spots her. A doctor? He is injecting something into the arm of another girl. Not Tiff. How many of them are they keeping in this perverse underground zoo? Will she one day wake in some country she doesn't know, slave to a man who will use her until she's too old to be valuable, then be culled like diseased bovine? Or will that happen, right here, in the underbelly of a London she never knew existed?

Jennifer is tackled to the ground by two burly men who weigh twice as much as her. A rib bows, complains, cracks. A needle slides into her arm, another violation, reality bending, warping, shifting until there is nothing.

Again.

That's when she earns her handcuffs.

"You're a troublemaker," said Mum when she stole red lipstick in tenth grade.

Jamie Weiss, when she kissed him for the first time and accidentally bit his lip.

Her first boss at a retail job she hated during summer breaks.

The man in the club with no name, who grabbed her arm.

The smirking guard that licks his lips after he breaks her rib as she lies on a cold, metal floor, the world swimming before her eyes.

You're a troublemaker.

She's had a lot of time to think about her mother. Of how she was right when she warned her that the world would be cruel. Of her desperate need to tell her that she finally understood, and that she was sorry for the things she said before she left. Before she ran away. She's spent hours trying to remember what, precisely, she said that made her mum's face first flame red in anger and then crumple with hurt. Then she spent days thinking about every bad thing she'd ever done, wondering if it was bad enough to deserve this.

She regrets longing for something to happen, because eventually it does. They open the door. Inject her with twilight drugs. Uncuff her wrists. Replace them in the corridor with manacles hooked to a long chain where the other girls are being attached. A long line, wobbling out of the rooms of this labyrinth. She doesn't remember walking to the van, but suddenly there she is, in a windowless lorry. Cattle for the slaughter. Pigs for the butcher. Fish for the monger. Each and every one of them knows it.

No one talks on the drive. They're too drugged to do much besides stare into the dark abyss as it takes them to their known, yet unknown, fate. Everything is unreality.

Whatever they gave the girls has worn off by the time they reach the destination—a castle by the sea.

How gothic, she thinks absurdly. There's a poetry, at least, that she will die in such a pretty place. The wind and the sky and the roar of the ocean is a delicious dirge.

They are led inside beneath the *chop-chop-chop* of a helicopter arriving, and then separated. The girl next to Jennifer— nameless—grabs for her hand as they are parted and unchained, a desperate motion, a *don't leave me*.

Primped.

Preened.

Perfected.

(Again.)

Somewhere outside comes the near-constant sound of helicopters arriving. Their bullet-staccato resonance runs through her like a live wire each time, a tiny electrical pulse. Every chop a machine gun vibrating through her skin.

The man dressing her is expressionless. He leads her from the room past a mirror where she sees a muted siren staring back. She looks alluring. She looks like she wants to be here. What a trick. What a deception.

The man leaves her alone in the corridor, nodding to a stone stairway leading up. She's going to run—going to jump into the sea. She saw it when they arrived, the tempting gray green through the window. There's something pure about a drowning, at least. And maybe she'll survive it.

The castle is labyrinthine in a way it's not supposed to be. This is like no castle she's seen before. Constructed to be lost in. To perplex and mystify and confuse. She tries to find her way out and ends up circling back to the beginning. Nothing is where it should be.

A man watches her from a shadowy corridor. She goes the other way.

Eventually, she comes upon a room glittering with gold, full of the other girls being fawned over by men in black tie. Something makes her go cold, and it takes her a while to put her finger on it, on why it feels so different from the club.

None of the men are wearing masks. That's it. They talk and touch and laugh, one glinting eye meeting another, hungry. They're not afraid to reveal their identities here. She knows instantly what that means.

No one will talk, or everyone will be dead.

She rubs her wrists, marveling at her sense of deep and confusing horror; that she feels more afraid now that her handcuffs are gone. Now that she is wandering freely. The man from the shadows in the corridor watches her from the other side of the room. She turns away and finds a door, slipping inside. Another corridor. He's at the end of it, smiling seductively. Cunningly. She turns down another set of spiraling stairs, and hears his chuckle below.

All these months, kept, fed, cared for...this was the reason. She has the strangest sense that she is in a shopping market.

She is the merchandise.

Though she runs farther from the grand, glittering ballroom, she ends up back there anyway. She tugs on the arm of a girl who is standing shivering in a corner.

"We have to go," she says. "It's not safe."

But the other girl is too far gone, too terrified to hear.

"Have you seen him?" she whispers. "I heard the men talking."

"What? What are you talking about?"

Then another girl hurries over. "They're talking about the host," she says, her voice dry as sandpaper, her hand a claw on Jennifer's arm. "Something's happening."

And then she tunes in to it. The low hum and hush of the men's voices.

"He'll be arriving soon."

"He's almost here."

"I wonder what he'll do this time."

"I wonder who he'll choose."

A man touches her arm and she rips it away, a snarl on her lips. His eyes flash and he raises a clawed hand—such a strange motion. One of the silent guards steps between them and murmurs, "She's for him."

The man lowers his hand, chuckling. "He likes them feisty."

He takes the shivering girl instead, and she tumbles away with her arm in his grip.

Jennifer steps forward without thinking. "You f—"

But the guard blocks her path, shaking his head. He is amused.

Another girl pulls her away. "Come on. It's not worth a swollen face."

Music spills from unseen places and the men liven up. Something is happening. She tries to find the quiet girl again, and—yes, there she is...through an archway partly concealed by a thick tapestry curtain.

It takes a moment to put the pieces together. Why she is bent backward like that, her back arched like an ogive, the man who took her with his lips pressed to her breast. He pulls back for only a moment to catch his breath and a river of blood rushes down her dress, gold to burgundy in seconds.

"Oh my God," Jennifer says, stumbling back. *"Oh my God."*

And how could she have been so stupid? How could she have been so blind?

They are not the merchandise.

They are the feast.

25

I've only just begun to drift to sleep when my phone vibrates on my nightstand with an incoming call, lighting up my room in an eerie blue haze.

I check the time—midnight. I see the caller ID and my heart stutters. "Lucy? What is it? Are you okay?"

She's breathless on the line, her voice soft, feeble. "Can you come over?"

"Now?"

"Yes."

"I'm on my way."

It takes me fifteen minutes to speed over, during which time I'm catastrophizing so badly that I'm sick with it when I pull into the drive. No sign of any other cars. I expect they have some fancy garage underground or a private driver. I walk up the gravel path to the front stairs, but Cariad meets me on the walkway. Ever-professional, no sign of fatigue from the late hour, she indicates the side of the house, so we skirt the main building and head to a thin louvered door just beyond the verge.

It opens into a narrow corridor, with a narrow set of stairs running up to the left. We climb them quickly and we're suddenly in a hallway on the first floor. The master bedroom is the first door on the left. It strikes me how unsecure this entrance is. Anyone could get out—or in—in a matter of seconds.

When Cariad opens the bedroom door, I find Lucy lying on her bed, dressed in a long silk nightdress that is almost the same pallid shade as she is. Veins protrude alarmingly on her arms, neck, and chest. The rash—the petechiae-like collection of holes—is overlaid like a thin spray of ink around her neck and collarbone. Like someone threw poppy seeds at her and they stuck. Even a few black holes litter her arms. It's spreading, whatever it is.

She looks bad, I think, staring at her beauty exhumed.

Lucy sits up and raises her arms for me. Cariad leaves us alone and it takes five long strides to reach the edge of the bed. I sit down and she pulls me to her, snuggling close. She's bony and sharp and it hurts when she presses her face to my shoulder, but I blink back horrified tears and hug her. She's freezing to the touch and so insubstantial I fear she'll simply float away were I to let go.

I won't let that happen.

Silently, she begins to cry.

"Shh," I whisper, stroking her straw hair. "It's going to be okay, Luce. I'm not going to leave you alone."

"Mina," she whispers, pressing tighter to me. She smells of nothing, like she's already fading. The shush of her breath is precious.

"I'm here. I'm here…"

"I'm so sorry to call you over here in the middle of the night, but… I think something's really wrong."

I shut my eyes, try to force back the terror that has come screaming into my body. No. *No.* This can't be happening.

"Shall I get help?"

Lucy shakes her head. "Arthur is next door. Mina, I'm so afraid."

"I need you to listen to me."

A small nod, heavy breathing.

"Do you know what's happening to you?"

A shake of the head.

I only have a moment's hesitation. Here in the night, here in the dark, I can say secret things out loud. "I've been looking into your symptoms. I have reason to believe that something...unnatural is happening to you. That your illness isn't happenstance. You're...a victim of something, someone. Do you understand?"

She begins to say something, but coughs. "Hmm."

"I've been working with Quincey Morris."

I wait for her astonishment, but it doesn't come.

"We care about you very much. We're trying to get to the bottom of this, but I need you to tell me. Has anything unusual happened recently? Have you seen anything strange?"

She closes her eyes for a bit too long, and then stares at me, not wholly present.

"Please," I urge. "Please try."

"I... I'm so tired, Mina."

"Have you ever met the owner of Cysgod Castle?"

She shakes her head. "No. I never go anywhere."

I glance at the balcony doors. They're shut, but are they locked?

I shudder, the pit in my stomach growing. I'd thought of this place as a fortress, but it's flimsier than my flat in London.

Her voice breaks as she says my name. "Mina...please save me."

Shadows sigh around us.

"I'm not going to let anything happen to you," I whisper fiercely. "I'm *not*. I'm going to save you."

Renée. Seren. Renée. Seren.

My failures thump like a cruel heartbeat in my head, and Singer's grief over losing her daughter adds to the rhythm.

Renée. Seren. Beatrice. Renée. Seren. Beatrice.

"I swear it," I whisper. "You and me against the world, like always."

I can barely hear her reply.

"You and me."

I leave Lucy sleeping in her bed just before 1:00 a.m., sneaking out the same way I came in. She doesn't stir, even when I bend down to kiss her forehead. I don't want to leave, but my head and heart are churning more violently than the Irish Sea and I need action, something to focus my mind on, some pathway to take that alleviates a little of this panic. I feel like I'm going to scream.

I'm standing in a fine mist of rain, lifting the knocker on his cottage door before I've fully realized what I'm doing. He's awake, but opens the door with a ruffled confusion.

"Mina?"

"Jonathan, hi. Can I come in?"

He stands back immediately and I hurry inside, feeling like something is chasing me over the threshold.

This cottage was always where I could find him, but it was never *his* before. It was his father's. It looks almost the same, but the energy within has shifted into something more Jonathan-like than when Mr. Harker was alive. It's a large farmhouse, more than a cottage, but the front section is thatched and so we always called it Fairy Cottage, and the name stuck. The walls and furniture are the same, but now there are books littering almost every surface. I peek at the one on the entrance hall table but can't make out the title.

Jonathan leads me into the kitchen and puts the kettle on to boil. "Unless you want something stronger?" he asks.

"Stronger, I think."

He nods, switches off the kettle, and takes me into the living room. He gestures to the sofas, which were always so big

and plush that I craved them when I was away. I allow myself
to sink into the pillows, letting my head fall back.

I'm almost dozing when I feel him nudge my hand with a
glass.

"Scotch okay?"

I take it. "Perfect."

He sits and watches me carefully. I down the Scotch in three
gulps and sigh.

"Better?"

"Mmm-hmm."

"Are you okay?"

I start to nod, but it turns into a shake. "No. No, I don't think
I am. I'm so worried about Lucy."

"How's she doing?"

"Not well. I feel like I'm losing her. I have to save her. I have
to."

"It's not your responsibility to save everyone," he says softly,
his fingers lifting to gently caress the back of my hand.

"It's my responsibility to save *her*."

"You always did what you set your mind to. You'll do this
as well."

"Jonathan… I don't know if I'm strong enough. I'm so tired
of fighting."

I lean closer to him and rest the top of my head on his chest.
It's firm and unmoving. A strong chest. A farmer's chest. I inhale him and feel my body tingle in response.

"Mina," he whispers, running his hand up my arm. "Why
did you come to me?"

"You're the only person I ever want to go to."

He lifts my chin and searches my eyes for the lie, but there's
none to be found. He presses his lips to mine, eyes still searching my face, and it is painfully soft. I moan and press into him
harder, and his eyes finally close and then we are kissing with
the same roughness and passion we used to share.

His hands are firm and strong as he lifts my turtleneck up and off, exposing my bra, pulling loose my hair from the comb holding it in place. It falls into the cushions, but I don't care—I don't care about anything except his lips, his tongue, his hands pressing me close.

I haven't been with anyone since the day I left. The psychiatrist in me knows it's because I craved control and safety. I've never felt safe with anyone except Jonathan. It's only ever been Jonathan.

He releases a sound, low and graveled in his throat, when I unbutton his shirt and slip it off, pushing myself against him, skin to skin. I haven't done this in so long. I haven't felt the touch of another human in years—it's almost painful how much I want it.

When he pushes me down into the pillows and presses himself to my body, kissing my neck with a force that scares me, I freeze—

And everything changes.

The sea was raging when I felt his teeth go in, breaking the sensitive skin of my neck with anesthetic precision. I could feel the ironclad strength of his hands locking me against him, his body like stone. His hair fell into my eyes and I tried to breathe. My vision was swimming like he'd dosed me, but I felt the terror, the pure undiluted panic, and could do nothing about it.

I gasped and some semblance of reality returned when I felt a pinch along my collarbone where the sharp end of the rowan branch amulet Mum had given me for my eleventh birthday pressed into my skin. This was a different kind of pain: clarifying. It woke me from whatever spell I was under.

He was strong...so strong, but as he pushed me to the wet sand, his hands roaming my body like it was his for the taking, I managed to slip my hand up and under him, grasping the edge of the rowan in a shaking fist.

The fragile leather thong broke, as though it had been waiting for this moment all along, and I lifted it up and around. There was no hesitation, no moment of doubt. I stuck it into his neck, shoving as hard as my failing body would allow, and felt it break into his skin with a disgusting *crack*.

His grip loosened right away and he sat up—mouth agape and bleeding, teeth sharp even as they retracted into his gums—and touched his neck where the rowan still protruded. He looked at me, then out at the sea, then at the sky, before he fell back and lay still.

Was I crying? Screaming? Where was Jonathan? He'd left me… Yes, I remembered. The fire had finally taken in the skip, but there were no other signs of life. I scrabbled back and away from the man, my body half wild and half dead—when I realized that he wasn't going to come after me. Because he wasn't breathing. Wasn't blinking.

Wasn't moving.

After a while, I don't know how long, I crawled over and checked.

The rowan still stuck out of him, marking the tender spot where I'd struck, like a macabre spotlight on what I had done. *Killer*. The word came to me then, unbidden.

I don't know what I was thinking after that. It was like watching myself from outside. I watched as I dragged him over to the fire—watched myself haul him up—watched as I collapsed time and time again with him on top of me, until finally I managed to drag a leg, then an arm, into the fire, and push him with every last ounce of strength I had left, into the skip.

His body caught like dry kindling, smoking like ancient coal, and within minutes, he was nothing but char. Even then I knew it wasn't normal for a body to burn like that, for blood to come spooling from his orifices and catch fire like pure alcohol, but I blotted it out—blocked it out with furious intention.

No. *This didn't happen.*

Only it did.

My neck was glacial where he'd bitten me. The dry blood crusted over already-healing wounds, smattered, I would later find, with a rash that his saliva, or venom, or *something*, had caused. I felt like I'd been abducted by aliens. My hands were shaking. I was covered in blood—his and my own.

What if Jonathan came back?

I knew very little in that moment except that he couldn't see me like this. I couldn't face him, or anyone else, after what I had done.

Killer.

I ran.

I ran, and I ran, and I ran, and I stopped seeing what was in front of me. When I came to, I was almost home, standing on the hill above the house, looking at a moon ringed in red. A moon glaring at me, telling me, *I know what you did.*

Blood. So much blood.

I took a shower. I scrubbed and scrubbed at my skin, the white enameled tub streaming with endless streaks of browns and reds. It was everywhere. I was so dirty. So unclean.

I scrubbed the tiles until I couldn't see it anymore. Until all traces of what had happened were gone.

I packed a bag, gathered the money I had saved for uni from working part-time summer jobs, adding the small stash I knew Mam kept in the gravy boats in the linen chest, and I fled. I left a note in the microwave. I wanted them to know I was okay, but not to come after me. I didn't want anyone to find me, because if they did, I feared what I might tell them…that I might somehow betray the truth of what I'd done, of who I had become.

I slept on a bench on the station platform, and when the 04:51 train to London Euston arrived, I climbed on and never looked back.

When I come back to myself, I'm curled into a ball on the floor, my arms wrapped around my head, rocking back and forth, sobbing. Jonathan is on the floor with me, holding me between his legs like a protective blanket.

"I killed him, I killed him, I killed him…"

I can hear myself saying it, over and over; I can hear Jonathan shushing me, whispering that he's here, that everything is okay.

Slowly, slowly, I tell him everything that happened all those years ago—and why I left without a word. The forgotten story. The *whole* story. The one I haven't dared touch or examine.

When I'm finished, we're both sitting close to each other on the carpet. He's draped a blanket around me and is stroking my hair.

"I'm a victim…*and* a murderer."

"You're safe with me," he says. "And what happened wasn't your fault. It was self-defense."

"I can see it clearly now. He wasn't human. He was…something else."

Jonathan doesn't argue with me. He takes in the knowledge with a kind of calm acceptance that reminds me of Mam. A true Tylluanian.

He raises his fingers slowly to the ruined side of his face, and when he speaks he sounds far away. "There are dark, evil things in these hills. That I believe. That I've always believed."

I lift my face and softly kiss his scars, and when I taste his tears, I kiss those too, craving comfort, familiarity, warmth. Lips find lips, gently now, and our hands seek each other's bodies, peeling away the last remaining layers separating us. His hands, big and warm, cup my breasts and I sigh and press myself against him again, climbing on top of him so that I'm straddling his body, his erection pressed patiently against my sex. The pain as I lower myself is sharp and brief, and I am full of him and he is sighing into my neck, pausing, allowing me to take him in, to ache with pleasure, and then we are moving slowly together in a rhythm I didn't realize I knew.

26

I can't sleep.

A storm has been rattling the downstairs shutters for an hour, and I'm tempted to go and see if I can secure them. But I don't. Outside isn't safe now. Darkness isn't safe now. Vampires could be anywhere now, in this new world where Mam was right all along.

I consider going to her room, like I'm five again and afraid that the rains have washed in the *afanc*, but I keep my own council. If she's able to sleep, then let her. I have a feeling things will get worse before they get better.

I think of texting Jonathan, but I only left his house a few hours ago, and if he too has finally fallen asleep, I don't want to wake him. My body still hums with the frantic energy of our coupling, the feel of his skin on mine, and I close my eyes, relishing the memory. But even that can't banish my worries for long.

Eventually, the tintinnabulation outside blurs into white noise, and my mind begins to drift.

When I awaken once more, it's fully daylight, the sun slanting in at an angle that tells me it's nearing noon. The shadows are gone from my room, but I know they lurk still.

After my revelations last night, everything takes on new shape. First, my history: a victim not of sexual trauma, as I'd so long assumed, but something equally violent and predatory, yet harder to understand. My attacker on the beach sought to violate me in a different way than I could have ever imagined...yet somehow, unbelievably, I fought him off. Returning to the long-repressed memory now, in the warmth of my sunlit bedroom, I attempt to reflect on it in a more rational way.

I try to look at it through the distance of years of training and therapy, to gain a sense of clarity. My young brain hadn't been equipped to process the many revelations of the night: that the folklore Mam had forced on me for so many years was actually true. That beasts *did* roam the night. That I had been attacked by one of them...and that I had somehow escaped.

Killer.

I was not the prey, but the predator. This final piece is one I still need time to adjust to, the one that, perhaps most of all, had made the teenage me so desperate to run from Tylluan and never look back. To cut ties with everyone I cared about, lest they learn what that night had done to me, what it had made me become. For years, I repressed the memory and its implications.

Murderer.

Jonathan's words come back to me, a warm, fleece blanket, a soft caress, a gentle kiss: *What happened wasn't your fault. It was self-defense.*

It was—that's true. If teenage Wilhelmina could sit on her couch, what would Dr. Mina Murray tell her? What would Dr. Murray say to any of her patients in a similar situation? *You defended yourself. You survived. Well done.*

Okay. I can work with that that. One foot in front of the other. I survived. And maybe...just maybe, knowing what I survived, what I conquered, gives me more agency—more power—than I thought myself to have, in this moment when I need it the most.

It's not only my history I see now in a different light, but the case before me: the fate of the other women, the other victims. Renée, Seren, Beatrice…their plight takes on new shape in the light of this almost incomprehensible development. Lucy, no longer in my mind a victim of a powerful predator wielding a designer drug or STI as some kind of weapon.

I know now that his weapon is far more sinister.

Lucy's illness is clearly the result of an attack, or multiple attacks—the same one I escaped, the same one that these women eventually succumbed to. *My best friend is being preyed on by a creature of the night.* Once my brain gets over the sheer shock of it, my usual practical sensibility takes over. When and how did he get to her? And how can I possibly protect her?

Is it too late to save her?

In this, my utmost challenge, I know I cannot work alone. I consider my possible allies: My mother is, strangely, my best hope at being believed. It would be so easy to walk the twenty steps to her room and tell her what I now believe to be true. But years of resistance hold me back; I'm not quite ready to admit to all the time I spent absorbed in righteous anger, unable to accept the possibility that my batty old mam might have the right of things.

Then there's Singer, who, for all her paranoia and conspiracy theories, would probably balk at the idea that the predator she's been stalking for more than a decade is not of this reality.

And finally, there's Quincey… Despite having spent her formative years in Tylluan, her logical, American brain makes gaining her belief an uphill battle. But I know a powerful motivator in belief is *need*. And if Quincey understood the depths of what we were dealing with, the gravity of the situation, she might be that much more likely to believe—to be ready to help.

One step at a time, I tell myself. Understanding doesn't come quickly. It didn't for me.

I pick up the phone, and I make the call.

★ ★ ★

Quincey almost doesn't come.

"She may speak more openly to you," I point out gently.

The muscle in Quincey's jaw works and she sighs. "It might make her clam up."

I told her just enough to convince her that the threats on Lucy have escalated. That we are running out of time, and that she needs to see it for herself.

"She might see me and freeze," Quincey adds.

"Maybe," I concede. "But I need you to do this with me, to question her one more time. To see what I've seen."

"Is the husband blocking access?" Quincey's voice is sharp, suddenly on.

"He's protective of her, that's for sure, but no."

I didn't mean to rub her the wrong way, but I can see I have.

"Okay, fine. I'll go to her house, take stock of the access points, see what I can see. But I'll decide if and when I see her."

"Are you just going to stand outside while I talk to her?"

"I don't know. Maybe."

I nod, wishing all of this was easier. I message Singer to let her know we're going to talk to my friend, one of the victims, and she insists on a debriefing afterward. I tell her we will message when we're through.

The drive is tense, neither Quincey nor I speaking. I park in the drive, and we traipse to the door. Cariad answers, smiling shyly at me. At least this time, I don't have to feel badly dragging her out of bed for my visit. She shows us into the same parlor where Lucy and I got sozzled, seemingly a lifetime ago.

"Has she had any doctors come to see her?" Quincey asks, pulling out a notepad from her top pocket. I know all of this, of course, but I also know that Quincey needs to take her own steps, conduct her own investigation, before I can let her in on what I've learned and why she's really here.

Cariad's eyes move toward the spiralbound notebook, then toward me. I smile, encouraging.

Cariad nods. "There have been several. They take blood, they do tests, they leave."

Quincey nods. "Okay. Thank you."

"I'll just go to see if madam is up for visitors," Cariad says, backing toward the door.

I wait with Quincey, who is staring out of the window with a faraway frown on her face. At least she's here.

Lucy is still too sick to be able to meet us downstairs, so Cariad leads the way to the bedroom. This route is far more secure than the external staircase—which suggests that whoever is targeting her is getting in the latter way.

Quincey follows, never taking her eyes from the carpet. In Lucy's bedroom, Cariad places a cup of watery tea on Lucy's bedside and whispers, "Try to drink, madam."

I can smell the verbena from here. For once, I am grateful for mam's forcefulness, for the fact that she's so clearly been over here. She never gives up on her beliefs.

Lucy touches Cariad's arm fondly. "Thank you, Cariad."

She doesn't touch the tea.

I sit beside her on the bed and take her hand.

"Hello, Luce."

She smiles at me wanly. "Bambi."

"Looks like Mam's given you verbena tea. Have you tried to drink it?"

"It makes me sick and I keep getting worse."

She's even paler today. How is she paler today? Veins lie delicate and blue along her arms and breasts; her mouth is cracked and crimson, somehow alluring and appalling at once, the terrible contrast so extreme.

Her eyes take me in and then snag on Quincey, who is hanging back by the door.

"Qu—" she tries, her voice not much over a whisper. She licks her lips slowly and tries again. "Quincey Morris."

Quincey stands frozen in the doorway, her mouth slightly ajar, jaw rigid with shock. I feel guilty for bringing her into this terrible knowledge, even though it's what we came here for. She blinks, swallows, and comes to the bed. She sits, taking my place, and reaches for Lucy's hand.

"Hey, Luce. Been a while."

Lucy smiles again, and it seems to take all her energy. "Look at you. Woman in uniform."

Quincey makes a choking sound that might be a laugh or a sob.

Lucy's eyes roll alarmingly back into her head, but she fights her way back to us. It's happening more and more now, and a surge of panic rises in me. Quincey jerks forward and grips Lucy's hand.

Lucy groans. "I'm okay."

Quincey straightens up, releasing a breath. "I need to ask you a few questions, okay?"

Lucy nods, her eyes closing and reopening. "Tired…"

"I know, love. I know. But this is important."

Lucy nods again.

"When was the last time you went to the beach? Can you tell me that, love?"

Lucy frowns. "The…beach?"

Her eyes close and don't open. Quincey touches her cheek, her voice tense. *"Lucy?"*

Lucy's eyes flutter open. "Qu-Quincey?"

"Hello, love. Listen to me carefully, okay? What do you know about Cysgod Castle and its owner?"

I watch with bated breath as Lucy processes the question. Is she alert enough to answer this time? She shakes her head.

"What?" she whispers. For a moment it doesn't look like Lucy knows who Quincey is.

Quincey pulls out her pad again and clicks on her pen. I note the way her hand shakes.

I brush away a tear and bite my lip. How is this happening? How is this creature getting to her?

Yet I know that the physical protections of Lucy's house mean nothing compared to the ancient force we're dealing with. True, we're two floors up, but who the hell knows what a creature such as the *Sugnwr Gwaed* is capable of? For all I know, every tale of a shape-shifting demon or devil-sighting is really a vampire, spotted through the ages, the actuality of his monstrosity warping down generations, twisted until no smidgen of the truth remains.

Or perhaps it's all true, and he can transform into a bird or bat and fly up to her window.

Lucy searches Quincey's face, a wan smile creasing her cheeks. "Quincey?"

"You're doing great. When was the last time you went to London?"

Lucy's eyes fall closed again. Quincey shakes her, but this time she doesn't wake.

I rush to the other side of the bed and check Lucy's pulse and breathing. She seems to have fallen asleep, but her heartbeat is not as strong as I'd like.

"I think I better call for an EMT to bring her into hospital."

Lucy's eyes suddenly roll and then open wide, staring at me. Her irises all but vanish, her pupils dilating in absolute terror. It's almost like she's screaming in silence, crying out for me, a desperate attempt to tell me something that I just can't understand.

"Lucy." I try to stay calm, but it's a whole other kettle of fish when the person you're doctoring is someone you love. I've never had to deal with that before; I can't do this. Without thinking, I press my mouth to her ear.

"Listen to me. We think you're being targeted by a vampire.

A *Sugnwr Gwaed* like Mum used to warn us about... Stay strong. Stay with us—"

"Is everything okay?" asks a voice from the bedroom doorway. It's Arthur, and he looks aghast, face red. His kind eyes flash with worry, his protectiveness kicking into high gear. He glances at Quincey, still holding her notebook. "Who are you?"

I straighten. "Arthur. This is Detective Sergeant Quincey Morris. We're here to help Lucy. To ask her some questions."

His eyes dart to his wife on the bed. "Lucy?"

He rushes over and Quincey moves out of his way. She watches, dead faced, as Arthur strokes Lucy's hair.

"Lucy? Lucy, wake up." He sounds panicked as he shakes her shoulders.

Her eyes flutter open. She looks disoriented for a moment and then finds Arthur and her face splits into a grin.

"Arty."

He buries his face in her shoulder. The love there, the anguish, is so painful to behold, I almost have to look away. "I thought... I thought..."

He strokes her head and I hear Quincey move toward the door. I suppose that's my cue too. I glance back to tell her we should go, and find that she's already left.

"Arthur," I say quietly, almost telling him the truth. Instead, when he looks up at me with tearful eyes, I say, "Keep her safe. Please."

"Always," he replies, and I realize that I trust him.

I nod at him. "Good day."

"Good day," he says.

I head for the door, hating to leave Lucy behind.

Outside, Quincey is standing by the hydrangeas, a hand pressed to her forehead. I touch her shoulder and she jumps.

"I'm sorry," I whisper.

"Jesus, Mina," Quincey says, angrily scrubbing away tears. "She's fucking dying."

And there it is. The truth I've been avoiding, but the one that will, hopefully, help me make an ally out of Quincey in the logic-defying world I now find myself in.

"I know."

27

Back at my house, I push open the back door. "Mam?"

There's no reply, so I herd Quincey into the conservatory, past the towering tomato plants and bunches of herbs swinging from the lintel. Rain sputters on the glass of the roof like impatient fingers.

On the way home from Lucy's, I invited both Quincey and Singer to come to Mam's house. We're all tired and sad, filled with an aimless purpose, an arrow loosed with no fletching to stabilize and guide it home. Now it's time to pull together, to bring all the women who want to catch this predator into one place—to put everything we know on the table.

It's time for everyone to get acquainted.

Quincey moves to the shabby sofa, sinking down with a grateful sigh and leaning her head back on the patchwork quilt. I think of how hard today must have been on her. If I had returned home to find Jonathan married to someone else and our past lingering over me like storm clouds that could never break into rain—I don't know how I would have dealt with it. And if I had then found he was dying on top of that? An impossible, terrible nightmare.

I sit next to her and lay my head on her shoulder, not meaning to be so intimate, but unable to stop myself. I think, even now, she loves Lucy as much as I do. That she understands my desperation. I see her begin to smile, and then swallow down a yawn or a sob or a scream.

I expected it to be some comfort, having an ally in my worry. Misery loves a little bit of company. Instead, it has made me anxious, like I've spoken the monster into being, made it real by letting others believe in it. Renée is gone, so is Seren. And Singer's daughter, Beatrice. Lucy looks not much far behind unless we can actually *do* something.

I feel a surge of rising panic, so I say their names under my breath over and over, a mantra to still the nerves, a promise to myself and to Lucy.

I will save you. I won't fail again.

A knock at the door breaks our reverie. I open it to find Singer dripping in a trench coat, looking quite peeved.

She comes in without being invited, nodding at me and then spotting Quincey in the conservatory.

Quincey folds her arms, taking Singer in. "So this is your hacker friend?"

"You're the copper, then?" Singer returns, eyeing her up and down.

The women stare at each other for an uncomfortable moment, and then Quincey breaks out into a laugh. Singer grins.

Singer smacks a vine out of her way and collapses into the wide wicker chair that Mam favors. I wince at the rainwater dropping everywhere. Quincey trades her spot on the couch for a wooden chair near the door as though she's merely here for an official visit. I notice her checking the exit points and realize that my own trauma has created in me a copper-like tic that she, of course, shares.

Mam hurries into the room with a giant basket of verbena: tall, ratty stalks with clusters of purple flowers. I remember from many, *many* years of lecturing that October will be the last chance to harvest them.

She pauses at the sight of us, her brows popping up.

"I invited some friends over, Mam," I say, feeling absurdly like a teenager again.

She gives me a sharp look and I realize I've reverted to "mam" like when I was a teen, my faux London "mum" dissolving.

"Hi, Ms. Murray. It's been a while," Quincey says, standing up.

Mam grins and sets the basket down on a side table. "I believe the last time we had a proper chat was when I caught you and Lucy breaking into my house yonks ago."

Quincey looks startled for a moment, then sprays out a laugh. "I'd forgotten that!"

"Never would have thought you'd end up on this side of the law back then. When Ffion told me you'd gone down the policing degree route, you might have knocked me over with a feather."

"Alas," Quincey says, mock injured, a hand pressed to her chest. "My rebel days are over. Anyway, it was all Lucy. She was a bad influence."

"She's certainly a lively chicken," Mam says before thinking better of it.

Silence seeps between us at the knowledge that Lucy is far from lively now.

Then Mam nods. "I'll get the kettle on, then."

After a few minutes, I get up to help her, and together we bring in two trays of tea and *bara brith* that smells so deliciously fresh my mouth fills with saliva at the merest whiff.

"So I think we should start by acknowledging that everyone is here for the same reason," I begin. Eventually I will need to ease everyone into the knowledge I possess, but for now, I want to start small: create a shared sense of purpose using our common goal. Put together the facts we have, or at least, the ones that everyone can agree on. "Either you've lost someone already, or are at risk of losing someone you love, if we don't get to the bottom of who is doing this."

The women look at each other and slowly nod.

"I guess I should start by introducing everyone," I say. "Quincey Morris you already know, Mam. And this is Helen Singer, a woman who's already lost her own daughter to these monsters."

I gesture to my mother, who gives a perfunctory nod. "And this is my mam, Vanessa Murray."

"Call me Van," she says. "You too, Quincey. Or Batty Witch on the Hill. I answer to either."

Singer leans back on the couch and chuckles. I have a sneaking suspicion those two are going to get on. But there's no time for chitchat. We're here to discuss how to get to the bottom of this—how to stop women from dying all over the United Kingdom.

"We need to pool our resources and information," I say, looking at each of them.

"I'll go first," Singer says by way of agreement. She tells the story she already told me, of how her daughter, Bea, went missing, only to be torn apart and thrown in the river, cold and alone. She says it all methodically, without emotion, simply stating the facts. My mother and Quincey listen without offering condolences, maybe sensing that divorcing emotion from the tragedy of her story is the only way to move forward, or at least the only way that Singer has found. I refrain from psycho-analyzing her out loud.

"When the police failed me," she says, glancing at Quincey, "I went underground. I found links between girls up and down the country, namely a list of common symptoms, which Mina discovered on my forum. That's how we met," she adds. "A location kept cropping up in the research—a private nightclub in London."

"The club with no name," I supply.

"Right. Several of the girls were linked to that location in my research, and Mina found that one of her patients who had the same symptoms and who fit the profile of the victims was also linked to the club."

"This group operates outside of London as well," I add. "There's a tie to Cysgod Castle. Right here in Tylluan. Rhiannon told me that Seren was due to go on some kind of date at Cysgod, and she had the same business card given to the girls who went to the club."

Singer nods. "I followed the pockets of murders and symptoms over the years up and down the country and discovered a pattern. One or two women every few months since my daughter went missing fifteen years ago."

She waits for that to sink in.

Quincey leans forward, elbows on her knees. "More than ten a year, for a decade and a half? That's...a lot. Harold Shipman territory!"

"You don't say," Singer says sardonically.

"Right, I guess that's my cue." Quincey claps her hands. "We've learned that official routes for information are being blocked. My access to information regarding Cysgod and its goings-on is severely limited, even at my clearance level."

"That's a bloody understatement," Singer says, scoffing. "This is an organized effort at the highest levels." She leans forward. "Vulnerable, young, poor women, all of the ones we know about, display the same symptoms. I have a list. Most of them go missing after a bout of illness. Some are never seen again. Others are found dead."

"What we don't know yet," I say, nodding at Singer, "is how Lucy slots into all of this. She doesn't fit the pattern—she's not young, or poor, or vulnerable, not someone whose symptoms are likely to get overlooked. She's also still safely at home."

"And we know almost nothing about the group itself," Quincey adds.

"Well, we know some things," Singer says. "Girls on the fringe are recruited to the club with no name. They are sexually abused—" she slides a piece of paper across Mam's glass-top wicker coffee table "—before they are either released so near to death that their passing is almost a certainty, or perhaps they die at the club before having their bodies transported to innocuous places, places that obscure the true way they died. Some turn up within a few days or weeks of going missing. Others seem to be held at the club for a while before being transported to remote locations across the UK, like Cysgod—about twice a year—before they vanish or turn up dead."

"How do you know all this?" Quincey asks sharply as she takes the paper and looks at it.

"With the Cysgod lead, I began looking for references in back forums on the dark web. These men, the ones involved, they're talking about it. Some of them are roped in by blackmail and are trying to get out but find that they can't. Others are willing participants until they prove themselves and are what they call 'converted.' They mostly talk in code, like it's some sort of cult."

"Did they know you were watching?" I ask quickly. "If they find out—"

Singer gives me a look. "I should be insulted. *Anyway*, they don't seem very worried about law enforcement."

"Nor do they need to be," Quincey says. "When my inquiries about Seren were blocked, I started checking records at the crime agency they sent it to. The search warrant for Cysgod wasn't even *issued*. And what's more—this has happened before. A body was discovered near Cysgod years ago on the beach. Looked washed up. Autopsy report was redacted, except mention of a minor rash, and no follow-up investigation was carried out. Both instances were signed off by the chief of police at the time. This goes all the way up."

"My God," I whisper. Then another thought occurs to me. "You said years ago—when, exactly, was this?"

"1956," Quincey says, and the room is silent, letting the magnitude of her answer set in.

"Just how far back does this go?" I ask.

"And just how wide?" Quincey chimes in.

I lean forward. "What do you mean?" But as the words escape my lips, I realize how naive we've been. We've been assuming this is contained to the United Kingdom. But really... who knows how far the web spreads?

I can't ignore it anymore. I can't deny it. This is not the work of a mortal man, but of an ageless creature. A creature who has needed to feed for as long as he's been alive...which could be more decades, centuries or millennia than I can fathom. Mam was right all along.

I glance at her to find she is already staring at me.

And if this really is...a *Fampir*, why would something as trivial as a land boundary contain his path of destruction? And the people that aid and abet him—why would they ever stop there?

I fiddle with my polo neck and force myself to think about something else. Anything other than the memory of his teeth in my flesh, of how close he came to—

Stop.

I get up and pace the room. The others watch me but say nothing. My panic is growing like a virus again. I have to stop it. Quell it. Crush it.

Keep it together, Murray. You're a doctor, remember? Reason and rationality, even in chaos.

"Are you ready to tell them, love?" Mam asks quietly.

I give her a pointed look. "Not now, please."

Quincey and Singer glance between us.

"What?" Singer says sharply. "What do you know?"

"You brought us all here for a reason," Mam says gently. "If we're going to do this together, then they need to know the truth."

There's no oxygen in this room. I hurry to the window and

throw it open, leaning out into the night; the wind is churning harder, the rain smattering into a storm. I can smell it like fog.

I take several deep, loamy breaths and then feel Mam's warm hand on my shoulder.

"It's time, love."

I shake my head, deflating. "I don't know what the truth is anymore. I don't know what's real."

I turn back into the room, hugging myself, and Mam smiles at the two women staring at us, bewildered. "Quincey has lived here long enough to be able to accept that there's more to life than what is conventionally known," she tells me. "You have to trust them, Mina."

I sigh and squeeze the bridge of my nose. I really don't want to do this. It goes against all my strongest instincts, the rules and barriers that have kept my life ordered and controlled, kept me safe all these years.

"Tell us," Quincey says, squaring her shoulders.

"My mother is of the opinion…" I hesitate, laughing.

"Spit it out, Murray," Singer says gruffly. "We've got a girl to save."

I give them an apologetic look and then I do spit it out. "My mother is of the opinion that Lucy is being targeted by what we know of here in Wales as a *Fampir*—more conventionally, a vampire."

I expect their silence. I expect their confounded expressions. I can tell, as Quincey searches my face, her frown so deep it's practically cutting her face in half, that she doesn't think I'm quite compos mentis—and, really, can I blame her?

"With all due respect, Mrs. M., you think Lucy—and all these other women—are being attacked by a *vampire*?" Quincey asks. I can tell she's trying not to openly scoff.

"The *Sugnwr Gwaed* are nothing new." My mother raises her chin and keeps her gaze full on Quincey. "Tales of those who consume the blood of the living have haunted nearly every culture around the world for centuries. The undead of the Grettis Saga; Sekhmet, the bloodthirsty Egyptian goddess; Lilith, depicted as surviving on the blood of infants." Her eyes dart to me. "Most people refuse to acknowledge—"

I feel my hackles rise. "There's a good reason, Mother. Are we to believe everything from offering tribute to King Vortigern's red dragon to gathering beneath the Llangernyw Yew to hear the Angelystor proclaim the yearly list of the soon-to-be departed?"

The heat rises in her cheeks, and she counts off her fingers. "The Greek *Striges*, the Hebrew *Motetz Dam*, the Icelandic *Draugr*, the Romanian *Strigoi*, the Hungarian *Izcacus*, Croation *Kulzac*, the Hindu *Vetaal*, the Spanish *Guaxa*, the *Asanbosam* of the Akan people, the *Adze* of the Ewe people, the Madagascan *Ramanga*—countless tales of the same creature over and over, but please, go ahead and dismiss them!"

She's breathing furiously, her eyes wide with a barely suppressed rage. I swallow and look away. I know now that there is truth to what she's saying, that there has been all along. But that doesn't make it any easier to accept.

"I've seen plenty of human monsters and the evil they do," Quincey says.

I sigh, my voice pleading. "Yes, but that doesn't explain the blood loss or the rash that looks like their body has been poisoned from the inside."

"You believe her?" she asks quietly, her eyebrows slightly raised.

I realize everything hinges on my answer. "I…" I trail off, not knowing where to start. "There's obviously a lot of folklore here, and some history. Until recently, I was the staunchest of skeptics—Mam can attest to the number of fights we've had over our clashing beliefs. But something…happened recently that's made me look at everything differently."

Unbidden, my eyes cut to my mother's. Her eyebrows rise in

surprise, but I can't read more than that in her face, and right now, I don't want to pause to imagine what's going on in her mind.

"Given the scope of what we're talking about here," I continue, "I think she's right that we need to think bigger. We know that this goes beyond any one man. We're dealing with an elaborate, well-planned conspiracy. We're only beginning to grasp its scale. Look at how far back this goes—we know there have been cases dating back to *1956*, and *that* may only be the tip of the iceberg. These dates…it suggests something beyond any one person's—any *human's*—lifetime. That timeline could be explained by a conspiracy spanning many generations…or it could be explained by something else."

Quincey's lips purse as she looks from myself to Mam and back. "I only care about saving Lucy," she says, and I can see her face shutter, the impasse setting in. It's the same look I've doubtless given my mother a million times before, and for the first time, I understand how she must have felt, faced with such instinctual disbelief. "I… I have to go. This is a lot to process."

"Quincey, wait—" I begin to stand up to head after her, but Mam grabs my arm, holding me back. She shakes her head, signaling for me to sit back down.

"I'm sorry, Mina," Quincey calls back as she leaves. "I just need some time."

The door rattles shut and we're quiet for a moment. What I don't expect is for Singer to get to her feet and say, "Right. I'll expand my search to include any vampiric references."

"Wait—what? I didn't think—"

She raises her eyebrows. "You know how I spend my time, Mina. I've seen and heard far stranger things on the internet."

"Fair enough."

"This might be among the strangest," she mutters to herself. "I'll also include hits on a global scale," she adds, matter of fact. "Mina, why don't you look into translating the words on the crypt? Those feel more relevant now. Let's meet back here in—" Singer looks at her watch "—eight hours?"

And with that, she heads out the front door, leaving Mam and I alone in the darkened room.

Mam looks at me then, her open, knowing glance an invitation, and for the first time, maybe ever, I take it.

"Can you make another pot of tea?" I sink down beside her on the couch, weary but also ready. "I have a story to tell you."

TODAY 6:04 A.M.

MINA MURRAY

Quincey, are you ready to talk?

MINA MURRAY

We're reconvening this morning.

MINA MURRAY

Listen, I know it sounds impossible to believe, but does it really matter if it's true? We still need to figure out who —or what—is doing all of this... Man or monster.

MINA MURRAY

Lucy will die if we don't.

QUINCEY MORRIS

What time are you meeting?

28

It's half past eight in the morning, and Quincey still hasn't shown up.

"I don't think she's coming, Mina," Singer says impatiently.

"She texted she'd come," I insist, staring down at my cold tea.

"She'll return when she's good and ready, love," Mam says gently. There's a kindness in her tone, in her gaze, I haven't seen in years—maybe ever. "You did."

It's difficult to face the years of ridicule I threw in her face. Difficult to admit to my own ignorance, and how I thought her crazy for so long, like everyone else in this village.

Last night, after I told her everything about why I ran away, we sat in the swirling darkness silently accepting the new shape our relationship was taking. I know one conversation can't possibly heal the years of hurt between us, but everything has to begin somewhere, and it's a start. In the meantime, we have a shared goal to bind us.

"Right, then, I've got a lot to update you both with." Singer pulls out her laptop. "Did you decipher the text from the crypt?"

I look at Mam and shake my head. After my confession, she and I stayed up late trying to decipher it. "We checked every language we could think of—I even pulled records from Oxford's online library. It's too ancient. Perhaps a dead language."

Singer sighs. "Well, I used images of Seren's rash to do an advanced search through sealed medical records around the world."

Mam shakes her head, but she's smiling. "Maybe it's a good thing Quincey isn't here. Who knows how many laws that broke?"

Singer shoots her a look. "I found girls and women across the globe. Clusters in Miami, Tokyo, Sydney…many major metropolitan areas. I honestly can't believe I never thought to look overseas before."

My stomach is twisted into knots. How can we fight something this enormous?

"Pretty much squashes Quincey's lone-serial-killer theory. This is *big*." Singer purses her lips as she keeps typing. "And what's more…it's always methodical. The girls come from impoverished or seedy areas dispersed throughout the city at even intervals. Of course, there are gaps—my abilities only take me so far—but that pattern is there."

I close my eyes, wondering just how far this venom spreads. How many innocent lives have been lost, swept under the rug to feed the system? How many of the women I've treated have brushed against this evil?

"I also looked into your theory about the assaults being vampiric rather than human. The symptoms, the blood loss, the confusion, the rash…" Singer closes her laptop then and looks long and hard at my mother. "I'm going to tell you something you probably aren't used to hearing. Frankly, I'm not either. You were right, Van. I believe you."

The corners of Mam's lips twitch, but she just stands up, her knees cracking, and shuffles toward the kettle at the Rayburn. While she's still turned toward the kettle, I think I hear the faintest "Thank you."

After putting the kettle on the stove, she goes to the mammoth oak chest that has sat under the window since before I was born. She hesitates, then takes a steadying breath like she's made a decision, and lifts the lid. She reaches into the bottom of the chest and pulls out a large book bound in leather, the pages rumpled like wrinkled skin. I frown, biting back my annoyance at another thing I don't know about.

I clear the table of used mugs and a bowl of fruit as she brings it over. She lays it down for us to see.

"This," she says, stroking the brown cover, "is the oldest Grimoire in Wales. It's been in my family for generations. We call it y Llyfr Gwaed."

I frown. "The Bleeding Book?"

Mam nods. "We've always just called it the Book of Blood."

Singer snorts. "Clive Barker would be thrilled."

Something stirs in my memory. A stormy night, howling at the window, many candles lit around the room. The outside gates banging like hammers, my father yelling and throwing something wet at the walls. Mam bent over a giant book, reading from pages scrawled with symbols.

I've seen this book before.

I reach out to touch it, but stop, sensing Mam tense. She clears her throat. "This book," she says, "describes old lore of women being preyed upon by monsters for centuries—maybe millennia."

She heaves it open, flipping to the last page. It releases a plume of musk as she turns the pages and I sneeze. An intrusive image of me snorting straight bleach—chemicals dissolving my sinuses—makes me flinch. Scrawls of numbers in two neatly inked rows litter the endpapers like kitten scratches.

"The monsters go by different names in different cultures and folklore, but the pattern you just described has been written here since before I was born. These creatures live forever, are all-powerful and alluring, and they prey on the vulnerable. They also share the venom of their master. When one *Fampir* creates another, it passes on its venom, binding them forever."

"You've known this all along?" I ask, searching her face. "You've had this knowledge and never told me?"

"You wouldn't listen," Mam says. It isn't a rebuke, but it might as well be. "You needed to get here on your own."

Had I been willing to hear this, could I have saved Renée?

Singer brings her hand to her face, rubbing her thumb across her lips. "Do you think this is one central group that moves across the globe, or many clusters?"

"There's likely one master who binds them all," Mam says. "A head of the snake, so to speak."

Renée's words come back to me now. She'd called for "Master" in the psych ward. Perhaps the maker of them all. Could it be possible that the head of the snake is here, in Tylluan, my own backyard? I lean my elbows on my knees.

"If these things are immortal—and if the master is all-powerful—then why hide? Why go through such great lengths to stay on the move?"

"'The greatest trick the devil ever pulled...'" Mam murmurs.

"'Was convincing people he didn't exist,'" I finish for her.

"Perhaps the movements are practical," Singer says, opening the book to examine the dates once more. "Not mystical. He moves so he doesn't overfeed in one area, like roaming cattle... As a bonus, it helps him stay less noticeable. He still has to do legwork to cover things up, stay unnoticed by the populace at large. But it helps to spread out the crimes across the globe, over time. He must think in centuries, not decades."

"This book contains everything I know about the *Fampir* and how to protect ourselves from it. The first step of which I have already done." She nods to the teapot. "Verbena. I grow it. A lot of it. It slows them down, taints the blood."

It all comes back to me. The first time she gave me the verbena to drink, how I complained and called it bitter poop-water, how I begged her for some honey to stir in at the very least, and how she said it was meant to be bitter to keep the *Fampirs* away.

I was eleven, had just started my period, and she had said it was time for protection now I was becoming a woman—an unfair burden my father never had to bear.

I remember how, after years of ritual drinking each morning before school, I had, when I was seventeen, stopped. Without telling my mother, I began brewing the tea and tossing it down the drain, untouched. My small act of defiance; a rebellious *fuck you*.

By the night of my attack, I had been verbena-free for several weeks. I close my eyes, hating my impertinent nature. It's my fault. All of it.

When I ran away, I took a supply of verbena, perhaps instinctively sensing the safety there. After the showering, it was my second tic formed. I've been drinking it ever since. Part of me must've known—always known—that it was keeping me safe.

Singer looks down at her tea with raised brows and downs the lot. Mam's mouth quirks up at the side.

"We need to make sure Lucy is drinking this," I say quietly, remembering the undrunk tea on Lucy's bedside table. I look at Mam desperately. "We have to try harder."

"I've been trying, love," she says softly. "I think I got it to her too late—she was already too sick."

It can't be too late. There's still time.

She clears her throat and continues, "There are ways to kill these creatures. Rowan wood blessed with an ancient ritual…" Her eyes meet mine and a kernel of understanding passes between us. The necklace I'd used on the night of the attack. It was a blessed rowan wood charm. My mother had saved my life and I hadn't known it.

She flips through several pages until she finds the passage she's searching for. "'Under the light of the moon, anointed wood, fashioned into a stake, can be used to dispatch the serpent and all its bearn back to Hell.'"

The door to the kitchen opens and Quincey tumbles in, looking disheveled. There are bags under her eyes and her hair is a mess. I wonder if she slept at all.

Mam pulls out a chair. "Take a load off, love. Have a cuppa."

Quincey shakes her head furiously. "No time. I almost didn't come here first. Mina, why didn't you pick up your phone?"

I stand up with my mug and walk over to my iPhone charging at the kitchen counter. I'd turned it on silent. Looking at the display, I now see I have seven missed calls from Quincey Morris.

"What's going on, Quince?"

Quincey takes a deep breath. "When I left here last night, I didn't want to accept a word that came out of your mouth, Mina. I know what folks here believe, but I've never bought into it myself, not even close. But then, when I couldn't sleep, I went to the station. I thought about the part of what you said that I could wrap my head around—how long this has been going on, the *scale* of it. So I looked through the archives—everything on-line, and all of the files in the back room. I searched hundreds, maybe thousands of documents, for cases that might fit the profile of what we'd discussed. Girls going missing, cases handed over to outside jurisdictions, the trail eventually going cold.

"There weren't many, mind you. There's no activity here like there is in London—otherwise small-town folks would notice. But I found a handful, and their similarities were striking… More than that, the timeline was just…astounding. I found cases fitting the pattern going as far back as our files go. As far back as the Tylluan police department exists. Which means this has been happening for a century and a half, at least. After that… well, I wasn't ready to believe, per se. But I was ready to dig as deep as I could."

Quincey says all of this in a rush. "Maybe this guy's made of smoke and mist, for all I know. But he has to have had help, human help, people incentivized to make these cases disappear. And these helpers exist in the real world, which means they can be tracked like the common criminals they are."

"And?" I prompt, eager.

"And… I did what I would do in any investigation, when I know where a crime has been perpetrated—draw a boundary, and work the clues." Her eyes are desperate, almost wild. "I reviewed CCTV footage of the main road all night. There's a turn-off just past the street to the beach. It's the only road that leads up to Cysgod Castle. It's the only way in, and the only way out."

I lean forward, zeroing in.

"I traced the plates of every lorry, every car, every fucking delivery that has ever gone up and down that road for the last ten years. Of the ones I could trace, there's only one company that supplies haulage logistics to and from the castle. Only one way girls are being carted in and out."

My heart sinks before she continues.

He's got his own logistics company. Lucy's airy laugh from our drunken reunion floats through my mind, haunting me.

"R. F. Holmswood Ltd.," Quincey spits out. "The company's been operating in the area for decades. These days, the proprietor is one Arthur Holmswood."

29

The mug falls.
Smashes.

A crash that should sound shocking but is somehow faraway. Verbena tea scalds my leg. I'm running out of the room, out of the house, heading for my car, my boots crunching through wet gravel, mobile in hand dialing Lucy's number.

After all this, after all our careful searching, the monster has been inside her house all along. With unfettered access to the victim. To Lucy.

Gravel crunches behind me—the others have rushed out too. They're heading for the car.

"Let me," Quincey says tightly, taking the keys from my shaking hand.

I get into the front passenger seat and she takes the driver's side. Mam and Singer are in the back, their faces taut in the rearview mirror.

The car careens out of the driveway and down the hill, pebbles spraying.

The line rings and rings.

Her answering service. "This is Lucy, leave a message!"

Words fail me, stick in my throat. No telling who might be listening.

I phone again.

Again.

I compose a text. Try to be sneaky.

Coming to visit. Meet me outside?

Someone says something. I don't catch it, but Quincey's hands tighten on the wheel.

"I'm assuming you know who this bloke is?" Singer says.

"Lucy's husband," Quincey mutters, pressing down on the accelerator. Hedges whip by and dimly it occurs to me that if we die, Lucy dies.

I don't tell her to slow down.

The windscreen fogs up, wipers whipping the rain away.

"It has to be a mistake," Mam says softly from the back.

"How could I have been so blind?" Quincey says through gritted teeth. "I always knew he was bad for her."

"But I went to their wedding," Mam says. "More than a decade ago, it was. He's been in the area ever since his father moved his business here, since he took over Ifori Estate. And I swear it, Arthur looked right young when he first came to town, not at all like he does now. He's been *aging*, I'll be hung if he isn't. And these creatures don't age a day—the blood keeps them young. Unless..."

"Unless what?" Singer says sharply. "What?"

"*Fampirs* can be made. It can be done. Maybe his transformation...maybe it was recent."

"There was mention of 'conversion' in the back forums," Singer says slowly. "But how are we going to even get to her? They're supposed to be strong, immortal—all-powerful? Your book said as much. So how are we planning to extricate her?"

Pick up. Pick up!

Horrible images of Lucy being savaged by Arthur—*Arty*—flash through my mind and I start counting. I try to reconcile it with what I know of him, with what I've seen of them together: his accountant-like demeanor, his thinning hair, his ruddy cheeks. The love in his eyes as he looks at his wife.

Was it all a ruse?

"Won't he follow her?" Singer says. "Going to get her is all very well, but what then? Where will you take her?"

One, two, three...

"I don't care," Quincey says. "I'll fly her to Mozambique if I have to."

"He'll follow her until he can't anymore," Mam says. "Bring her back to the cottage. I've had protections around the property for decades. He won't be able to cross over the lines unless invited."

Four, five, six...

"What if he sends human thugs?" Quincey mutters. "Powerful men always have thugs. We know enough to know these... *things* have human accomplices. We're up against a whole network here."

"I'll shoot them in the head," Singer says bluntly.

Seven, eight, nine...

Quincey side-eyes her and Singer shrugs. "A necessity."

"I'm assuming you don't have a firearms certificate?"

"How about we save your ex-girlfriend and *then* you ask me questions?"

Ifori Estate looms up as we speed down the drive.

I've opened the door and jumped out before the car has fully stopped—and then I'm running across the wet slate gravel and up the limestone steps, but I slip on the top one, landing hard on my knee. The pain is sharp but distant. I try the door handle, praying it's open, but it resists, so I ring the doorbell and knock incessantly until Cariad answers.

I shove past her and rush up the stairs, her voice calling after me, "Mrs. Holmswood is too ill for visitors—"

I hurry into Lucy's bedroom, my sentence half out already. "Lucy, come with me, we—"

My knees buckle and I fall onto the plush carpet as if in supplication, my mouth hanging open in a silent scream of horror.

Lucy's skin is riddled with the hideous black holes; they are *everywhere*. Her face, the part of her chest I can see, her hands— she is dissolving. Her eyelids flutter open when I drag myself to her bedside, unable to look away even as my skin crawls and my mind screams, warning me of the lip at the edge of sanity yawning blackly close by. The rash is even on her eyelids.

Itsy bitsy spider, went up the water spout…

My voice trembles. "Lucy…"

Her eyes focus on me for a fleeting moment and she smiles, teeth huge and grotesque. "Bambi…you came back. It's been… so long…" She closes her eyes, then forces them open. "Mina… you came back…"

I swallow down the illimitable horror and take her hand in mine.

Went up the water spout…

"I'm here, Lucy," I choke. "I'm so sorry I left. I'm here now." I press my lips to her hole-riddled forehead, smell a carrion rot. "I love you."

She takes a breath to say something, sticky white saliva stringy between her lips…and doesn't move again.

Down came the rain…

A howl behind me lets me know that I'm not alone. Quincey's footsteps thunder as she runs across the room and throws herself at Lucy.

Not at Lucy, who is no longer with us. At Lucy's lifeless body.

I don't shriek. Quincey does that for me.

"Lucy!" she cries, shaking the frail body with gross force. *"Lucy!"*

Quincey falls on top of her, burying her head in Lucy's chest, sobs racking her body. Singer is here now, and she puts a hand on Quincey's back; there are tears on her cheeks.

And washed the spider out…

Warm hands wrap themselves around my upper arms.

Mam's voice is in my ear. "Come, love. It's too late."

It's too late.

I'm too late.

Too late.

Too late.

 # VII.

Jennifer is calm in the face of this knowledge. Everything has clicked perfectly into place. They are the consumables, here for the taking, for the slaughter.

They delight with their beauty, they arouse with their sex, and satisfy with their consumption. Each part of them a tasty treat for men who are monsters and monsters who are men. This is the why. The why of the delicate food and drink, the why of the pampering—the why of the careful, tender care. To make her plumper. Juicier.

It's also why her "feistiness" sets her apart. It makes her better prey.

She forces herself not to scream.

Swallowing, she turns to her handler, the man who has been trailing her all night. "I need to use the bathroom."

He eyes her warily, but leads her there nonetheless.

She locks herself inside and looks for escape routes, but there are no windows. There don't seem to be any windows in this place. She uses the toilet to have somewhere to sit, but she has no ideas. The guard bangs on the door and tells her to hurry it up, so she stands and flushes.

A piece of metal is poking out of the wall near the drain—

part of a previous installation. She yanks on it, pulling it off the
wall with some help from her shoe. The guard bangs on the door
again, and when she unlocks it and steps out, no one would be
able to tell that a shiv is hiding in her bra.

"Time to go," the guard tells her, and her face must tell him
she knows he isn't talking about going home. He grins and leads
her to a side room off the main hall. She can't see any of the
other girls. Have they all been taken to separate rooms?

Are they already dead?

The guard opens the door and once she's inside he closes it behind her. The room is small and intimate, a study elegantly fitted
in deep greens, burgundies, and leather. There's a deep walnut
built-in lined with bookshelves and a wet bar in the center. A
leather chesterfield couch sits opposite a chaise longue. There
are no windows, but that adds to the coziness of the room. It's
the perfect man cave.

"Good evening."

The man himself steps forward, smiling gently. He looks to
be in his late forties, maybe early fifties. On the surface, an ex-
ecutive type who's spent enough money on trainers and stylists
to look young for his age. For the briefest of moments, she wonders if he might be someone who could help her out of here.
That perhaps he's someone who has nothing to do with the carnage happening in the rest of the house. He looks unassuming,
harmless, though she knows he must be anything but. Then
she looks closer and sees the sharp edges of him. The cold glint
in his eye. The ancient bearing of his frame. This is a monster
in disguise, and he is shedding the sheep's clothing even as she
watches, the predator shucking free.

This is *his* party.

She gulps and steps forward. She's not going to meet her fate
cowering in fear. If she is here to die, she is not going to go
down quietly.

"Good evening," she replies, squaring her shoulders, feeling the jagged pipe pressing into her chest.

"I've been looking forward to you since I first laid eyes on you."

She is certain she has never seen this man before, and yet, he knows who she is. A distant memory surfaces: a security camera at the club, the guard listening to an earpiece and escorting her away. He must have been watching this whole time. Had he "selected" her? Is she meant to be flattered? Another memory…a shadowy figure in a car.

Bile rises in her throat.

He throws his jacket on the chesterfield and begins unbuttoning his shirt, taking several lazy steps toward her. Her heart pounds in her ears.

"Would you like a glass of wine before we get started?" He gestures toward the wet bar, which houses two crystal decanters of deep red liquid. He starts in on his cufflinks and smiles up at her. Innocent, boyish, intimate, like this is a date. Peeling off his disguise.

She resists the urge to spit at him.

He shucks his dress shirt, revealing chiseled abs.

He catches her staring and smirks, pleased. Then he turns away, reaches for the decanter. When he begins to pour, she knows this is her chance. She races up behind him and brandishes her makeshift knife, swinging. It meets his neck with a dull thud. There's not a trace of blood, only a faint line where the rusted edge met his skin. As she watches, the skin heals before her eyes. The shiv falls uselessly beside her, and she clamps her jaw tight to keep from screaming.

He laughs with riotous mockery, and finishes pouring his drink. "You found it."

She stares dumbfounded as he turns and glances down at her shiv.

"I was hoping for at least three stab wounds." He winks and takes a long swig of his drink.

Her hand is shaking now.

"You're...almost perfect," he says, his eyes filled with lust. With longing. And something else...something entirely ancient, inhuman, and predatory.

For all these weeks she's been primped and contained—all this preparation, yet she realizes that the thing he likes most is her *resistance*. This is all a game to him, to keep him entertained. He reaches up, pulling a lock of her hair to his nostrils. He inhales deeply, then smiles.

The sight is the most terrifying of all. His smile is stained, dripping, with blood.

She doesn't realize she's already screaming.

"You taste so sweet," he says, his eyes flicking to the glass. Hyperventilating, she takes in the decanter and she realizes that the vials the doctors have been collecting...they were an appetizer. "I'll give you ten seconds' head start."

The door to the study swings open, an invitation for her to run. She stumbles backward, her heels catching on the makeshift knife, tripping her.

"One," he begins, taking another sip. "Two..."

She hurries to regain her footing, and doesn't look back.

She flies through the door and toward the spiral staircase. It looms downward, a vertiginous abyss, and she stumbles down on deer legs, bruising herself against the walls. She doesn't know her way toward the exit, but she figures she should just head down as long as she can. Her breath shallow, she looks behind her. He hasn't found her yet. Or maybe he hasn't even started, true to the ten-second head start, relishing the game.

Her ankle twists and with a sickening lurch, she's tumbling—Alice in fucking Wonderland—coming to a painful stop at the bottom. She rips off her heels and throws them aside with a cry, scrambling to her feet and running full pelt. She's now in a long corridor—she races ahead, her eyes blurred by involuntary tears, until she trips over something else...a pale, slender arm.

It is another girl. Her eyes are lifeless, and her skin is a wrong kind of pale, a yellow, gray, *dead* kind of pale.

Jennifer takes a deep shuddering breath and stumbles back to her feet. Turning a corner, she ducks into the folds of a heavily draped window, the only one she has found thus far. There is a small wooden door three stories below on the opposite wing of the castle, but she knows if she jumps, she'll be long dead before she ever reaches it. Beyond it, there's a courtyard and just beyond that, a low point in the wall that looks scalable. If she could just get to the wall...

She eyes the crenellated roofline and decides it's her best chance. Unlatching the window, she gingerly steps out into the blustery night, crouching to keep her center of gravity low.

A blood moon hangs low in the sky. *How apropos*, she thinks bitterly. She makes her way toward the edge, looking for a way down. There's a drainpipe at the far end, but she's not sure it will hold her weight.

A shadowy figure steps out from behind the chimney. He's grinning, his white teeth glinting horribly in the thin moonlight. She can't help but realize she's played right into his hands. She's now trapped, defenseless. Goose bumps cover her arms and legs, and her silky dress whips in the wind as violently as her hair.

She skirts the lip of the castle wall and makes it, with white-knuckled terror, to the drainpipe, managing to shimmy herself down. Something cold and sharp tears at her thigh, and she gasps, but does not stop. She's doing it. She's going to make it!

She is almost at the ground when she sees him above her, up by the window, clinging to the wall like a demonic Spider-Man, crawling toward her, his neck twisted impossibly around, grin wide and delighted.

"You were hoping to reach the gardens?" he taunts when he is no more than a foot away, his fingers clawed into the hard rock as though gouging rubber.

With barely more than a flick of his wrist, he has hit her,

pushed her, and she goes flying through the air. She lands with
a sickening thud, the air whooshing out of her and jamming
her lungs firmly closed. Something cracks and she hopes, prays
wildly, that it isn't bone. She opens her mouth, willing her lungs
to inhale, desperately seeking oxygen, and slowly—painfully
slowly—they yield.

"You really are something," he says, almost kindly. He is already beside her—how is he beside her?—crouching, caressing
his erection and violating her with his gaze.

The break in the wall is only a few feet away. If she could
just get over...

He seems to sense this, and crawls on top of her, the fullness
of his naked weight pinning her to the ground. He is breathing like a man in the heat of passion and she has never felt such
revulsion.

"Do you have any last words, Jennifer?" he asks, caressing her
throat, tracing the spot he intends to strike.

Blinking back tears, she tells him the one true thing in her
heart: "My mother... I hope someday she'll find out what happened to me. That she'll forgive me. That she'll understand."
Her mother, who loves her more than anything—who taught
her how to be bighearted, fearless, risk-taking, strong.

Thinking of her gives her courage, makes her final moments
unafraid.

"And my name isn't Jennifer," she adds, a newfound fire in
her eyes. "It's Beatrice. Beatrice Singer."

30

I walk without a destination in mind, trying to hold myself together, trying to understand what has just happened.

I always thought, in those dark midnight moments when I worried over Mam's eventual passing, that grief would be a slow sort of madness. A shadow crawling over my life like a sunset. But this...this is a sudden, horrible magnitude. An overwhelming and all-encompassing presence, wholly here all at once. How can one fragile human heart bear so much?

Quincey was inconsolable. When Cariad found us, she stood staring until she realized what had happened. Then she cried. She didn't call for help. Lucy was beyond that now.

Eventually she left, closing the door behind her.

Bits of Mam's and Singer's words reached me as my mind yawned with the impossibility of a world without Lucy in it. Even in London, in all those silent years, knowing she was there, somewhere in the world, I realize, was an unconscious comfort. Now it was gone.

Lucy started getting sick a year ago...

Must have been turned recently...

I tuned in to reality and looked at my mother.

"I'm telling you, that man has aged a decade since he arrived here," she was saying, shaking her head. "If nobody noticed anything strange about him, it's because there was nothing to notice, at least not until recently."

"But a vampire was getting to her, and we could never figure out how."

"Yes."

"So he's the vampire. He's got to be. It's the only thing that makes sense." Singer glanced at Quincey and grimaced. "She didn't fit the pattern. Because *he* didn't fit the pattern."

Quincey's voice was hard and definite. "If she's been sick for a year, then we need to find out what changed a year ago. Either Arthur was turned, and he started feeding on her, or he started giving access to someone else who was. So look at anyone, anything new. Any emails you can hack, any phone calls. If Holmswood Ltd. has been involved with Cysgod Castle and its operations for years, I want to know what changed. Any new business contacts, any new companies—all of it."

Singer hesitated. "Do you want to rest? Take some time—"

"Fuck time."

Singer nodded like she got it. Like, *Yeah, I've been here.* She looked like she didn't wish it on anyone.

I got to my feet and staggered to the door. Mam tried to reach for me, but Singer held her back.

"Let her go. Let her process."

Jonathan finds me in the old stile on Eithin Hill where we used to secret ourselves away. We used to meet here when he was supposed to be doing chores or Mam and I were fighting over some silly thing.

Of course he knew where to find me. I don't know which of them contacted him, told him the news...

Jonathan holds me tightly in his arms, but I'm still breaking apart. Tripping and tumbling upward and outward, the fabric of me unraveling, the seams of me unstitching, cracking open like some terrible tsunami breaking on a beach of glass. Grief is insanity, crushing me while pulling me away from myself. A bottomless, stygian pit of raw despair. And then rage blossoms and I hate that I failed her.

I failed her.

I lost her.

Grief is love persisting. I read that somewhere. *Grief is love with nowhere to go.*

Well fuck that person, whoever they are.

"I can't breathe," I say, or sob, or scream. *"I can't breathe!"*

Jonathan holds my face, stares into my eyes. "You're breathing right now." He makes sure I hear him. "You are alive and you are breathing."

"It feels like I'm dying."

A text pings onto my phone. Jonathan hesitates, then pulls it from my pocket.

He frowns. "'No sign of Arthur.' What does that mean? Where is he?"

I bury my head in my arms again, shaking.

"Mina, someone has to tell him his wife…"

"He killed her," I mumble, and even to me it sounds crazy. Impossible.

"What are you saying?"

I lift my head and spit it out, the rage making it waspish and cruel. "He fucking *killed* her, Jonathan! Can I make myself any clearer for you?"

He swallows. "Okay, let's just calm down. I'm sure—"

"That man is a monster, and he finally killed her because I was too stupid to see. How can I call myself a fucking doctor? How could I call myself a therapist—I've failed at everything! Renée's dead, Seren's dead—now Lucy! What good am I? I'm bloody useless!"

Jonathan falls silent, taking some of the wind out of my rage, and I begin sobbing again.

"You are the cleverest woman I know. You're always so careful. You don't jump in, not like Lucy. And it keeps you safe. If
you're right about Arthur...then I'm glad you're okay."

He means to comfort me. But he's cut me deeper than anyone could.

You're always so careful.

I'm the reason Lucy is dead. That quality in me. My careful, mousy, timid fucking bullshit is the reason I lost Renée
and Lucy. I am to blame for them. And any other girls who get
hurt while I sit here crying into the earth will be on my conscience as well.

"You're right," I whisper. "You're absolutely right."

He smiles at me. Kissing my cold hand.

"I need some time," I tell him. "I need to process this."

"Of course. I'll be here when you're ready."

You don't jump in, not like Lucy. And it keeps you safe.

Lucy climbing through my window at sixteen.

Lucy getting Jonathan to admit he liked me.

Lucy gate-crashing parties like a pro.

Lucy nicking boxed wine and getting me to do the same.

Lucy being the raging, chaotic, beautiful light in my life.

It's time for me to be like Lucy and take from life what she
believed it owed her.

It's time for me to jump into the lion's den.

VIII.

MINA

Rain lashes the shop windows, long since closed for the evening. In my miniskirt, I feel every icy sting. My makeup, so carefully applied, will no doubt run soon, leaking ivory and crimson into the puddle at my feet. They are both veneers—one hiding my fear, the other draping the world in moonlit crystals, obscuring the ugly parts.

"It's a fucking suicide mission," Quincey had said when I told them my plan, laying Renée's business card on the counter. I'd go to London. I'd call the number. I'd get picked up. Mam crossed her arms—she was against it too. I could feel them ganging up on me.

"It's the only way."

"But they could kill you long before you find him!" Mam had said frantically.

"Maybe I'll take him with me."

"Mina, stop this! Stop it! I can't lose you again."

"It's too late."

I had failed at everything anyway. I might as well go all in, and if I died…then I died.

She begged me to consider other options. When I doggedly refused, she clutched at my shirt and yelled and screamed and sobbed into my face. But I was immovable. It took time. Days and weeks to convince them.

"I'll do it with or without your help," I said at last. Mam knew I meant it. I didn't really give her a choice.

"If we want to kill the master, to cut the head off the snake, we have to find him first," Singer said. "The only way is from the inside. He's too well protected, too difficult to pin down."

With Singer's support, I won them all.

The black 4X4 arrives with a whisper of tires. The door clicks open, a maw of darkness.

I can't see the man inside but know he is there. Can sense him watching me.

Staring into the unknown, everything in me screams, *Run.*

My heart screams, *For Lucy.*

I glance back only once, then take a breath and climb inside.

31

Chaises longues. Crystal decanters. Low, intimate light splashed over oak paneling and heavily draped curtains. All of this should murmur of luxurious conversations, delicate foods, and expensive drinks. Rich cologne and silky pearls. The promise of a safe, cozy place to relax and mingle with the finer things and people in life. But then the incongruities and oddities stick out. Curtains draped over walls, not windows. Crystal decanters glinting a little too scarlet. A door in the far corner opens and I glimpse a couple having sex, darkly perdu, while two docile, scantily clad women drink champagne on a chaise longue. Men sit at a table nearby and leer, the habitués of a sordid baroque spectacle.

The men are masked, raucous, and deviant, infatuated with themselves and their power—relishing their own clever wickedness.

I hike down my skirt and cover my stomach with my arms; my skin feels as thin as tissue paper. Never in my life have I felt more like my nickname: *Bambi*. I am a deer in a decadent lion's den.

The malignant glamour of this parlor—part gentleman's club, part trading ground—sickens me. It's tempting to buy into the

illusion of louche opulence, of consenting adults just having a
little fun, but then I remember the cover-ups, the payoffs, and
the deaths. What goes on in this club might not reach the levels of what happens at places like Cysgod Castle: here it's mostly
powerful human men, enjoying the sexual pleasures they believe
can be theirs for a price.

And yet, this is where women's fates are sealed. This is, for
some of them, the last place they'll ever see. For others, an even
worse fate looms.

Those who *please* are kept for the real depravity: the parties
that happen at even more secluded places around the globe,
where the real predators—and the worst violations—take place.
Singer didn't even have to look very hard to find the dark web
forums where they bragged about it…getting confident. And
sloppy. I have to make sure I'm chosen.

I tongue the bead in my mouth. A safety blanket.

When I think of it I quake with fear and rage, but instead,
I work on channeling Lucy. Seventeen-year-old Lucy. Brave.
Loud. Confident. Transgressive. Wild. I clock the security cameras in each corner. The difference between the club and the
castle is striking. At the castle, there are no cameras, no digital
trail. Here there's a constant reminder: they are watching every
encounter. I expect the men here are little more than pawns,
objects for blackmail when the time is right: want to clear your
conscience and go to the authorities—the ones we don't already
control? I think not. Remember this little clip of you and the
underage girl in the back of the club with no name? Yes, we
remember too.

Of course, that means there is now a video recording of me
too.

We are being sorted. And I know my next move might seal
my fate.

I force myself to drop my arms and walk, force myself to
smile at men who grin at me. I ignore that most of these girls

are fighting for their lives and don't yet know it. I ignore how filthy I feel, lean into my big doe-eyed youthfulness, which has hindered my professional life for so long—I make it my asset instead.

Come get me. I am a young, vulnerable mark.

Some of the men who were leering my way before, when I was scared little Mina, have lost interest. My timidity aroused them, I realize. I almost laugh at the absurdity of it. At the horror of it.

The girls don't seem to notice *who* these men are, but I can venture a guess, having spent my entire professional life observing people. And I recognize a few of them. From the news. From think pieces. From high-profile articles. Ministers. An archbishop. Businessmen and captains of industry. Men we see on the news, informing us about the running of things. Men who are supposed to be leaders, who are supposed to keep us safe. Equal parts reckless and afraid. Their masks prove it.

It's one thing to suspect this. It's quite another to see it with my own eyes—to see the powerful men involved.

I wander past the bar and see a man in an expertly tailored suit kissing a woman's arm. She is passed out on a chesterfield. His hand wanders underneath her dress. I almost throw up.

When he sees me looking, he grins and drinks, toasting to me first, a glint in his eye.

I look away, but there is another shadowy area and a woman is screaming as a man forces himself on her.

"Come now," he says. "Be good."

A round of laughter, almost bored. A security guard with an earpiece closes a heavy wooden door, sealing off the girl's screams.

I try to leave. This was a bad idea. What was I thinking, coming in here like this? How can I possibly expect to succeed, alone in a sea of predators? And not even the ones I'm most interested in taking down. Most of these men are just that: men. Monstrous, yes, but human. I head for the door.

A man in a black suit stops me. He has an earpiece. Guards. Of course there are guards.

Beatrice. Renée. Seren. Lucy. And so many more.

My mantra. My reason.

I take a breath, square my shoulders, and turn back to the room, bumping into a man who was standing behind me.

"What's your name?" he asks with a devilish grin.

I smirk. "Bambi."

"You're older than my usual type," he says. "But I think we could still have some fun."

I step away and he grabs my wrist. "Not so fast."

My throat closes and my vision splits, spinning on one half, twisting on the other.

Stay here, I warn myself, feeling that familiar dissociation, the memory of my attacker ripping and tumbling upward from my past like an unholy abomination. And then a spark. Which turns into a flare. Which spreads into a raging inferno.

I shove him in the chest so hard he stumbles and falls. At the same time a "respectable" man close by whispers into the ear of a young woman.

"I want to go home," she whimpers.

Instead of pulling away, he throws his brandy in her face and she splutters. The men nearby roar with laughter.

I'm running before I realize it, the man behind me ignored— "You little cunt!"—and I'm shoving my way through the men, turning to face them, a broken bottle somehow in my hands, the young girl behind me.

"Fuck off!" I yell. I scream. I rage.

The men are surprised into stunned silence for a precious moment. Then one of them grabs for me. It's a casual grab, as if to say, *Don't be ridiculous*, but I swipe with the bottle and he swears, pulling away. Bleeding.

"Bitch!"

I spit in his face, daring the others to try me. The girl I'm protecting grips my skirt like I'm a buoy in a turbulent sea, sobbing.

"Break it up," one of the guards says, stepping between the men and me. "She's coming with us."

The men look like they want to argue, but only for a moment. Then they chuckle and step away, slapping one another on the back.

"She got you nicely, didn't she?"

"Fuckin' hell, mate, not had one like that for a while, eh?"

"Good sport," another drawls as the guard leads me away.

I clock another security camera and look straight at it. A red light blinks twice.

I only hope I've done enough not to die.

32

They keep me in a basement area with at least six other rooms off a main corridor. I never hear any other girls, and begin to wonder if I'm alone. After three days, they give me a change of clothes—a set of thin gray cotton pajama shorts and a matching top. Nothing to protect my feet from the frigid metal floor except the heels I was brought down here in. The food is good. I didn't expect that. They don't let me shower.

I scratch at my skin until it bleeds, yearning for the feel of bleach, the tang of Clean in my nostrils. A guard cuts my nails below the quick, shoving me back when I bite him. Pours orange antiseptic over my cuts; frowns when I sigh with relief, a junkie with her fix.

After a week, they send in a doctor.

I'm sitting in the corner, my head between my knees, wondering where I go from here—and whether I've made a deadly mistake—when he comes in.

"Don't struggle and it'll be easier," he says, bored, a syringe with a large needle dangling from his hand.

I look up. "Oh my God."

John Seward is standing in this basement room, in this hole in the world, under the club with no name.

The shock is mutual for a split second.

Then he laughs.

"You just couldn't keep your nose out, could you?"

"Seward," I whisper, choking on his name. "What are you doing here?"

As if we've bumped into each other on Kensington High Street rather than this brothel. He is still laughing. Breathless.

I'm reeling. This can't be real. This can't be happening.

He's laughing. *Laughing.*

I shake my head, trying to clear the shock, the gelatinous disbelief. *"John?"*

"Ah, you stupid bitch."

I get slowly to my feet. "You motherfucker."

"Dr. Murray! Language. So much for the 'consummate professional.'"

Everything clicks.

"That's why you were so interested in Renée," I say in realization, the unreality of the moment like sticky egg yolk sliding down my body, head to torso. "I thought it was negligence, but you actually killed her, didn't you?"

"There you go again. So earnest. You know how it is in our field, Murray. Patients die all the time."

His calm, casual, languid confidence enrages me.

I raise my chin, taking some of that back—force myself to smile. "You fucked up. You lost her. Of course you did."

He pauses. "Can't let the perfect be the enemy of the good." His smile is rigid.

I shake my head as I put it all together. "She was here, wasn't she? For days or weeks, being preyed upon, which is why her mind was so far gone. She must've escaped somehow, smart girl. You probably had paid-off police looking everywhere for her, and then, once she was found, you made sure she was placed under *your* care so that you could clean up your loose ends. But how did she even make it out of here alive?"

His smile fades for a moment, then returns. "We all make mistakes."

"Not good enough."

He grips my arm tightly now and pulls me so close I can smell his breath, can feel the spit from his mouth as he talks. "Most of the patients go quietly, but some cause more trouble than others. Especially since it's the feisty ones who are brought down here. They're the ones he wants for the feasts—they survive longer, and make it more interesting. When Renée escaped... I only had a limited window to clean up the mess before they came for me too."

I soften my voice, try another tack. "John...why are you doing this?"

He searches my face, then blows air through his lips, looking away. "I don't have a choice."

"They have stuff on you," I realize aloud, remembering the cameras upstairs, the system of blackmail Singer discovered they perpetuate.

He runs his hand through his hair. "Photos." He looks at me and shrugs. "I'm fucked, Mina."

"What happened?"

"There was this girl... I didn't know she was underage."

"You could prove that you didn't know, that they were black-mailing you."

"Oh, come on. You know better than that. You know how it is. The moment an accusation is made, it's over. I'd be black-listed. Lose everything."

I glance at the needle in his hand. "You could be the whis-tleblower. The one to bring it to an end."

He laughs mirthlessly. "You don't know these people. They're more powerful than you can imagine. You don't even know the half of it."

"Vampires."

He's taken aback. He didn't expect this from me. "I have

to admit, I'm impressed. They're extraordinary creatures. The science…we haven't even begun to crack the potential of their DNA. Their saliva alone contains an enzyme that breaks down human tissue, while their own repairs itself. So you see. I can't escape."

"One person speaking up from inside could make the whole thing crumble. Who's at the head? Who's running it? Give me a name, anything."

"You're not getting out of here. It's too late for that."

"We can leave right now. We can go together."

"They're everywhere. They can make things happen. Open and close doors at will. I can't risk it."

"Unbelievable," I say, shaking my head.

"I'm not a monster," he says desperately. "I'm the victim, don't you see?"

Revulsion bubbles up my throat. "How many have there been? How many women have you had come through here?"

"They're druggies, criminals—they're nobodies."

"We can't save everyone, is that it?"

He looks relieved. "Exactly."

"And me? Am I a drug addict? A criminal?"

He looks almost regretful. "You're just stupid, Mina."

I fold my arms, dropping the act. "You know, I always wondered how someone so completely incompetent could be published all over the place, could have accolades coming out of his arse. Now I know. You're no victim here. You're complicit. *They* make sure your career thrives, so you can keep doing—" I gesture at the room "—what you do." I scoff, shaking my head. "I always thought you were a mediocre pillock, and now I know it's true. You're sloppy and unprofessional and flippant. No wonder Renée escaped. You're pathetic."

He hits me. Hard.

My head jerks to the right, cricking my neck. Then he's got

me pinned against the wall, a big hand wrapped around my throat. He breathes hot and fast into my face.

"You bitch," he says, his eyes wild.

He presses himself into me then, and I feel his erection growing. This is exciting him, I realize with revulsion.

"Remember," he murmurs. "I'm the one with the power here." His thumb caresses my chin. "I could end your life right now."

He's so much bigger than me. He can do anything he wants, and I wouldn't be able to stop him. He probably *has* done anything he wants countless times.

Itching in my neck and the familiar panic rising—I force it down. He presses himself into me again, breath hot in my face, his hardness against my crotch, insistent. Bile rises in my throat.

I pretend to yield for a moment, my lips parting. I picture Jonathan, remember his lips, his skin, his scent, his body. I relax my stance, remember how to be soft and inviting. How to be vulnerable.

"I always wondered what you'd be like," he murmurs into my mouth.

I hold my breath and press my lips to his. He looks surprised for a fraction of a second, then he's kissing me, moaning, his hand leaving my throat to grope my breast.

I bite down. Hard.

Through his lip.

A crack, then sudden warmth. My upper teeth meeting my lowers, a clean cut.

He yowls, scrabbling back, the flap of his lip where I bit it off on one side dangling over his chin, blood pouring everywhere. The syringe is on the floor. I make a grab for it as he keeps screaming, holding his face.

He comes toward me, but I'm faster.

The bevel is in his chest, needle up to the hilt. I depress the plunger. I don't know what's in it, but I know a large dose to the heart can't be good.

I always wondered what you'd be like.

"To men like you?" I whisper into his face. "I'm poison."

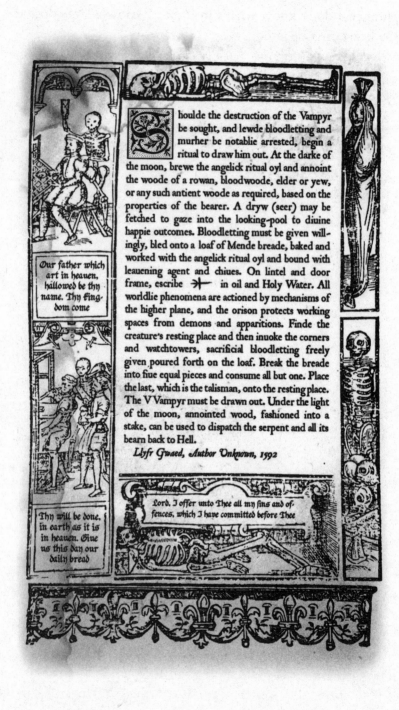

houlde the destruction of the Vampyr be sought, and lewde bloodletting and murher be notablie arrested, begin a ritual to draw him out. At the darke of the moon, brewe the angelick ritual oyl and annoint the woode of a rowan, bloodwoode, elder or yew, or any such antient woode as required, based on the properties of the bearer. A dryw (seer) may be fetched to gaze into the looking-pool to diuine happie outcomes. Bloodletting must be given willingly, bled onto a loaf of Mende breade, baked and worked with the angelick ritual oyl and bound with leauening agent and chiues. On lintel and door frame, escribe ⟐ in oil and Holy Water. All worldlie phenomena are actioned by mechanisms of the higher plane, and the orison protects working spaces from demons and apparitions. Finde the creature's resting place and then inuoke the corners and watchtowers, sacrificial bloodletting freely given poured forth on the loaf. Break the breade into fiue equal pieces and consume all but one. Place the last, which is the talisman, onto the resting place. The V Vampyr must be drawn out. Under the light of the moon, annointed wood, fashioned into a stake, can be used to dispatch the serpent and all its bearn back to Hell.

Llyfr Gwaed, Author Unknown, 1592

Our father which art in heauen, hallowed be thy name. Thy kingdom come

Thy will be done, in earth as it is in heauen. Giue us this day our daily bread

Lord, J offer unto Thee all my sins and offences, which J have committed before Thee

33

The guards must have been watching this display on a camera I can't see, because they're opening the door before Seward has hit the ground. They restrain me, but I'm not punished.

It occurs to me that my blood is worth more than his life.

They leave me handcuffed for a long time—hours, days, it's impossible to be sure. There is nothing to do except pace and think and lie on the floor and wait. After a while, when my shoulders have begun to ache and my wrists are chafing with the friction of the restraints, a new doctor enters.

"Good morning," he says, not looking up from a clipboard in his hands. "Time for bloodwork."

He pulls out a syringe, much like the one Seward wielded, and lays it on a tray that a guard wheels in.

"Will it be necessary to sedate you?"

I shake my head.

He nods, that same bored air that Seward was dripping with until he recognized me.

I don't fight him when he removes the handcuffs. I don't resist when he takes my blood for some unknown tests. I don't make conversation. What would be the point? Instead, I watch. I watch through my pliancy, hoping to glean more information.

I've already learned that I am important. More important than Seward, certainly. They are feeding me, keeping me healthy—making sure that I am in peak condition. For the feeding party. So I'll make sure I reach it in the best possible shape.

It's hard to keep track of time. They let me wash by bringing a bucket of warm soapy water and a soft cotton cloth. I yearn for strong astringents, never feel clean enough. I count one, two, three, three hundred times and then begin again. Again. Again. My addled mind focuses on the discomfort; it gives me something to do. Something to focus on. I run through old lectures on intrusive thoughts, muttering out loud.

"Compulsive cleaning is a manifestation of a fear of contamination, a perpetual engagement in compulsive acts of decontamination. Mental contamination includes rituals like counting to a certain number to neutralize a bad thought."

I count again. Again. Again.

They bring a change of gray clothing every few days and a pair of slippers when I comment that my feet are cold. I complain about the hard floor bruising my hips and they move me into a room with a bed. Whatever this game is, I'm moving up the ladder.

Hours.

Days.

Weeks.

I fantasize about home. About Mam, about Singer and Quincey. I wonder what Lucy's funeral was like. Did they put her in a white dress? Make her look pure and angelic? Or did they go for blue lace, like some kind of royal? Did Arthur attend, still pretending to be a high society gentleman? Or is he too ashamed of what he's done? Too afraid to come out of hiding?

Will he ever face justice for what he's done, or will he, like so many before him, be able to carry on like nothing has happened?

My thoughts turn to Jonathan, despite the fact that I've been trying not to think too hard about him. I miss him differently than the others. It's more a yearning. A deep longing. He didn't even know I was leaving...not like this. And even through this ache, it's nothing compared to the hole Lucy left in me. Her absence is a pit I carry inside.

I try to remember why I'm doing this.

Beatrice. Renée. Seren.

Lucy.

My name is Mina Murray.

My name is Mina Murray.

My name is Mina Murray.

My name is Mina.

My name is...

I tuck my head into my hands, face the wall, and cry.

A day comes when things are different. Breakfast is larger: eggs, bacon, homemade chips, fried tomatoes and mushrooms, and freshly squeezed orange juice. Have I graduated? Or does this signify something more ominous? I eat everything. If they are feeding me like this, it must mean I need my strength.

Some time later, the door opens and two guards gesture for me to go with them. I'm led into the corridor where all the other doors are spitting out girls who look as terrified as I feel. The girl in the room behind me rushes to my side and grabs my hand. I hold hers back tight as we are prodded with batons to follow the guard at the head.

"What's happening?" the girl whispers. "Do you know what's going on?"

I shake my head. "No idea. But keep your eyes open."

We are led up, via a narrow staircase that isn't the one I came down when I first arrived, to another corridor that ends in a fire escape. The guard at the head of the line opens it onto the cold London night—the alley behind Cloth Fair. The girl in the lead makes a break for it, but the guard was expecting it. He presses his baton to her back and it makes a horrible electric sound as she falls like a stone. Deadweight.

The guard chuckles as he lifts her onto his shoulder and opens the door of a waiting van, tossing her inside. She rolls off the seat and flops awkwardly onto the floorboard.

"In," the guard says, poking the next girl until, crying, she climbs into the lorry.

It is so tempting to run. To try to get away. I'm fast enough...

And then I realize that my legs are weak beneath me.

The breakfast... They put something in the breakfast.

I am already passing out when I climb into the truck.

I am jolted awake as the truck judders to a stop. The engine dies with a rumble. Doors slamming. A moment of silence. Muffled male voices. Footsteps. Then the metallic rattle of the rear door abruptly rolled up, admitting a blast of brilliant daylight.

As the tailgate is unfolded and whines into operation, it is with grim satisfaction that I see the cobbled courtyard of Cysgod Castle. I was right. The castle is linked, perhaps central, to their game. There must be something to ancient addresses—easier to conceal illicit activity when the estates have not changed hands in a string of generations.

I feel a tug on my wrist and my arm lifts up as my neighbor tries to rub her eyes. She smiles weakly, apologetically. While we were out, our wrists have been ziplocked together: my right wrist to her left wrist; my left wrist to my other neighbor, a brunette who can't stop shaking. We are all still groggy, half-dazed, and addled.

Here we go.

I fiddle with the ampoule between my molars. A grim source of comfort.

I spent my childhood basking in the shadow of Ifori Estate and Cysgod Castle, wondering about their interior and about the kind of people who enjoyed such luxury. Now, as the guards herd us into the castle, a chain of premium chattel, I realize it was I who had enjoyed the luxury—of ignorance.

"We're going to die," one of the girls is muttering over and over. Her voice jangles my nerves, but I can't correct her.

We're led through a small side door into an adjoining chamber—*straight*—then left down another corridor, right, right again, up a set of spiral stairs, and left into another chamber. My brain clicks like a metronome, memorizing. A flash of Oxford uni, sitting in the Bod, learning complex strings of chemical formulas. I can do this. Now reverse it: *right, down spirals, left, left, right, straight.*

Seven stylists await us. One for each girl. They are sinuous, blank-faced Ken dolls, readying ointments, sprays, and utensils to fluff-up their Barbies. A rack of exorbitant garments hangs in the corner. Our bodies are scrubbed, our skin moisturized, our hair coiffed, our faces decorated and optimized. They don't bother to check my mouth. They're focused purely on beauty.

I force equanimity as invasive combs chomp through my hair, licentious hands manipulate my flesh, insolent fingers tug my chin this way and that. So impersonal. So deeply personal. Expert. Mechanical.

This is what you wanted, I remind myself. *Right, down spirals, left, left, right, straight.*

"If you're doing this, then we need to have a plan," Singer had said. "There's no sense in wasting our one chance to get this bastard."

"Get all these bastards," Mam clarified. The Book of Blood was clear. If we could manage to kill the creator, all its spawn would be unmade. That's why it was essential to infiltrate the center of the web.

We had huddled around Mam's kitchen table for weeks planning it out. Singer would use a bug planted in my phone to connect to the club's Wi-Fi as soon as I arrived. She'd hack into their system. If it was successful, she'd try to let me know.

"I'll blink the cameras twice, if I can," Singer had said. "It really depends on how much access I can gain. We'll know on the day."

If she was successful, then they could keep tabs on me, keep me alive. Quincey was ready to go nuclear and storm the club if I found myself in harm's way, although I reminded her that "harm's way" was the point.

We did the blood ritual in St John's church's thousand-year-old graveyard during a waxing moon, three weeks before I went to London. Each of us pulled free the wooden stakes that Mam had carefully crafted for the purpose. Elm for Singer, for the death and rebirth of her daughter. For vengeance. Elder for Quincey, our powerful protector. For balance. Cedar for Mam, boundless and eternal. For protection. And bloodwood for me, killer of *Fampirs*. The only wood for someone with blood already on their hands. For justice. With any luck, however, the ampoule would do the killing for me.

Mam broke open the bread roll she had baked that morning. It had the scent of garlic and chives, and something bitter that I couldn't place. Not verbena, but a substance equally caustic. She put it in the center of the circle she'd drawn in salt and squeezed a dose of verbena oil onto it from a small pipette in a vial.

A hysterical impulse to laugh hit me as I took in the moment's surreality. Here I was, Dr. Wilhelmina Murray, scientist, performing blood magic in a graveyard, with my mother, the batty witch up on the hill.

"It's your turn, dear," Mam said, nodding at Quincey.

My stomach lurched. Something about this felt so very wrong. Like playing with fire.

Quincey nodded and before I'd even blinked, she'd nicked her finger with a lancet from her glucose monitor bag.

"Diabetic," she said, pursing her lips and raising her eyebrows at me. "Diagnosed ten years ago."

"You were fated to this role, it seems. Although it's less impressive than an athame," Singer agreed.

"On the bread," Mam directed. "We need a fair amount."

Quincey squeezed her blood onto the bread. When it wasn't enough she pricked herself again and again until the blood soaked the whole loaf on both sides.

"Well endowed with collagen, dear copper," said Singer, then muttering sardonically, "The athame would have been faster."

"Repeat after me," Mam said firmly, and enunciated words in what sounded at once Welsh and not. Quincey repeated each phrase diligently, and I shuddered.

Mam took the two halves and broke them apart so that five soggy pieces now lay in the grave dirt.

"Now eat."

Singer's eyebrows shot up. *"Pardon?"*

"Eat the bread. One piece each."

"Even me?" Quincey asked, her nose wrinkling.

"Even you."

"No one said anything about eating blood," Singer said. She looked a little green.

"It must be done."

"What about fucking hepatitis?"

"I'm clean, you cunt," Quincey said, laughing.

A memory of Renée rose, sharing her masticated flies with me, and I choked back a sob. With shaking fingers, I picked up the bread and bit into it. Every instinct I had screamed for me to spit it out, to rinse my mouth with bleach and then bathe in a tub of it until I was clean again. I chewed, and chewed and chewed, trying to ignore the soggy mouth-feel and coppery tang in my nostrils, the knowledge that I was ingesting Quincey's DNA, and forced myself to swallow.

Singer and Quincey glanced at each other, then did the same, gagging behind closed fists and scrunched eyes. Singer almost vomited hers back up but managed to hold it down, retching into the dust. Mam ate last.

"What about that piece?" I asked, eyeing the remaining soggy chunk.

"This one is for you," she said. "And it will need all of our blood."

I groaned. "Why is it always blood?"

Mam shrugged. "Blood is life."

Quincey rummaged in her pocket again and held out a handful of lancets, and we all eyed them with distaste. "Doesn't hurt, you big babies."

It took less time for us to add our blood to the final piece of bread. Then Mam picked it up and began crushing it between her fingers. It squelched wetly, turning her hands crimson.

"This piece is for the ampoule."

"Are we sure this is the best plan?" Quincey touched my arm. "Can you keep a plastic bubble in your gob for an entire month?"

I tongued the gap in my teeth where my front molar had once been. "If I can't it'll be me and Lord Cysgod in boiling excrement for the rest of eternity."

Mam looked less than pleased.

Singer barked a laugh and slapped me on the shoulder. We all chuckled for a moment. Fleeting conviviality in the depths of horror.

"How will we know it worked?" I asked.

"As soon as we speak the words for Invocation, it will. I'll seal it in the ampoule, then, once you've broken the capsule and it's in your bloodstream—" she looked at me, her expression unreadable "—you'll be protected."

Now the moment has come.

As the stylist fusses about my hair, I take a breath and bite down on the ampoule. Bitter, concentrated verbena mixed with the spellbound blood of me, Mam, Singer, and Quincey is released in my mouth. It is a vaccine against fear. And against what is to come.

Please...*please* let it work.

When the priming up is complete, the guards steer us through labyrinthine hallways and twisting staircases—keeping a route in mind is impossible—until we are ushered into a grand foyer.

Every imaginable luxury is on display. Immense, richly patterned tapestries, Lucullan sofas arranged around a massive inglenook, crown molding on high ceilings, tufted detailing in every medieval splendor—nothing less than flawless for this thirteenth-century aerie. I imagine the blood of generations splattered unseen on the walls.

I keep my eyes open.

Five men sit languorously on sofas, while one leans against an adjacent column, conversing calmly among themselves. When we're ushered into their presence, they turn in unison like a six-headed beast to scrutinize us with predatory cunning.

A seventh man with a vulpine aspect and shoes shined to mirror polish, seated in a high-backed chair steepling his fingers, gestures for us to approach. Dark hair combed back, his strange eye glints as he regales us with a smile. The other men seem subtly deferential: a nod here, legs crossed to face him, heads tilted to listen.

"Welcome to my house," he says.

There is an easy politeness to him. An almost boyish charm. He's not young—his features have something of a salt-and-peppered quality, suggesting an established man in middle age—but there's nothing pompous in his manner. Nothing sinister. If I didn't know better, I'd suspect the other men were the monsters.

And yet, I am certain this is the man I have been looking for. The head of the serpent. At last.

My waning energy lifts its head like a mole scenting air.

Our ties are cut, one by one. We rub our wrists, each of us

scanning the room for opportunities for escape. I watch the leader.

A ginger girl at the end of the line breaks away and rushes for the door. In the blink of an eye, the blond man by the column has cut her off with a wolfish grin. He snaps his teeth at her, and the other men laugh. The man in the high-backed chair watches, impassive.

Ginger lunges away from Blondie with a panicked shriek, and he catches her wrist with unnatural speed, laughing as he licks it with a tongue too long to be human.

"I like this one," he says, sly eyes trailing over her flesh, nostrils flaring with the scent of her. "I think I'll start here."

"Now, now, Rodney," says the vulpine man. "You will have your chance to bid, as always."

The girl holding my hand cowers close to me.

"They're not human," she whimpers.

"No," I say coldly. "They're not."

The vulpine man turns to us and smiles again. "You have been selected for a special celebration." He inhales, closing his eyes, and I have an impulse to press my arms close to my body. "Such fine flowers. Don't be scared. You're my invited guests," he says to the girl standing next to me. His eyes are kind, unassuming. If I didn't know what he was, I'd almost believe him. What perfect camouflage.

I watch him, even as the other men move to survey us.

"And what purpose do we *guests* serve?" I ask, stepping forward. The girl beside me gasps at my audacity and tries to pull me back. I shake her off. I know what I am doing. I have to make certain he chooses me.

I clench my teeth to stop them from chattering.

He regards me with interest. His eyes are so penetrating I wonder if he can read my mind. I make sure to think something vulgar just in case.

"You are the sport," he says with graceful charm.

"And you're the monster, ready to pounce."

He shrugs. "No use lying to the dead."

"If you can catch me first," I mutter, eyeing the door.

He cocks his head at my response and gives a sheepish, almost apologetic smile. "Indeed."

With this he turns away, beckoning to his aides to prepare for what comes next.

A small team of men in suits—human by the look of it—shuffle around us setting up a small block, readying the television above the fireplace and handing out tablets.

Then it begins.

The bidding is degrading. Each girl is shoved forward for auction like we're a Modigliani or Renoir, and the men bid by the hundred thousand. It doesn't take very long. Our stats are shown on the main screen above the fireplace—blood count and type, muscle makeup, diet, features, and behaviors. When my own data litters the screen I watch the men salivating and a weird sense of violation comes over me. Even clothed in this gown, I have never been more naked.

I catch a glimpse of my profile. My name is listed as Bambi, next to my blood type—AB—along with other stats. I frown. My blood is O+. I'm absolutely certain. I wonder with panic if this could make or break what happens next.

Several of the men bid for me, but I keep the leader's eye, my chin defiantly raised.

But it's the worst possible outcome.

Blondie wins after nine rounds.

The creep is exultant.

"Yes!" he shouts, punching the air.

"Dickhead," murmurs the long-haired man next to him.

Blondie turns, smirking. "First pineapples, then tulips, then the South Sea, then the Japanese stock market, then the dotcom bubble…at this rate, you're going to be living off rats!"

His target, frowning, inhales to speak, but the vulpine man raises his hand.

"Rodney."

Blondie's smirk dribbles away.

The long-haired man chuckles as their leader raises his hand and waves Blondie to the side like so much debris.

Blondie, sulking, grabs the ginger girl and pulls her away with him. The other men follow suit, dispersing with their weeping "winnings."

Mr. Vulpine stands and smiles at me.

"Mine," he says, and offers me his hand.

34

He is so confident, so absolutely sure of his power over me, that he walks ahead, leading me out of the drawing room and along shadow-veiled, sinuous corridors without looking back. He doesn't expect his prey to have fangs. Centuries have proven him right.

My fury is acid—how I wish I had the power to drain him of the lives he has stolen. How I long to give that life back to Lucy. *My fault*, my mind taunts. *And yours*, it adds, staring at the creature leading me to my death.

Right, down spirals, left, left, right, straight. I add in the new turns in reverse as I follow; they are a new tic, an obsessive song. *Left, left, spiral down, right.* The castle is more like a hedge maze—no doubt carefully built and added to over the centuries for this specific purpose. We are mice in a trap.

His eyes follow me as I enter the room he has chosen. A private study at the top of a spiraled staircase. I don't know how far I am from the ground, how far from the sky. It feels like a terrarium, deep underground, hermetically sealed. It screams *no point trying to run.*

Mine.

"Wine?" he asks.

"Always," I reply with mock enthusiasm.

My tongue probes for the ampoule, my companion for so long, forgetting I already cracked it open and swallowed. A momentary sense of loss, then buoyed by the knowledge that I *am* the ampoule now.

My reply gets a smirk and a raised brow. How he enjoys the mock civility of this game.

My reckless, furious rage returns as he pours wine from a glittering crystal decanter. It obliterates any fear.

Lucy will never drink shitty boxed wine again.

My eyes bore into him as he wanders over, holding out the glass. I force a smile. "Changed my mind."

His jaw works, a flash of irritation quickly hidden.

Fuck you, I think, and almost sneer.

"Drink," he insists, handing the glass over.

"No."

He sips from it instead, his eyes never leaving mine. "Delicious," he says, lips stained red. "It's a shame, really. I bet you've never tasted yourself before."

I jerk, startled. It's my blood. But I force outward calm.

A long sigh, as though this is the real tragedy. "So few people get the chance to really drink deeply of themselves." He puts the glass down and unbuttons his shirt, hands moving slowly from one button to the next, taking his time. *Pervasive pattern of grandiosity...* My brain is spitting diagnoses. *Lack of empathy... excessive need for admiration...* Does psychopathic narcissism occur among the undead? Or is it a situational hazard?

We haven't even begun to crack the potential of their DNA...

Seward's vile fascination.

I want to spit at him. I want to scream. To claw. *Not yet.*

Instead, I force myself to pick up the glass and take a sip. "I must admit it's a first," I manage, my revulsion disguising the fear contaminating my reckless anger.

He grins. Am I the first, I wonder, to willingly drink of her own blood? He looks back at me, shirtless, as he takes off his belt. He kicks off his shoes, followed by his trousers.

"Not a fan of clothes?" I quip, an edge creeping into my voice. I wonder just how many ways he plans to use my body before he's finished with me.

"Oh, don't go all prudish on me now," he says, tilting his head to one side. "Your innocent look doesn't fool me for a moment. We could have a lot of fun if you'd loosen up a little."

Loosen up. He sounds like a uni lad, out on the town for a "bit of fun." I can't even count the number of women who've entered my office because they weren't *loose enough* for a man's liking.

Playtime is over. I swing my legs down and make a move to stand. But with inhuman speed, he's pinned me down on the chaise. He's fully naked now. One arm immobilizes my torso, while another holds the wineglass between us. I can't move. He is a stone megalith. An arresting monster.

"Drink," he says, and he isn't asking. His pupils dilate, feeding on my fear and humiliation. "A benediction in blood."

His weight grows heavier at my silence, my refusal, crushing me down until I feel my ribs creak in protest. All the easy manners of before, the facade, are now gone. His eyes lick themselves over my face, and his grin is more a sneer. Flurries of panic litter my body.

I remember why I'm here. What I'm doing this for. *Who* I'm doing this for. And slowly I open my mouth and close my eyes, a deliquescent form.

The soupy, clotted gore fills my mouth as I feel his erection grow against my leg.

Seizing my moment, I spit my own blood back into his face.

He's startled for a moment, but that's all I need. I slip out from under him to the door.

I glance back once and mouth, "Fuck you." Then I'm running, leaving behind his sibilant anger.

Left, left, spiral down, right; right, spiral down, left, left, right. And then straight.

I race through one room draped in shadows after another. The entire castle is under a pall of gloom. I almost stop when I stumble on Blondie feeding on the ginger girl from the back of the line. She is limp in his arms, her throat entirely missing. The vampire looks up as I pass and grins, her flesh dripping from his teeth.

I hear howling in the distance and a dog—far too large to be normal—rushes past after a screaming girl in the opposite direction. I haven't heard footsteps running after me, his inhuman speed chasing me down. I don't slow, won't wait to be found.

My eyes flick to the next turn in the hallway.

"Once you've taken the potion, you'll have some advantage," Mam had said. "A circle of protection that will make you harder to smell—and harder to trace. This might give you more time, but not much."

Quincey had crossed her arms. "But you're still on your own finding your way out of the castle. And we don't have blueprints for you to study."

"I'll memorize the route when they take me in."

Singer had glanced at Quincey, and I had seen their small disbelief, their yawning worry. *Left, left, spiral down, right, right, spiral down, left, left, right. Straight.*

I fly down the second flight of stairs, knowing that fresh air is near. Except... I should be outside now. I spin around, checking my formula.

Left, left, spiral down, right, right, spiral down, left, left, right. Straight.

I should be at a door now, a door that will lead me outside. Instead, another corridor unfurls before me. Heart hammering, I check the next corner and see nothing. I continue forward, and through the next set of doors, entering the kitchens, which are more of a relic than a room; after all, no one here eats regular food.

On the far end, a layer of mortar dust that lies in faded moonlight beneath the window alerts me to a small gap in the lower wall where the bricks blocking the window have been pulled out. I glance behind me to make sure he's nowhere near, then I slither through, ripping my dress on a jagged edge of masonry.

Getting outside had been one of the greatest, most insurmountable hurdles. Something inside me loosens and threatens to unravel knowing that this crucial piece of my work is done. "Get him outside" had been my mother's command. It seems I have done it. But I'm his prize; he won't be far behind. Terror spurs me on when I imagine him surging forward, rushing after me like carrion crows.

The night air is a susurration on my fevered skin, but there's no time to linger. I've come out on the back end of the castle, which opens onto the woodland where I found Seren's corpse. I run for the trees, trying to silence my brain as it pulses with every desperate step—*grave dirt, grave dirt, grave dirt*. Above me the moon is full and red—an omen if I ever saw one—and the wind plucks at the dress they put me in as though trying to pull me back.

He catches me in an open patch between a copse of Japanese larches.

I turn to face him.

"No one has made it to the gardens before," he says. If he is unsettled by this, he doesn't show it. To the contrary, he seems pleased—by the newness, the challenge. He isn't even out of breath. My blood still smears his face and I feel a pang of victory at that, at least.

"I had help."

He cocks his head to the side. "Oh?"

I nod. Force myself to smile, knowing it will irritate him, even as a plume of icy wind rips through the air, cold fingers on my flesh. I shiver.

He takes one menacing step forward. "What kind of help?"

I put my hands behind my back. Innocent. Unassuming. How odd that I should notice, in this moment, that he has no goose bumps. He is immune to the cold.

"Has one of your own betrayed you at last?" I wonder aloud for him.

He grins. "What caustic wit!"

"Someone you trust, maybe?"

He scoffs. "You're not what I expected from the evening."

"I expect not. My mother is *Swynwraig.*"

He laughs again, my dry blood cracking, flaking off like moth wings. His teeth are a shocking white in the night, predator's teeth. Wolf's teeth. His naked body should shock me. Affect me in some way. But I find that my capacity for horror has been exhausted. All that is left is sheer will.

"I've known many a *Swynwraig, Dewines, Gwyddan, Hudoles,* and *Consuriwr,*" he says, curling his words with vulgarity. "They all made excellent meals."

"They don't have your talent for immortality," I admit. "Nor for murder, or mayhem."

The muscles bunch around his mouth. "It *is* a talent. Your witch mother may have spellworked your way out of the castle, but I still have you. No one will hear your cries."

"Who said anything about my cries?"

He is standing in front of me in the blink of an eye. "There was never any chance of your getting away from here without my bite."

His hands are cool on my neck as he reaches for me. There is a strange magnetism I can almost not resist. I can sense that there is a biological function at work here that turns him into the flame for a moth. Pheromones?

I let him draw me nearer, watch with horror as his tongue elongates from the chasm of his mouth by several inches, licking dried blood from my cheek. My skin tingles and then burns where his saliva sits. Then he opens his mouth, revealing a second layer of hundreds of little needle teeth behind his human veneers. And at last he is drinking from me, long and deep.

I remember this feeling.

It swims up from the umbra of my locked memory box to burn bright.

Hard flesh pressed against mine, a viselike grip impossible to break. The shock of it, quickly quelled by some sort of anesthetic property injected into my body from his bite, disguising the way his saliva dissolves and breaks down my DNA, something meant to calm and subdue...followed by the warmth of my life leaving me. My feet leave the ground as he lifts me closer, squeezes me tighter. A perverse embrace.

Except the verbena-and-blood-spelled ampoule has done its job. My *mind* is intact. While I feel the physical effects of his bite, and gain a vertiginous glimpse of my mortality, I am fully present and aware of it.

I feel him falter. He doesn't realize what's happening at first. He continues to drink. More blood than I can spare.

And then he jerks away, spitting my blood from his mouth, a look of stupid incredulity washing over his nacreous face.

"What have you done?" he gurgles, vomiting blood into the soil.

But it's too late. Already his legs are failing. Now his arms. He drops me and I stagger away. He collapses, then scrabbles in the dirt the way I imagine Seren did, gasping. "What...have...?"

"I told you," I say, looking down on him through fractured vision. *"Swynwraig."*

With beautiful timing, the trees move with the shadows of three women.

Mam. Singer. Quincey.

I close my eyes, woozy from the loss of blood, the world fragments and shafts, and fall to my knees in relief. The final piece of the puzzle. Quincey had promised to survey the property for any signs of the bacchanal. Of any lorry shipments heading off the main road. Of any choppers overhead. She had promised they'd be ready. The days and weeks in the metal cell had been an excruciating exercise in trust. But I believed.

"Mina!" Mam screams, rushing to my side.

I blink my eyes open, wondering if I'm hallucinating the axe dangling from Singer's hand. My would-be killer, lying mere yards away, opens his mouth to scream, but his voice is no longer there to serve him either. With the plants of the land, a bit of freely given blood, and a well-evoked bind, my mother, the batty witch on the hill, has brought a centuries-old monster to heel.

She takes my hand, touches my face, strokes my hair. "Are you all right?"

I nod and sit up, though I still feel dizzy. "It worked."

Singer and Quincey beam at me, and Singer hands me a rowan stake.

I shake my head, handing the stake to Quincey. "You should do it. For Lucy."

She looks at me for a long moment before taking it. "For Lucy," she agrees. She looks at my mother, and at me, and finally, at Singer. "For Seren. For Renée. For Bea."

I lean into my mother as I watch Quincey ram the wood into his chest with a heavy cry. His mouth yawns open in outrage, those pikes-teeth pulsing outward grotesquely. A last precaution: Singer lifts her axe and hacks away at his head.

It.

      Takes.

            A.

                Long.

                      Time.

Finally, Quincey lights what remains of his body on fire, as my mother holds me, rocking me back and forth, murmuring spells. His body turns to dust before our eyes.

Earsplitting, plangent cries rend the air from within the castle, a jagged collection of demonic howls from the doomed vampires being unmade…and then nothing.

An eerie silence.

Just as I think I have nothing left in me to spend, nothing left to give, I realize my cheeks are wet with tears.

35

I stumble to my feet. My mother, Quincey, and Singer pepper me with questions, fussing. Quincey drapes a tartan blanket over my shoulders and Mam hands me a flask of tea and a cling-filmed bundle of biscuits. Singer wraps me in a hug so warm and earnest, it feels like she's hugging her own daughter. I imagine in a way, she is.

"I'm going to see if any of the girls made it," Singer says stiffly.

"There were men in there too," I tell her, remembering the stylists. "Human men."

"I'll go with you," Quincey tells Singer.

"If you call it in, they'll only suppress it," Singer says drily.

"We'll see," Quincey mutters, eyeing the castle. "With the head of the snake gone, maybe not."

Mam shuttles me to Quincey's car to rest, parked a few yards down the road. We don't talk, but I let her hold me and kiss my head like she did when I was a little girl, before I knew that the world wasn't safe.

Eventually, when Singer and Quincey return, both shaking their heads, Mam goes with them to burn the bodies of the vampires. The Book of Blood had been right. Blondie and his friends were unmade along with their master.

"You should take the car back to your mum's," Quincey tells me. "Get some rest."

"Yes, love," Mam agrees. "I can walk back. We all can."

"Could use the time to think this whole thing over," Singer adds.

Quincey claps Singer on the shoulder. "Could grab a pint to help it slide down."

Singer grins. "A pint of that shite verbena, maybe."

Mam tsks and hurries them on with a flap of her hands.

I watch them return to the castle, these brave women, this unlikely trio that helped carry me into the viper's den. I watch them until they've vanished behind the castle walls. I so wish I could have saved the other girls in the cells. Hopefully, they will be the last.

The moon's red glow has faded to an eerie yellow, illuminating the roads I know so well with a pallid, bloodless light. I can't count the number of times Lucy and I walked these lanes as girls, daydreaming about the women we would become. She should be here. Her absence in the world hits me again, and I wonder if there will ever be a time I can think of her without pain.

I grip the thermos, white-knuckling it.

I should feel relieved. I should feel glad that I was able to walk into the snake pit and cut the head off the serpent, killing the entire line of evil spawned there. I should feel proud of myself for overcoming all of my tics and traumas to do so—for saving who knows how many girls from a similar fate. The therapist in me knows it.

Instead, I feel numb.

Instead, I feel like there's more to do.

I need to be sure that Arthur was vanquished alongside the others. That he paid for what he did to Lucy.

I crawl into the driver's seat, and turn on the car.

★ ★ ★

When I turn into Ifori's drive and my headlights splash over a woman howling over a body lying on the ground at the gates, it doesn't hit me for a full five seconds.

Lucy. Vibrant, alive, *glowing*. A vision I've yearned to see for weeks…yet almost grotesque to me now, in its impossibility.

I stumble out of the car.

I leave the door open.

My headlights drape them in glitter.

"Lucy?" I murmur, stepping forward.

Lucy howls again, her hands balled into Arthur's shirt.

My best friend, alive and well, sobbing over the body of her dead husband.

Everything is muggy with the shock of it.

I choke out a sob that is a laugh.

"Lucy!"

She looks up at me and my entire being sinks into the floor, dropping away. Because, of course her skin has the same pale, vaguely nacreous quality of those men in the castle. Her lips have the same strange ruddy luster. Her eyes, even as she sobs, have that same feral glint. The rash is completely gone.

Lucy Westenra-Holmswood is a vampire.

"Mina," she sobs, reaching for me. "He's dead!"

Under the light of the moon, anointed wood, fashioned into a stake, can be used to dispatch the serpent and all its bearn back to Hell. How is Lucy alive? How is Lucy alive, when all the others aren't?

I want to race to her side, to hold her in my arms, to tell her, finally, how much I love her. How thankful I am that she's here, that she's alive. That I will protect her this time, and never fail her. How sorry I am for a life of sins, and any that were made against her.

"What has he done to you?"

Arthur's corpse lies between us.

It begins to rain, a smur that shimmers as Lucy shakes her head. "You don't understand. He truly loved me, Mina. More than anything."

"He changed you!"

"He saved me. *And* he changed me." She swallows. "The first time he fed on me, I think it truly was an accident. You have no idea, Mina...the thirst..."

"He killed you," I say, fighting my rising urge to scream. "He *killed* you, Lucy! I watched you die!" And I choke on the last words, unable to hide my grief any longer.

"Yes. I hated him for it at first, until I understood that he didn't want to lose me. Couldn't bear the thought of a life without me. He didn't want to be alone. And I understand that now. The thought of living as a monster without him...it's too horrible to fathom." She lowers her head to his forehead for a moment, then hands me an envelope I hadn't seen she was holding. "Read it," she says softly. "After I'm gone."

I shake my head, pushing the letter away. "Don't say that."

"The hunger gets worse by the moment, Mina. There's no escaping it."

A sob chokes its way out of me. "I *won't* lose you. I failed you once, and I'm not going to let you die. Not again."

She pushes the letter in my hands, and then lifts something from the ground. A stake. She knew I would come. She knew she would ask this of me. "I don't want to be a monster. Please, Mina. Please."

I'm crying now. I realize with horror I don't care what she has become. I only care that my friend is here with me now. Whole and complete. I would do anything to save her again, even as I know it's impossible. "You could change me too. Lucy..."

She places the stake's point against her heart and wraps my hands around it. "Don't become a monster for me. Please. I'm already dead." Her eyes meet mine, and there is a hint in them of the old Lucy: girlish, carefree, alive. "We made a pact, remember? We'd both escape here, together. You owe me, Bambi. Set me free."

"I love you," I whisper.

She smiles and mouths the words back at me. I push the stake in and scream into the night. My friend slumps over her husband, dead and finally free.

My dearest Lucy,

I know that as you read this, you are changed and that you must hate me for it. I also know that I am likely already dead. Master tolerates no dissent, and if he finds out about you, your life—immortal or otherwise—will be at an end. And I cannot accept that. I won't tolerate your destruction.

I first met him when I took over the estate from my late father. My father had left me a note in his will, a confession of sorts. The finances of our family's estate had been in trouble. My father was desperate. Then he'd met the man who owned Cysgod Castle—for your safety, I won't write his name—through a mutual acquaintance, a wealthy yet secretive financier. The man offered him a contract. He owned the castle here in Wales and several others across the United Kingdom. He wanted a trusted haulage supplier. It had seemed innocent enough, and it was an offer my father couldn't refuse. The money was ridiculous. At first he thought the role was to oversee a logistics firm—the transport of goods. But soon he realized, as did I, the real job was to not ask questions, to sign on the dotted line. When I inherited the estate, I was given no reasonable choices. To keep my estate and you safe, I'd have done anything. The less I knew, I supposed, the better.

Yet then, a few years ago, a prick of my conscience caused me to look into what the operation really was. It was far more terrible than even my worst fears. I tried to get out. But it was too late. Along with other "colleagues," I was turned so that I'd be forced to aid and abet my master in perpetuity.

Unlike some of the other men, I never wanted to attend the parties, never wanted to feed on the beautiful young girls. I hated what I was, and I only had eyes for you. I didn't want to live without you. To be a monster without you.

The first time I fed on you, it was an accident. The lure of blood is stronger than you could imagine, but which I am certain you understand now. I cried for days. Tried to kill myself. My wounds healed. I didn't want to take your blood, but the urge to feed was impossible to resist, and when it came over me, there was nothing I could do. Eventually, as I saw you grow weaker and weaker, I realized soon there would be nothing of you left.

In my cowardice facing eternity without you, I performed the ritual that would turn you. The same one done to me.

I've been watching Mina and her friends closely. I believe they are planning to infiltrate the web, so I am going to help. I am going to ensure that she has every chance to defeat this monster. I am going to ensure she is chosen.

If I am vanquished, any vampire I create will be unmade. But if I am unmade myself—if my creator is vanquished—then my creation will live on. You will live on. All of this for the chance to save you. My darling. My beloved.

Forever loving you,
Arty

36

A week later, I wake up in my childhood bedroom.
Mam is asleep in the bed beside me. I watch her for a while, stroking her hair, and bask in the familiar Welsh light of early morning. It is a buttery light, warm in a way that the light in London never was. I let myself fall back into a peaceful sleep, and when I wake a second time, Mam is gone.

I find her in the kitchen toasting and brewing tea. Black, not verbena.

"Good morning, love," she says, and her voice is warm honey.

"Morning, Mam," I say, giving her a hug from behind.

"Go relax. I'll bring this through when it's done."

"You sure?"

She nods, smiling. "Go rest."

I wander through the house, taking my time, drinking in all the familiar but overlooked details that, in my pain, I forgot I loved. Mam's patchwork quilt draped over the wicker chair that Dad made before I was born, the heavy oak chests that are dotted all over, full of linen, blankets, and a wide variety of talismans and old books. The mismatched knickknacks on windowsills and sideboards, each precious, with a tale to tell. The uneven curtains Mam made herself, even though she can't sew to save

her life, the framed paintings on the wall, some floral, others
nautical—no theme or pattern to speak of. All of the small things
that make up our lives. I smell each bunch of dried herbs as I
pass. Lavender, bird's-foot trefoil, staghorn, motherwort, and
meadow sage. Scents that occupied my memory for so long in
London, and which smell even sweeter for it now, being home.

Home.

I realize that it feels like that again. Something has changed.
Something fundamental. The thing that sent me running, the
Mina I was, no longer exists.

My tics and ablutions have left me. Now I spend my days with
my hands in the soil, helping Mam to plant winter vegetables.
I'm planning to open up a practice right here in Tylluan, but in
the meantime I'm focusing on rebuilding the life I lost.

Mam brings the tray into the conservatory, and we sit on the
floor around the coffee table to eat and drink.

"This is nice," I say, sipping the black tea. "I forgot how good
tea can taste."

"You and me both," she says, grinning.

She adds honey to hers and a splash of lemon, and I opt for
milk. Everything is so blessedly normal.

"I miss her," Mam says softly, putting down her *bara brith* and
licking butter from her thumb.

"I do too. I hope she's at peace."

We're both quiet for a moment, thinking about Lucy. In
time I know the horrors of what transpired will fade, leaving
the happy memories untouched. I find already that my rage toward Arthur has softened, becoming closer to something that
resembles empathy and understanding. I've reread his letter at
least a hundred times, thinking of his torment, his love for his
wife, and his determination to set things right. I ponder all the
unseen ways he might've been helping us. If he had anything to
do with us finding Seren's body. Or gaining access to the castle.

I'm almost certain he was the one who changed my blood type in my medical records. All to help me get chosen.

I sigh and turn to my mother. "Let's sit in the conservatory and finish this," I say. "Like we did when I was younger."

Mam smiles, and we get up and head to the conservatory, each cradling our teacups. It is a balmy day for November, and the brilliant autumn colors are still vibrant. They are already falling, leaving the trees bare for the long journey through winter. Transformation and hibernation. But for now, the cool autumnal sun and the blue sky high above us are a reminder that we are alive. We made it.

There won't be anything that keeps us from being honest with one another ever again. I won't let that happen.

Later, Jonathan picks me up and we walk to the village to get eggs, bread, and milk. We talk about what we know—about my time in the club, what happened with the bacchanal, and how his own attack was part of it too. We wonder how many of the Welsh legends are true, linked to the vampires who preyed on us for so long. I kiss his scars and tell him he is beautiful.

When we get to the shop, I hold his hand when we go inside. This time I have the change I need for a plastic bag.

Mr. Wynn nods. "Morning, Wilhelmina."

"Good morning, Mr. Wynn."

"Jonathan."

"Sir."

I spot the paper and pop it onto the counter. "This too."

The biggest story is about an oil spill in the North Pacific and some new scandal involving a local MP.

We take the long way home. The sun peeks over the hilltops in the distance and I feel myself smile.

For the first time in over a decade, I don't know what the future holds. I don't feel in control. There are no guarantees in this life.

But my life is mine to live, and I'm going to make the most of it. For Lucy. For all of them.

HELEN SINGER
11:49

Just found a report of a missing girl in Madrid. Same symptoms.

They are still out there.

MINA MURRAY
11:50

Quincey's?

★ ★ ★ ★ ★

ACKNOWLEDGMENTS

When I was asked to write a *Dracula* retelling in 2019, I knew that it would be a mammoth task with a huge responsibility. *Dracula* is a beloved work of gothic fiction, and I hope that I have kept the spirit of it alive in this modern, feminist retelling. I couldn't have done it without the incredible people mentioned in these acknowledgments.

First, to my husband. You cheered me on, encouraged me with enthusiasm and fierce belief, and never wavered for a nanosecond. You are my rock in a stormy sea. I love you to the googolplex. To my mother, thank you for your faith, your strength, your love, and your warmth. For showing me what a badass woman is and how powerful survivors are. I adore you beyond words.

To Polly Nolan, who put me forward for consideration for this project, and to Sarah Davies, who continued to support me even after she retired. Thank you to Victoria Marini for your passion, your enthusiasm, and my absolute favorite thing about you: your booming, vibrant, tenacious voice! I could laugh with you for hours. I know we'll keep making bookish magic for years to come. By extension, thank you to the entire High Line Literary team and Sheyla Knigge for additional support and cheering from the sidelines. What a fantastic group of people. Thank you also to Chelsea Eberly of Greenhouse Literary for your kindness and support.

A huge thank you to Laura Barbiea, Joelle Hobeika, and Josh Bank for being an incredible creative team. You three could run the world. I mean it! The tenacity, vision, and genuine care for your authors is very much appreciated. When you all get in a room together, Mount Olympus can feel it! I am honored to have been a part of it. Another thank you to Romy Golan for your passion behind the scenes.

Thank you to Sara Rodgers, my brilliant editor. Your passion and advocacy for this novel have been humbling, and I am so grateful to have you and the Graydon House team behind me. I love how often we get sidetracked chatting about creepy shenanigans when we ought to be discussing edits! Wouldn't change it for the world.

Thank you to the entire Graydon House team who have shown genuine care and passion for *The Madness*. Greg Stephenson for your careful copyedits, Kathleen Oudit for your brilliant art direction and for talking me through specs for the *Llyfr Gwaed* illustrative page. Thank you to Mary Luna for the gorgeous design, Kezia Weerasooriya and Amanda Roberts your incredible work in production. A massive thank you to Diane Lavoie, Sophie James, Pamela Osti, Ambur Hostyn, Brianna Wodabek, Susan Swinwood, and Margaret O'Neill—chatting to you all was such an honour. I am truly blessed because of you all. A big thank you to everyone else behind the scenes that I would love to list individually by name, but which space doesn't allow.

I am blessed to have incredible friends. Special thank you to Kat Ellis, literally the best human friend alive, someone I adore more than I ever tell her (because we are far too British for that), but to whom I owe much of my sanity and the protection of my fragile heart; Ann Davila Cardinal, my *hermana* from another mother, who always cheers me on no matter what, and whom I would walk into battle (or eat churros) with any day of the week; Claire Hawksmoore, my Kiwi cutie; and the brilliant UKYA Discord gang: Joshua Winning, Melissa Welliver, Georgia Bowers, Kathryn Foxfield, Gina Blaxil, Andreina Cordani, Holly Race, and Cynthia Murphy. I truly adore each and every one of you, and the laughs we share every day. Thank you also to the Trifecta. You know who you are, and you are all incredible.

To the authors who read and blurbed an early version of the novel at the time of writing this: Amy McCulloch, Emily Lloyd-Jones, Gwendolyn Kiste, Paulette Kennedy, Amelinda Bérubé, Evelyn Skye, Wendy Heard, Joshua Moehling, Hannah Whitten, Juliet Marillier, and Samantha Downing. Thank you all, so very much, for lending me your eyes and time. Thank you also to Heather Brooke, who took the time to chat with me when I reached out in the early days of the novel to pick her brain about life as an investigative journalist. Though the book ultimately went in a different direction, I am thankful for the time and generosity she gave me. Thank you also for the lovely book gift, which has become a fast favorite! Anna Rose James and Lauren James, thank you both for your enthusiasm for all things gothic. Chatting with you was a blast!

Thank you to Imogen Church for the incredible audiobook performance. I was so happy when I learned you were narrating at my request that I almost fell off my chair. Thank you to the audiobook team behind the scenes as well.

To the London Writers' Salon, Matt Trinetti, and Parul Bavishi. I wrote much of the first draft of *The Madness* in the morning writers' hour, huddled over a candle and cup of tea, among a group of dedicated, passionate, warm, and talented individuals. Thank you for holding space.

Thank you to the reviewers, Bookstagram influencers, podcasters, and BookTokers who have taken the time to reach out to me and to shout about my work. Book people truly are the *best* people, and I'm so grateful to be one of you!

To those of you reading this book, thank you for picking it up, thank you for reviewing it, thank you for going with Mina on this journey. And finally, to Bram Stoker, thank you for the source material. I hope you don't mind that I gave your ladies a little more agency.

THE
MADNESS

READER'S GUIDE

GRAYDON
HOUSE

WELSH FOLKLORE IN *THE MADNESS*

Welsh folklore is weaved through *The Madness* like the threads in a tapestry. Here are some cool tidbits about the folklore that appears in the story.

Y Gwyllgi (Welsh pronunciation: [ˈɡwɪɬɡi])

Y Gwyllgi is a massive dog, or hellhound, or dire wolf, usually depicted as a giant mastiff the size of a bull, with baleful breath and red eyes that blaze like fire in the dark. The name derives from the Welsh *Gwyll*, meaning twilight or gloom, or possibly *Gwyllt*, meaning wild, and *Gi*, meaning dog. Often depicted haunting lonely roads, *y Gwyllgi* preyed on unsuspecting travelers who wandered alone after dark. Many view the hound as the devil himself. Reports of the beast persist today.

Pwca

A mischievous little creature known for leading travelers astray and generally causing mayhem, but can also be very helpful if properly motivated. *Pwcas* in legend occasionally attach themselves to a particular family to help with chores in exchange for food or milk, but if their payment is forgotten, they can turn quite nasty. Tales abound of beatings, destruction of property, madness, and stoning when proper payment was not made. They can take the form of horses, goats, rabbits, and even, if rarely, humans.

Ellyllon
Miniature, solitary Welsh elves. They are depicted as having varying temperaments—either great helpers or very malicious. Ruled over by Queen Mab, they have a fantastic appearance in Shakespeare's *Romeo and Juliet*.

Y Tylwyth Teg
The fair folk/the fair family. These otherworldly beings are a race of Welsh fairies who hail from the otherworld, though they have also been described as living in lakes, streams, and hill hollows, as well as being inhabitants of Annwn (the Welsh underworld). These folk are tall, fair beings who are quite mischievous, and they interact with humans and the human world fairly frequently. Legends abound of kidnapped mortal children replaced with changelings, humans getting trapped in the fairy realm, and even marriages (consensual or not) between the fair folk and humans.

Toili
A spirit funeral/phantom funeral is a shadowy funeral that portends a real one.

Canwyll Corff
The corpse candle (or the death candle). Tangentially similar to the will-o'-the-wisp, the corpse candle is more related to funeral processions and death than bogs and drowning. Legend has it that the corpse candle traces the route from the home of someone about to die to their grave. If the flame burns white, the death of a woman is foretold; if it burns red, the death of a

man. If it burns only faintly, a child. It has been written to take the form of a flame, a floating skull with a candle, or a vision of the soon-to-be departed. Also described as a "stately flambeau, flaming bluely and stalking about uninvited from place to place" (T. R. "Popular Superstitions of the Welsh." *The Cambro-Briton* 1, no. 9 (May 1820): 349–351. https://www.jstor.org/stable/30069263?seq=2).

Cyhyraeth

A skeletal wraith or ghostly spirit. It is an ill-portent that manifests as a disembodied wailing. Those who hear it are marked for death. Legend has it that they moan three times, each one getting fainter and fainter.

Gwyllion

A hag spirit, occasionally tied to witchcraft. Like many Welsh creatures, they haunt lonely roads and lead travelers astray, and are said to be hideously ugly with a disturbing laugh.

Cewri

Giants!

Nos Galan Gaeaf

Samhain, or the day before November 1.

Ysbrydnos

May Eve/*Nos Galaf Haf* (April 30). This night, known as "spirit night," is one of three when the veil is thin and spirits may wander and divination is possible. The other two are *Nos Galan Gaeaf* (October 31) and *Nos Gwyl Ifan* (June 23).

Angelystor

In Llangernyw, a rural village in Conwy, North Wales, there stands an ancient yew tree, estimated to be around five thousand years old. Every Samhain, or *Nos Galan Gaeaf*, a demon (or entity) known as *Angelystor*—or the recording angel—appears to read the names of those who are to die within the next year.

Swynwraig (feminine) / Swynŵr (masculine) / Swyn (gender neutral)

Witch, sorceress, magician, enchantress. Can also use *Dewines, Gwyddan, Hudoles, Consuriwr*. These witches would often keep a *Llyfr Cyfrin* (a Book of Secrets, akin to a Book of Shadows).

QUESTIONS FOR DISCUSSION

1. Mina performs daily rituals to keep herself calm and safe. Do Mina's rituals hold her back? Do they help her?

2. The illness that plagues Lucy and Renée haunts Mina, sending her back to Wales as she hunts for the root cause. Why do Helen Singer and Mina's mum have such different views on the illness? How does it affect their search for answers?

3. Magic isn't real...or is it? Mina's mum is known as the batty witch on the hill. What role does witchcraft and ritual play in the story?

4. Beatrice's story shows us what happens to the girls who go missing, and the ones who fight back. What surprised you about her journey? What were you hoping would happen? What would you do in her situation?

5. Beauty and youth and naivete are all prized traits in the vampires' chosen victims. Why do you think this is? How

does Mina subvert these expectations while still playing into them?

6. The wealthy and powerful men who attend parties at the club with no name do so in hopes of attaining even more power and influence, and, for a select few, immortality. Would you make the same bargain that they did? Why or why not?

7. Dr. Seward works behind the scenes to fix things for his masters, going as far as covering up deaths and disappearances. Do you think his punishment was fitting? Why or why not?

8. Mina went through an experience in her youth that changed her. Do you think she would have been able to prevail against the vampires if she hadn't? Would she have approached things differently, and if so, how?

9. Lucy makes an impossible decision at the end of the book. How does this affect the people in her life? Would you make the same decision?

10. The moody Welsh countryside and its rich folklore are as much characters in *The Madness* as the characters themselves. How does the remote setting add to the atmosphere of the story?

11. Did you catch all the parallels between the classic Dracula story? Which character changes surprised you most?

12. Vampires have been popular subjects for fiction, art, and mythology for a very long time. How does the portrayal of vampires in *The Madness* differ from other popular vampire depictions in stories? How are they similar?